SAVAGE

A Novel

James W. Cameron III

DEDICATION

This Book is dedicated to my friend and retired USF&WS agent
Monty Halcomb.

Acknowledgments

Many thanks to Margaret who waded through my draft
and fixed my oversights.

CHAPTER ONE

Something evil creeped into the southern Cumberland Plateau like low rumbling thunder. It reverberated off the forests and down through the canyons flowing out of the hills like a torrent. Perhaps it arrived in the form of soft warm fur, or something as commonplace as a cowboy hat. Perhaps it was there all along existing in a parallel universe, resting quietly and unseen waiting for the opportunity to present itself in wondrous glory, waiting to feed its own ravenous hunger with the soft flesh of weaker men. Later they wondered if it was something they did, a mistake so primal they never saw it coming like stepping over a venomous serpent that rises and strikes at your soft underbelly.

Molecules collided with one another bouncing like balloons of scent against the walls of his container so small and invasive they could not be stopped only misdirected momentarily. Like the bubbles of a Microsoft screen saver, lazily the perfect orbs floated in the air and into his nostrils where the nerves in the hairs of his nose vibrated a warning. It was a scent he knew. Then, he heard the blood running with regular throbs through the series of the man's vessels like liquid race cars on a Monte Carlo track. Lub, squish, Dub, Squish. The heart muscles contracted and expanded. Wait. He sensed there were two men, their blood pulsing at minutely different rates. It was his nature to know these things. Patiently, he remained as still as death and simply stared ahead, his breathing low and soft. He was confined like this for who knew how long, where days and nights were the same since there was no light in the place he was confined. He was not aware why this was done to him. None of it made sense, but it angered him and therefore made him dangerous. Running free and wild was his nature. The confinement churned anger deep inside him like a dormant volcano. If it was the last thing he ever did he would get even with these men whose scrawny arms who treated him roughly. These puny black and white morons underestimated his strength. His mind began to clear and with each advancing hour he regained the sharpness of a predator. Two compelling decisions now formed in his mind. The order of their execution was insignificant. He would escape and then he would kill the men. He would taste their salty blood, and it wouldn't be the first time.

He did not know where he was since the inside of the sterile cage presented nothing he could use to set his bearings. It was very cold and the noise surrounded him making it hard to sleep. He heard engines like this before, and they were always driven by men. Bouncing up and down there were times he felt almost weightless and other times when the rolling almost made him sick. There was little water and even less food.

Moments before, the noise and the cold were interrupted by a hard thump which shook the place he was being kept as the container slid and then crashed against the side of something hard and cold. Whatever form of transportation he was in came to a stop. Then the men came for him and that is when he smelled them. Each beat of each man's heart was registered and remembered. Whatever language they were speaking was not familiar to him. He heard their grunts and swearing as the container in which he was lying was moved and reloaded onto something else. Engines started again and he once again sensed he was being moved.

Still, he had not moved or given any indication He was awake. He told himself to be patient and could think of nothing other than escape and revenge. This anger and hatred pulsed with every beat of his big heart. Anger drove him to do dangerous things, even to kill. Killing came natural to him and caused him no remorse.

For some period he felt the rocking movement of whatever they loaded him onto, then came a sudden crash and he was thrown around again but this time his container bent and changed its shape. Something was draped over his container preventing him from seeing what was happening but he could hear the men yelling outside.

"You stupid, mother fucker, you went into that

ditch," He heard one of them say.

The other one yelled back, "It wasn't my fault. I didn't want to run into that deer."

"You should have hit that sonofabitch. Now look at this. The damn axle is broke and we are stuck in the middle of fucking nowhere. If we don't show up with this guy, you know the Boss Man is going to go nuts. Do you know the reward for this one?"

The second man did not seem to be able to fight back against the other man. Both of their hearts were pumping very fast, and he heard that very clearly. Such a rapid heartbeat meant panic.

"Ah, shit. This lock's been damaged too, when you hit the ditch. Good thing you gave him the extra shot when we landed at the airport," said the first man. There was a pause, then, "You did give him the additional sedative didn't you?"

He could tell the first man was very agitated and that the second man was apologizing for not having done something. He began to sense fear growing in the men which welled up in him like the excitement of locating the day's first prey. Their fear was palpable to him and fed his strength.

The first man screamed, "You didn't give him the second shot?"

"No, ah, guess I didn't," mumbled the second man.

He heard the slap and then the first man saying, "You are a fucking idiot. If that guy wakes up there will be trouble. Help me rig something up here."

Then he heard man hands rattling the outside of the container. Now, he decided it was time to act. With all his power he leapt at the door and put his shoulder into it. The force of his shoulder as he thudded against the metal sprung the door snapping it open, driving the men back and knocking them off their feet. Instantly, he was through and on the ground in a strange place. He could taste the fear in the two men, one black and one white, who were starting to feebly crawl away. Except for the headlights of the truck pointing down the hill, it was dark and smelled wet and green like no place he had ever been. Similar to a jungle but not quite. Casually and with one swift stroke he cut the throat of the black man and then stood watching as the man's twitching ended and the blood spurted in ever weakening pulses from his neck. He turned his big yellow eyes and just stared at the white man who vainly tryied to back crawl away afraid to take his eyes off him. The man's eyes contained the knowledge that death came for him in this form. The man stopped crawling because his leg lay beneath the big paw and he was trapped. One more lightening flash and the white man's throat was cut, so deep his head almost fell off.

The killer stood there for a moment staring at his two victims who were both now dead. He could have walked off, but he wasn't finished. He would leave his mark. His anger boiled over at the indignities he had suffered, so he reached out and with one movement tore through the man's clothes, leaned over him and bit off his genitals. Man tasted just like he remembered. Not bad, not bad at all, especially if you hadn't eaten a decent meal in days. With blood dripping from his mouth he shook his mighty head, cleared his throat and walked down the mountain into the place the locals called Savage Gulf, the sound of his kill echoing down the canyon.

CHAPTER TWO

It was a long day for Deputy Sheriff Yogi Baker of the Sequoyah County, Tennessee Sheriff's Office. After responding to and resolving a domestic dispute where the wife beat the holy shit out of her much smaller husband, and then threatened to beat the holy shit out of Yogi, he was called to investigate a trailer explosion that was likely a former meth lab over near Beersheba Springs. The explosion completely demolished the trailer, its occupants, and two old junk cars that probably looked better with the paint bubbled up or completely burned off, the "champagne look" as the Kingfish once told Andy. The lack of employment in Sequoyah County drove more and more locals into the meth business. Once proud moonshiners were replaced by red necks who fried their brains on methamphetamine then blew themselves up since they were never real sharp in high school chemistry class anyway. The tragedy of it all were the children, who did not ask for this life but who came into it with little chance of escaping their birthright. Yogi remembered a "Slow Children" road sign near the site of the latest disaster and considered that about summed it up. The sign, a sad reminder of their fate, was scorched from the explosion and the children's swing set in what used to be the yard was twisted grotesquely.

On the way to the blast sight Yogi passed

numerous hand painted signs advertising auto repair services, bail bondsmen, medical remedies provided by tea and herbs, and Big Dave's Market. He noted that one "For Sale" sign had the "S" written backward. Yogi assumed the writer did not know the difference. The front yard of almost every house or trailer was a parking lot for every car or truck the inhabitant ever owned along with washers, dryers, refrigerators and miscellaneous children's toys. Everyone was borderline surviving.

As the only detective employed by the Sequoyah County Sheriff's Department, Yogi was required to visit every crime scene. Page after page of reports would be filed so the County could justify its police work and qualify for state and federal money to support the department. Yogi's life became an administrative nightmare. Gruesome as a trailer explosion could be, it broke the paperwork monotony and got him out of the office. Some referred to these meth lab explosions as "thinning the gene pool", but since Yogi was raised in Sequoyah County he knew in spots the gene pool was only ankle deep to begin with. Nothing good came from cousins marrying cousins. Everyone he knew was looking for a little extra work, even deputies.

Darkness set in by the time he taped off the explosion, the coroner retrieved what was left of the cookers, and Yogi completed his routine photographing of the site. He rubbed his eyes and thought "just another ho-hum day in paradise." The remote location of the explosion meant that he would have to navigate the mountain road in the dark to get back to Northwoods, the county seat where he shared a modest home with his girlfriend, Rachel, who worked at the University up the road on the Mountain. Roads that followed the escarpment of the Plateau did not run in a straight line. Each proceeded in a serpentine crawl around the outline of the Cumberland Plateau taking corners widely with all the caution possible because the grade was so steep a vehicle built up speed before the driver became aware of the danger. He always heard the sharp turns referred to as "the Devil's elbow." In one of those precipitous turns on State Route 56 he encountered his third crime scene of the day.

A box like cargo truck sat off the inside of the turn its nose down in a ditch. One of its rear caution lights blinked intermittently and the other not at all yet the headlights were both on and working. Yogi radioed in the accident to dispatch and looked for a pull off so his department SUV would not be a hazard obstructing the road. The dispatcher acknowledged the call and instructed him to report back after his initial reconnoitering of the site. Gravel crunched beneath his feet as Yogi walked across and back up the road to the truck. The blue flashers from Yogi's patrol unit created a dusting of pulsing light along the road and trees back to where the truck listed. There were no markings on the truck to identify its ownership and no one was in the cab. Yogi recalled that none of the commercial trucks that worked locally bore identifying marks, especially vehicles involved in logging operations, and he wondered why. Around the rear of the truck he found a large container or crate of some kind splayed on the ground with its door open and a tarp that once covered the container ripped and torn on the ground. It looked like a large cage. His flashlight beam searched around the truck and then panned out in an ever widening radius away from the road. The arc of light stopped and froze on what appeared to be a human form. Yogi ran to the body of a black man and realized he knew this person from high school. The man's throat was slashed and there was blood pooled all over the ground. This victim was clearly dead. Yogi stood and continued to scan the area with his high beam flashlight and that's when he saw the next body but he didn't run to this one. Instead, Yogi turned and wretched up everything he ate all day. The throat of this victim was also cut but what was most disturbing and shocking to Yogi was how the body was mutilated. The man's entire groin area was cut or torn out. Because the head seemed at an odd angle, almost as if it were detached from the body, Yogi couldn't get a good look at the face from where he stood to identify this guy. He decided it was more important to call this in and get back up before he investigated further. Besides, he was ready to throw up again.

Within thirty minutes two more deputies arrived with generators and lights illuminating the horror Yogi stumbled onto. Although he searched no other vehicle tracks or tracks of any kind appeared since all the events occurred on the partially reinforced shoulder that was covered in gravel where the asphalt ran out. In one direction the ground fell off into the Savage Gulf Natural Area, and across the road the Plateau gradually sloped away to the valley containing Northwoods and other small communities. After the lights were set up and more photographs were taken the EMT's arrived to claim the bodies and take them to the hospital morgue. Each of the other deputies threw up just as Yogi had.

"Jesus Christ, Yogi. What in the hell could have done that?" Deputy Andrew Sparks asked not wanting to watch, but unable to take his eyes away as the EMTs got the bodies into bags. Sparks was in his early twenties, almost a decade younger the Yogi. While Yogi was slender, Sparks was almost "wormy" as Yogi's mother would have said.

"Don't know, Sparky. I know I haven't seen anything like it," Yogi answered.

"Do you recognize either of them?" The third Deputy asked. He was from a small town about thirty miles away and didn't know any of the locals yet.

Yogi answered, "I went to school with the black dude. Name is Buster Crockett. Haven't seen him much in the last year or so, but I heard he was just doing odd jobs for folks."

"Aren't we all?" Sparks answered. "I think the other guy was Larry Glower. Just a local guy doing whatever he could to make ends meet."

"Horrible damn way to die." The third Deputy whose name was Aaron Burns declared. The three deputies stood there staring off into the vast darkness below that was the wilderness area.

The Savage Gulf Natural Area encompasses approximately 20,000 acres of wilderness cut into the southeast corner of the Cumberland Plateau. High walls ring the canyon through which flows the Collins River, Big Creek and Savage Creek. Spectacular overlooks provide an exposed view of thousands of acres of true wilderness containing five hundred acres of virgin forest area that have never been logged in the history of the country. Hardwoods older than the nation itself towered in this area. The Gorge was so rugged access by vehicle was almost impossible although the remnants of an old stagecoach road could still be found traversing the valley. Savage Gulf was perhaps the most primitive, most wild area left in the eastern United States and certainly in Tennessee.

Yogi and Rachel had hiked and camped in the Gulf several times with their friends Emily and Jack Mathews. Jack was the Dean at the University and his wife, Emily, was an artist. Although Ranger Stations were located near a parking area on either side of the expanse of the Gulf, once you left the familiar Ranger Station there was nothing but wild woods and high rocks. Echoes of banjo music swirl as you descend into the Gulf. Students and faculty from the nearby University often hike and camp in designated areas in the Gulf and Boy Scouts make annual pilgrimages to the area as well. In the peak season from April to November more than three hundred people visit the Park each day. One popular spot is The Stone Door, an access point leading into and out of the Gulf that was used by Indians who passed through the area for thousands of years travelling from north Georgia up to the common hunting grounds in Kentucky. Above The Stone Door itself is a wide rock outcropping that serves to launch rappelling and rock climbing expeditions.

It was long past midnight when Yogi got home and found Rachel sound asleep. As quietly as possible he got out of his clothes, placed his service weapon on the dresser and slid into bed. Rachel snuggled into him and the lemony scent of her hair filled the room. He put his arm over her and tried to sleep but he could not run away from what he had seen that night.

Still exhausted the next morning Yogi began the tedious process of completing his reports and assembling the preliminary file known as the Murder Book. What he stumbled upon the previous night was definitely been a double murder but there were few clues as to who or what the murderer was. The disembowelment was most unusual and savage indication to Yogi that the murderer was either seriously deranged or some kind of animal. Yet, in all the years he hunted deer and other wild game he never witnessed such mutilation in the game world or such violence inflicted on a human corpse. As other department personnel reported for work, all the talk was about the double murder. Yogi caught Sheriff Mark Brown as he arrived at the station that morning and briefed him on what they knew so far.

"So, Yogi," the Sheriff said, "Both of those men had their throats cut?"

"Yes, sir. Or more specifically, their throats had been slashed with a long sharp object. There was no weapon left at the scene," Yogi reported.

"You are thinking some animal may be involved?" Asked the Sheriff.

"It's a possibility. If something was in that cage, it could have attacked and killed those men, but I have no clue as to what was in the cage, or why it was in the cage to begin with," Yogi said.

"What do we know about the victims?"

Yogi said, "Both are local guys early to mid-thirties. Crockett was married but Glower wasn't. I plan on talking with Crockett's wife later today. There was no marking on the truck and of course, no registration. The tags were reported stolen six months ago by a local farm."

"I understand the coroner will be in this afternoon after he has examined the bodies," the Sheriff said. "Why don't you try to speak with the Crockett woman and let's talk again later."

"Sure." Yogi said and as he walked out of the Sheriff's office he heard someone yell, "Newspaper is on line one, Chief."

Very few Black people live in Sequoyah County and Yogi knew they were all clustered in an area referred to as "Hard Bargain." What little prosperity ever existed in the County completely overstepped this area. You could smell the poverty. The neighborhood supported about a dozen very modest frame homes each with aluminum siding and yards littered with Big Wheels and other children's toys. Lola Crockett worked part time as a night waitress at the Truckstop Café on the Mountain just down from the interstate entrance to I-24. She met Yogi on the concrete stoop at the front of the house as he pulled up and got out of his Department Explorer.

"Mrs. Crockett," Yogi said as he approached the porch, "I am so sorry about Buster and your loss. I am Deputy Baker. We are trying to investigate and find his murderer. Have you got a couple of minutes to answer a couple of questions?"

"Come on in Deputy," Lola said opening the storm door and then the metal front door of the home. Yogi could see she had been crying since she was called as soon as her husband was identified. He also saw evidence that one or more small children also lived there.

Lola saw the Deputy look around the room to see the children's things in disarray. She thought he must wonder where the kids were.

"The kids is next door with his mama," she said before Yogi could ask. "She's all the family we've got here. My people are from Mississippi." Lola stepped into the kitchen and returned with two mugs of coffee, black. She thought all policemen drank coffee black and wanted to be polite.

"You know, Buster and I were in high school together Lola, but I haven't caught up with him in at least a year," Yogi began. "What kind of work has he been doing recently?"

"Just odd job stuff. A pickup here and a drop off there," Lola said almost as if she were in a trance.

"What kind of pickups and drop offs?" Yogi asked.

"He didn't say much about it. I think him and Larry picked up things at the airport on the Mountain and took them someplace," Lola said.

"There's no regular freight delivery at that little airport, is there?" asked Yogi.

"No, nothing regular at all, just special planes that came in. Always seemed like it was awfully late at night," she answered.

"Like last night?" Yogi asked.

"Yeah, him and Larry were supposed to pick up something real special. Buster and Larry were splitting a thousand bucks for that delivery," Lola said mentally counting the cash that would have bought food and clothes her kids needed. Gone now.

"Do you have any idea what it was they picked up?" Yogi asked.

"No, but I know it wasn't no kind of drugs or anything. My Buster never did anything like that," Lola said defensively. Lola was now a little suspicious. She didn't need the Sheriff thinking Buster was smuggling drugs and therefore would want to come search her house. Lola did not want the law to see the special birds Buster gave her either.

"Do you have any idea who Buster was working for? Or, who owned the truck?" Yogi asked probing a little further.

"I heard him talk about the "Boss Man" a couple of times, but never no names. Every now and then Buster hauled something for Mr. Pierce so he let Buster use the truck," Lola said.

Yogi was familiar with the name, Pierce. That referred to Richard Pierce who owned one of the two large and magnificent homes in Sequoyah County. Yogi wasn't sure what kind of business Pierce was involved in before he came to Sequoyah County but he was familiar with Pierce Farms a few miles away. Pierce Farms raised belted cattle, or Belted Galloway cattle to be more precise. This beef cattle breed was imported from Scotland and were a hardy lot. The Belted looked similar to Angus, except they had a two foot white stripe that circled their back and stomach. Yogi's mouth gaped open the first time he saw the herd in the field. The sight was so unusual he initially dismissed it as a high school prank.

Since the conversation with Lola, Yogi thanked her not wanting to intrude further on her grief, gave her a hug and took his leave. Standing by his patrol unit he thought he sensed a change in the weather coming.

CHAPTER THREE

Jonas Rodgers was the Ranger assigned by Tennessee Parks to manage the Savage Gulf State Natural Area as part of the South Cumberland State Recreation Area which consisted of several different areas geographically linked to each other. He was assisted by four assistant Rangers, one who worked primarily at the South Rim Station, one who worked mostly at the North Rim station where Jonas maintained his office and where The Stone Door was located, and two who rotated from the Visitor Center on top of the Mountain. Whenever possible the Rangers hiked through the Gulf themselves looking to see that open fires were contained to established fire pits and that campers remained in designated areas. The North Rim station attracted most of the visitors because it provided the easiest access to The Stone Door and therefore the Gulf. Before anyone could go into the Gulf they had to register with the Ranger Station on a punched sheet that was attached to a clipboard kept outside the Station beneath a topographical map of the Gorge. Later the punched pages would be transferred inside to a big note book that tracked the visitors.

The Ranger Station was typical of similar structures throughout the country. No more than thirty feet by thirty feet, the Station housed a desk, a couple of chairs, radio and computer equipment and the local maps and guides which could be purchased for a two dollar contribution. Over his career Jonas was stationed in many similar stations, but this was likely his last posting since he approached the mandatory retirement age of 62 for Park Rangers. That was ok with him since he put in almost thirty years with the State of Tennessee and at least ten years before that with the U.S. Fish and Wildlife Service. Besides, it was getting harder and harder to haul his big ass down into and back out of the Gulf. Almost everything about the job was accomplished on foot. Jonas stood six feet tall and pushed two hundred eighty five pounds. He kept his hair short, military style, to honor his father, a decorated Marine from the Korean War.

Jonas leaned over the Registration Book and read the names of the campers and hikers who entered the Gulf either late yesterday or early this morning: *Emily Mathews, Jack Mathews, members of the University Outing Club, Ron Coleman, Oren Parini, Keith Russell, Toby Lucas, Mary Beth Ford, Lisa Sweeney, Marcia Probst, Boy Scout Troop 45, Nashville, Tennessee, Parker Jones, Scoutmaster"* Only the adult leaders for the Boy Scouts signed in. A few of the Boy Scouts entered from the South Rim and planned to hike down the old Stagecoach Road to camp near the Collins River then climb out through the Stone Door the following day. The bulk of the Scout group camped at the top by the North Rim Ranger Station and expected to spend the day rock climbing and rappelling at The Stone Door. Jonas liked to keep up with how many visitors were in the Gulf and where they planned to camp in case the weather turned bad, as it was threatening on this day. Weather forecasters that morning mentioned torrential rains and even the remote possibility of a tornado or straight line winds. It was not tornado season but Jonas was cautious anyway. The U.S. Weather Service channel was on and broadcasting at both the Ranger stations.

What began as a typical fall weekend for Jonas was interrupted by the appearance of a Sequoyah County Sheriff's Department Vehicle in the No Parking Zone outside the Ranger Station. Jonas saw the vehicle pull up and stepped out to see what was up. Deputy Yogi Baker got out of his Explorer and put on his patrol cap. After introducing himself and shaking hands with the Ranger, Yogi explained,

"I don't want to alarm you or exaggerate anything but last night on the edge of the Gulf we came across a double murder where both of the victim's throats were slashed. At this point we don't know who or what did this but I wanted to give you a head's up and ask you to be on the alert."

Just as the old Ranger started to respond a gust of wind whipped up and blew off his hat and Yogi's as well. The trees began to sway in their uppermost branches as if they were waving and in such action created the wind itself. He and Yogi looked up at the flailing canopy.

"Front's coming in," Jonas allowed. He never wasted words. From his south Alabama roots Jonas retained a gravelly voice so resonant some called him "Bear" comparing his voice to former Alabama Coach Bear Bryant. Dark clouds began to dash across the sky and the air temperature dropped ten degrees in twenty minutes. "No one has reported seeing anything yet or anything unusual in the Gulf but it's a big place. Not hard to hide out down there."

"Just keep your eyes open. I was on that gruesome scene last night and I have never seen anything like it," Yogi said. Jonas could hear that Yogi was a local and the phrase "Nice night for a knife fight" came into his mind. All the "I's" intoned the letter "y".

"We've got a lot of visitors in there this weekend. There's at least thirty from the Scout Troop in Nashville, six or ten from the Outing Club at the University, a group of Foggies, a few couples, and I am sure some that found a way in without signing the Registration," Jonas said.

Recalling that his best friend Jack Mathews was a faculty sponsor for the Outing Club, Yogi asked, "Is there a guy named Jack Mathews registered with the

Outing Club?"

"Yes, and an Emily Mathews as well," Jonas recalled.

"That's his wife. Jack's the Dean of the College over at the University. Any idea where they are camping?" Yogi asked.

"I didn't pay any attention to that, but we can look on the Registration," Jonas offered.

"What are 'Foggies'?" Yogi asked as they walked toward the Station.

"Friends of the Gorge," Jonas said. "They do a lot to support the Area." Yogi nodded. Every State Park or wilderness area was usually supported by some group of "Friends" who assisted the Rangers and Savage Gulf was no different.

Inside the Weather Service Radio was blaring, "A tornado watch with winds approaching eighty and gusting to one hundred miles per hour with heavy rainfall and hail is predicted in the Sequoyah County vicinity by one pm central time. Residents are advised to take shelter in place." The same warning was repeated over and over drowning out all other ambient sound.

Jonas brought the Registration pages inside and saw that the Scouts coming in from the South rim were registered to stay at the Sawmill Campground. Under normal circumstances camping was limited at each campsite but exceptions were made for regulars like the Scouts and the Outing Club. He did not see a designated campground reservation for the Outing Club that Jack and Emily Mathews led.

As the Weather Service warning was blasting its monotonous understatement in the background, Jonas picked up the transmitter of his short wave radio and called the South Rim Ranger station.

"Stephen, did those Scouts leave out of there this morning?" Jonas asked Assistant Ranger Stephen Slydell.

"Yes, sir. Eight Scouts and two adults," reported Ranger Slydell. "They should be to the Sawmill Campground in about three hours."

"I am very concerned about that group of Scouts if they get down to the Sawmill Campground because this system looks like it is bringing in a lot of wind and rain. Big Creek and Savage Creek are both running underground into the sinks but we could have a flash flood and those kids could get cut off by the water from those creeks or the Collins," Jonas announced. Already a plan was forming in his mind to pull that group out. Protecting kids and campers was paramount for Jonas.

Jonas looked over at Yogi who was listening intently. "You up for helping me get those kids out?" Jonas asked.

"Sure. What can I do, and can we contact the Outing Club group as well?" Yogi asked.

"No cell service in the gorge. Plus, the problem is we don't know exactly where the Outing Club group is. There is one rough way into the Gulf up a dry stream bed and across an old stagecoach road. It leads to within 100 yards of where the Sawmill Campground is. If we can get there without all of us getting cut off, we may be able to get that Scout group out. Maybe they have seen or heard something about the other group," Jonas said as he pulled on a heavier jacket.

Reflecting on his plan, Jonas said, "Let's go get the rest of the Scouts off the bluff above The Stone Door first and get them packed up and safe. I saw that a couple of the adults with the boys drove four wheel drive vehicles so they can come with us."

There is a large rock outcropping just above The Stone Door that spreads out flatly toward the rim and provides the most expansive view of Savage Gulf. From there the sky reaches on forever and the entire Gulf spreads out panoramically eight hundred feet below and across to the other rim. Savage Gulf is actually three different gorges that come together formed by the three major creeks and rivers that cut through the sandstone over millions of years. Soon enough the tall giants that grew in the Gorge would reach with bare arms to the sky in supplication for spring as their leaves dropped to the forest floor, but now they lifted clouds of red, orange and yellow that painted the canyon like a sea of foamy color. It was here on the flat surface of the rim rock the Scouts rigged their rappelling lines with anchors hammered deep into the rock cracks. From below other Scouts were free climbing the face of the bluff. The younger ones wore harnesses and were tethered to a belay line but the older boys who climbed this rock face many times scrambled up the rock like monkeys.

As Jonas and Yogi walked off the asphalt trail to the overlook and onto the rock, they saw that the Scout leaders meticulously set safety lines with anchors and watched as kid after kid crawled over the edge and down at least a hundred feet in the sport of rappelling. Their mothers would have been horrified, as well as many of their fathers. However, Jonas knew this troop and its leaders and appreciated their training, skills and preparedness. Not long ago, boys from this Troop rendered first aid and carried out of the gorge an injured adult climber from another troop who fell without a belay line or harness. While he was confident these guys knew what they were doing, Jonas was alarmed by the weather conditions and his authority empowered him to evacuate everyone from the Park. He spoke with the Scout leaders and explained the situation. Quickly, orders were given and the older Scouts from the bottom collected gear and the younger ones and climbed back up through The Stone Door while the other leaders and boys disassembled the top ropes leaving the anchors in place for their next climbing adventure.

Back at the campground Jonas explained to the Scout leaders that he needed to evacuate the other Scouts who were hiking down from the South Rim. Conditions threatened due to the storm and the potential tornado were too dangerous. The Scoutmaster, Parker Jones, was with that group along with another adult, Bob Penske. Bob's Land Rover was still in the parking lot and an extra set of keys was left with Bob's friend, Rufus Cockerham. Yogi knew both Bob and Rufus since they were whitewater paddlers like he and Jack. Atop Bob's Land Rover stood permanently mounted canoe racks so that several open boats and kayaks could be hauled. With Rufus in Bob's red Land Rover Discovery, Yogi in his Explorer, another leader in a four wheel drive GMC Yukon, Jonas led the group out of the campground in his green Park Service Ford 250. The remainder of the Scouts and leaders broke camp and loaded all the gear into the other vehicles. As the storm raged around them and whipped the trees with fury, the group that remained behind huddled inside the other cars because there was little waiting room inside the

Ranger Station. Some of the parents wanted to drive off the mountain but others were willing to hunker down in the parking lot and wait. Within the Ranger Station the Weather Service radio still blared its unchanging warning like Will Robinson's robot. *Danger, Will Robinson!*

Conditions began to deteriorate as Jonas and his party left the parking area. The skies grew blacker by the minute and more threatening, thunderhead building upon thunderhead. The wind tossed the trees even more furiously like tall grass when it suddenly began to rain mixed with sleet. At first it was just a drizzle, enough to trigger an intermittent windshield wiper, but then the liquid fell in sheets. Jonas knew in Savage Gulf water accumulated fast, drowning the sinks and restoring the raging creeks and river. Jonas led the group down the mountain on Highway 56 through its endless series of twists and turns until he signaled a right hand turn into an old rutted mostly dirt road. Two miles into this part of the adventure Jonas stopped and stepped out of his truck to remove a strand of barbed wire connected to a pole that served as a rudimentary gate. When he removed the wire to the side he held up four fingers signaling everyone should go into four wheel drive operation. From there the dirt road that was already sticky played out, and became a dry creek bed littered with river rocks of various sizes. The Ford 250 had plenty of clearance as did the Land Rover but the other two vehicles were having more difficulty maintaining any speed at all. Jonas sped up slightly and Rufus attempted to keep up with Jonas while the other two bounced around and came along as best they could.

The creek bed narrowed as it climbed into a stand of trees reaching like gnarled arms on both sides of the creek bed. Suddenly, Rufus, in Bob's Land Rover, who forgot the canoe racks stuck out at least an extra foot on either side, slammed into and hung the racks on a tree, twisting the rack into an unrecognizable shape which forced Rufus to jam on his brakes. Shit, shit, shit he thought, Bob is going to kill me. A quick examination of the Discovery showed that the metal roof was not ripped but the racks were beyond hope. The other two trucks caught up with Rufus as he backed into the creek bed and readjusted to follow Jonas again. The tail lights of Jonas' truck were barely visible up ahead and the boulders in the creek were so large Rufus was forced to stop. Even the Land Rover didn't have adequate clearance. Rufus figured it was one thing to knock off a roof rack, and something entirely different to knock off Bob's transmission and strand his vehicle in a soon to be raging river bed. Rufus, Yogi and the other Scout dad jumped out of their vehicles and started running up the creek bed after Jonas.

They didn't have far to go because around the next bend even Jonas was stopped by a boulder as big as a house. He was climbing out of his truck as the other three men ran to him.

"Come on," Jonas shouted over the roar of the wind in the canyon, "campground is just ahead." The four men picked their way over the rounded creek rocks that now became slick from the rain until they came to the camping area beside the creek. In fact, two creeks and a river bed converged at that point with the campground to the inside of the convergence. It was easy to see how the campers would be trapped by rising water before they would realize it. When the water rose choking the sinks, or swallets as the geologists called them, the water courses would fill again and become unsafe to cross.

The men stood in the rain at the campground for less than five minutes when the rain became so heavy you couldn't see the edge of the woods. Their coats repelled some but not all of the water and each of the men now felt the chill and the wetness penetrating to the bone. Where were the Scouts?

Rufus began saying, "Shitomighty! Just Shitomighty!" which didn't slow down the rain but perfectly captured and expressed what they were all feeling. Just then the first figure of a small boy carrying a much larger pack on his back emerged from the trail and soon the campground was full of Scouts and their two leaders.

"What are you guys doing here?" One of the adults asked.

"We got to go. Bad weather is coming in and we've got trucks just past that big rock," Jonas yelled over the roar of the wind and water. "Come on. Got to get you out of here."

Even though the boys were chilled and tired from a several mile hike, it was mostly a downhill slog and they had gas left in the tank. As a group they moved back down the creek bed to the four wheel drive trucks and loaded gear and boys into the vehicles.

When Bob reached the Land Rover he immediately saw the twisted snaggle-toothed roof metal art that was formerly his rack. He raised his eyebrows at Rufus and thought "you hairy peckerwood" and just shook his head. Not much sense in arguing about it now. With everyone loaded the drivers maneuvered in the creek bed and proceeded back the way they had come. The rocks were as slick as gorilla snot now and the river bed began to hold water. Slipping and sliding the trucks took it slow since they were bottoming out on the rocks. Three of the boys climbed into the big Ford with Jonas. He reached over and popped the glove box and out fell a box of Goo-Goo Clusters which he tossed around to each of the kids. Jonas had been a Goo-Goo fan since he was their age listening to the

Grand Ole Opry on WSM radio. "Legend is that "Goo" was an acronym for the Opry," he told the Scouts but the history lesson was lost on the kids who were focused on inhaling the candy.

Back at the Ranger Station all the Scouts reloaded into the other waiting vehicles and headed back for Nashville. Jonas and Yogi walked back into the Ranger Station shaking off as much dampness as possible and listened to the weather alert that still droned from the radio. Both were worried because they knew hikers were still down in the Gulf that night and there was no way to find or help them.

CHAPTER FOUR

It wasn't until they passed through The Stone Door and were halfway down the trail at the foot of the cliff that Jack Mathews remembered he forgot to put the campground they would stay at on his reservation form. Too late now he thought. Jack and his wife, Emily lead a group of eight students from the University Outing Club on an overnight hike into the Savage Gulf Natural Area. The University where Jack served as Dean of the College was perched on the high rim of the south Cumberland Plateau in southeastern Tennessee. The fall semester was underway and since Jack was the faculty sponsor for the Outing Club, he and Emily decided to bring eight freshman on this trip as a plan to jump start the Club for the new academic year. The proximity of this wilderness area and others like it to the University was one of the not to be missed opportunities for the University experience. Jack thought if they could light the fire early, these students would tell their friends, and so on. Normally, a loop trail down into the Gulf and back up through Alum Gap could be hiked in a single long day, but Jack wanted to explore more of the Gulf and to show the students some of the magnificent waterfalls and sinks. Unless the students were from an area with karst geologic rock formation, they would not believe a river would disappear underground and then reappear later in the same stream bed.

But the water features were only one part of the Gulf experience. From the rim, the Gulf appeared as a wash of trees of so many varieties you could not name them all. The Gulf was as wild and diverse as any place in the country abounding as well with most known American mammals. Rumor was that campers reported hearing the call of a wolf and that cougar returned to the area as well. Round black bears were also spotted on a more frequent basis these days. The Outing group met at the campus and were off to an early start from the University placing them on the trail by eight in the morning. From the parking area down a partially paved path, The Stone Door lay a mile distant and was impressive in its own right. Stones seemingly cut or placed like the steps of a giant's palace unfolded and led down into the gorge. From the foot of the Door, the trail down followed a series of switchbacks which deposited the group at midday near Big Creek. Crossing the creek they hiked on up to Ranger Falls and ate lunch. The students were evenly matched as to gender, but it didn't appear to Emily or Jack that any of them really knew each other. One was from Illinois, two from Mississippi, one from Memphis, a couple from Alabama, and two from Texas. As they ate Emily talked to them about Savage Gulf.

"For millions of years the water from the three streams cut into the sandstone formations creating three different gorges that compose Savage Gulf," she said holding her hand out to resemble a bird's foot. "On a map it almost looks like a bird's foot. Gulf is just another word used by locals to mean 'gorge.' The 'Savage' part comes from one of the early settlers to this area who owned this land at one time and not because this area is wild and wooly. More recently, the family who owned the Gulf made a very favorable offer to allow the State of Tennessee, the Nature Conservancy and others to purchase the property. An estate tax fight arose over the potential taxes due when the principal owner died and the Head of the Forestry Department at the University served as an expert witness to contest the extreme value the IRS was trying to put on the land. One of the Savage descendants still leads trips into the Gorge today."

Emily swallowed another bite of her sandwich and continued, "One of the reasons the family wanted the Gulf preserved was to keep it together as it was when immigrants came from Switzerland to this area. You may not have heard about the communities of Gruetli and Laager yet, but a long time ago a promoter convinced a group of Swiss immigrants to come to this area on the representation it was just like their homeland, Switzerland."

"You mean like the Alps?" One of the students asked.

"That's the bill of goods they were sold," Emily said. "Some of those families are still around here."

As Emily continued her story Jack noticed that his Golden Retriever, Rocket, was standing at the edge of the pool beneath Ranger Falls staring intently at the water. That dog is fishing again, Jack thought, and he was correct. Jack's buddy, Deputy Yogi Baker, taught Rocket how to fish on the banks of the Hiwassee River as a pup and she was hooked for life. Rocket knew that if she stood in the water very still fish would approach to see what she tasted like, and thus the game began. Jack looked up and noticed the sky was getting progressively darker and the clouds overhead seemed to be chasing each other across the sky and piling up into dark clusters. Jack explained they should go ahead and get to the campground so everyone stood up, grabbed his or her backpack and they headed off toward the Stagecoach Road Campground which was still miles ahead.

The trail from Ranger Falls led to the Sawmill Campground and then on to Stagecoach Campground. They passed through Sawmill Campground no more than thirty minutes before Yogi and the Ranger picked up the Boy Scouts. Within an hour later they reached their camping area and it began to rain harder. Jack and Emily raised a tarp over the fire pit and everyone pitched their tents facing into the covered area. The last tent was raised just as it began to rain even harder. Sheets of water cascaded off the tarp and tents forcing everyone to the center of the tarp area to stay dry. As darkness approached Jack fired up his backpacker's gas lantern as the students used their camp stoves to heat water for the freeze dried packages of food they packed in for dinner. Even down in the gorge the wind whipped the trees to and fro and the rain came down heavily like buckets of water thrown by titans off the rim of the gorge. They heard Big Creek roaring as it filled with water, but the campsite was high enough they were not threatened by the rising water directly. The problem was that as the river and creeks rose they were cut off from the paths back to the top of the North Rim. The only way out the next morning might be back up the trails to the South Rim which was miles away from where their cars were parked.

Everyone bedded down early to the continuing hammering of the rain, the roaring of the river and the high wind whistling through the tree tops in a constant drone like that of a giant electric fan about to throw a bearing. Sometime that night, Jack felt a low muffled growl coming from Rocket as she lifted her head from her position snuggled in between him and Emily. A clump of hair stood out from between and just below her shoulders signaling she was not happy about something. Most of the time when Rocket's hackles were raised she had simply heard something strange, something out of the ordinary not encountered in her normal daily routine. This growl was deep and more of a warning than a call out. Somewhere in the night a branch snapped and so did

Rocket. Suddenly, she was standing up barking as loud as possible waking up all the campers.

"Easy girl," Jack said petting her head and massaging her shoulders. "It's ok. Nothing to worry about." Rocket wasn't calmed at all. She stood facing the door, tensed and her barking echoing into the darkness. Jack and Emily were both wide awake and they heard the students talking.

Somebody said, "Tell that dog to shut up."

Jack heard the tent fly unzip on one of the tents as someone opened their door to look out. The interior of a couple of the tents glowed as flashlights came on. Then Jack heard a scream and now he was pulling on pants, his shoes and a jacket. His own flashlight was in a pocket sewn into the tent at the end by the door.

"Emily, hold Rocket for a second," he said.

Jack crawled through the tent flap and zipped it back up so Rocket couldn't follow. Although the rain stopped, big drops fell off the trees and in the distance Jack heard the river, interrupted by the sound of something crashing in the woods.

"Are you ok?" he asked the girl whose scream alarmed everyone. "Did you see something?"

The student was crying in her tent. "I saw eyes,"

she said. "Big, orange eyes."

"Where?" Jack asked as he flashed his light around the perimeter.

"Out there in the trees," she cried.

Jack walked to the edge of the tents and swept his light moving side to side. "There's nothing out there now. Everybody go back to sleep."

As he crawled back in to his tent, Jack knew Rocket was still not happy and her hackles were still in full display.

"What do you think?" Emily asked.

Now back in his sleeping bag, Jack said, "It was probably just a deer or something. You know Rocket can hear a mouse fart."

Rocket snuggled back into place but the growl continued for a while. She knew what she knew, and her instincts told her something was out there and it was dangerous. Neither Rocket nor Jack could fall back to sleep so they lay there just listening for the next hour until it was 5 am and time to rise. What little firewood Jack gathered upon their arrival at the camp site was mostly dry and laying near the fire pit. Within minutes he had the fire popping and crackling as the rest of the campers climbed out of their tents, stretched and went off to the brush for an early morning pee.

Once the sun was up Jack realized they would never be able to dry the tents or other gear in these conditions, so the best they could do was to shake off the loose water and pack it up for the hike out. Emily left for her personal time in the bush when she called out to Jack,

"Jack, you better come see this. I'm serious."

The tone of her voice sounded serious enough, so Jack walked over to where her voice came from.

"Stop!" Emily said. "Not another step. Look down." Jack stopped and looked down to where she was pointing. In the wet mud before the campground changed into scrub brush and then the forest began was a huge print easily eight inches wide of an animal that looked like a large cat. He went down on one knee for a closer look and pulled out his cell phone. He tried to measure the print by holding his own hand over it and took multiple photographs with his phone.

"I would say from the position of the print the animal was standing looking at the tents," Jack said.

Emily agreed, and said, "There's more prints over here leading back into the woods." Jack rose and following Emily's directions as the prints turned and then moved off.

"This must be what the girl saw," Jack said, thinking, this was one huge cat. Rocket sniffed furiously at the tracks but her tail was not wagging. When everyone was packed up, single file they proceeded up the South Rim trail, constantly climbing over the rocky terrain switching back and forth as the trail made the long climb out of the gorge. Emily continued looking around as they climbed higher because her instincts kept flashing warning signs.

"Jack," Emily said, "Something's watching us." She stopped and was scanning up the rock bluffs and down into the forest.

Now having caught up with her, Jack asked, "Did you see something?"

"No. It's just a feeling. Like we are being hunted," Emily said.

"Let's just get out of here," Jack said and took the lead.

About a third of the way up, Jack looked ahead to a disturbance of black vultures and the body of a slaughtered deer. Flies buzzed around the carrion as soon as the buzzards moved off. The deer's entire stomach and groin area were torn out. Since the carcass was in the middle of the trail there was no way to avoid it. Emily looked at Jack and just arched her eyebrows. They kept moving in silence as Rocket continued her investigation around the carcass. Everyone was unsettled, eyes darting left and right for whatever might be out there. The group was silent or spoke in muffled whispers. Jack heard a couple of the students say "Holy shit." Climbing out was much more challenging than the hike down into the Gulf. By the time they reached the South Rim Ranger Station everyone was bushed.

Jack's Outing Group dropped their backpacks outside the Ranger Station and came inside where it was warmer, completely filling the small office. Jack introduced himself to Ranger Tommy Yager and talked him into driving him and one of the students back around to the North Rim where they could get their cars. Emily stayed with the remaining students. On the way over Jack said,

"We found some awfully big animal tracks in the gorge this morning."

The Ranger just looked over at him and said, "How big?"

"Bigger than my hand," Jack offered, extending his hand and demonstrating.

"We've got someone missing down there. Maybe more," Ranger Yager said.

"Who is it?" Jack asked.

"Student from over at the University. Two of them went in, but only one has come out. Neither of them registered like they were supposed to," the Ranger said. "The kid who came out said they got separated in the storm and he couldn't find his friend."

"Have you got a name?" Jack asked.

"Callicott, or something like that," said the Ranger.

Oh crap, Jack thought. President Callicott had a nephew enrolled at the University. When they reached the North Rim Ranger Station, Jack saw that Yogi's department vehicle was in the parking lot.

As Jack stepped into the Ranger Station, Yogi turned and put a big bear hug on him. Yogi was several inches taller than Jack and with longer arms he was able to wrap Jack like a straight-jacket.

"Thank God you guys are out of there," he said letting Jack loose from the hug.

"That water came up fast, so we could not come back up through The Stone Door. There was no way we could get across the creeks," Jack said. Then he continued, "Last night one of our campers thought she saw something in the woods, and this morning Emily found a huge paw print of something that looks like a big cat. Let me show you." Jack went to the photo gallery on his cell phone and showed Yogi the prints he photographed.

Staring at the pictures, a cloud came over Yogi's face and he said, "You don't know the half of it. Last night two local truckers were killed on Highway 56 just outside the gorge. Their necks were slashed and something tore the guts out of one of the men. I was afraid we might be dealing with some kind of beast that escaped into Savage Gulf. Looks like I may be right."

Jack filled Yogi in on Emily's concern about being watched and the deer they found killed on the trail. "On the way over here the Deputy told me there was a missing student and perhaps others still in the gorge."

Yogi said, "I am waiting on backup now. We have one missing student and a group from the Friends of the Gorge organization that were also hiking through yesterday. They have not reported in either."

"Do I need to email you these pictures?" Jack asked.

"Please. Ranger Rodgers has been in contact with Tennessee Wildlife Resources Agency and the U.S. Fish and Wildlife Service. Those prints may help us identify what we are dealing with so I will forward them on to those agencies." Yogi paused, and said, "Where's Emily?"

"She's waiting with the other students at the Ranger Station. I need to be getting back over there. Let me know if you find out anything on the Callicott kid," Jack said and headed for his Jeep.

CHAPTER FIVE

Special Agent John Jarrett put in more than twenty years with the U.S. Fish and Wildlife Service and was closing in on his mandatory retirement age. Over his career he received many commendations from the Department of the Interior for his service and skill in apprehending wildlife criminals whether the perpetrators operated a wildlife smuggling ring or were importing products into the country in violation of the Lacey Act, The Rhinoceros and Tiger Conservation Act of 1998, or other federal statutes designed to prevent illegal trafficking in endangered species. He especially enjoyed apprehending smugglers who traded in animal parts used as aphrodisiacs. To him, they were the dregs and deserved an old fashioned ass kicking. Prior to his long service with USFWS he flww helicopters in Viet Nam, and lied about his age just to get into the fight. Although he maintained his flight rating, Jarrett flew little these days. When the call came in from Ranger Jonas Rodgers, an old acquaintance from the Federal Law Enforcement Training School in Georgia, Jarrett's interest was piqued and he responded. After so many years he grew bored with the routineness and never ending pursuit of criminals whose methods were almost predictable. Two dead men, their throats cut, and one disemboweled was not an everyday occurrence, especially in a place as remote as Sequoyah County, Tennessee. Jarrett was presently assigned to the Ranger in Charge Office in Nashville.

The USFWS Agency heard rumors of an illegal animal operation in the remote southeast Tennessee hills but nothing concrete was discovered that justified assigning the manpower or launching an investigation. Since there were only a few hundred special agents covering the entire United States, agents often worked alone and had no backup. The workload was always overwhelming and often dangerous. However, the facts the Ranger reported pointed to more than just a random encounter between humans and wild animals. The photographs of the animal tracks were impressive in comparison to the man's hand in the picture. From the size of the imprints Jarrett did not think this was a mountain lion or a Florida panther who wandered north. Cougars once lived all over the eastern United States and were making a comeback, but there were no reports of such sightings in the Savage Gulf area. A mountain lion had been shot in Kentucky a year or so earlier but this animal could be as much as three times the size of the mountain lion based upon the paw prints.

Pouring over the crime scene report and pictures provided by the Sequoyah County Sheriff's Department Jarrett noted the ferocity of the attack on the humans and the presence of what looked like a large cage. Most big cats attacked from the advantage of surprise and jumped on the back of their prey gripping the victim's neck in their mighty jaws. But this cat, if that's what it was, cut the men's throats then took a bite out of the groin area of one of the men. The fact that the man's genitals were found several feet away led Jarrett to believe this beast was a man-killer, a very rare circumstance in the cat world. The mutilation was a statement and not formed out of hunger. Could it be a tiger of some variety? There were fewer than 5,000 tigers in the world and they were listed as an endangered species. Since their natural habitat was India and Southeast Asia, such an animal would not have come to Tennessee on its own. One of the most interesting facts about tigers, Jarrett recalled, was how large their brain was. It compared to the larger primates making these animals fierce hunters and adept at avoiding capture.

Special Agent Jarrett saw enough in the reports to realize that he needed to get to Savage Gulf and as quickly as possible. The Rangers and local law enforcement had no idea what kind of adversary awaited them in that remote country. Jarrett packed his SUV to be away for a few days and loaded whatever specialized gear he thought might be needed as he drove east on Interstate 24..

By 1pm Jarrett arrived at the North Rim Ranger Station overlooking the wilderness area where three Rangers and an equal number of local Deputies were waiting for him sitting around a picnic table outside the Ranger Station finishing lunch. It was warm day in early fall on the Cumberland Plateau, the storm having blown through leaving a robin-egg blue sky overhead where hawks patrolled on high thermals. Jonas Rodgers introduced Jarrett to Stephen Slydell, Tommy Yager, Andrew Sparks, Yogi Baker and Aaron Burns. After they shook hands all around, Jonas suggested they move inside the Ranger Station. The Fish and Wildlife Officer, Jarrett, began by summing up what he learned from the file materials and photographs.

After the summation, he asked, "Deputy Baker, I understand you were first on the scene night before last?"

"Yes, sir," Yogi said deferentially to the older and more experienced officer. Jarrett was slender but tough and stringy from years of outdoor work. Yogi was taller, and also lean. It occurred to Yogi that he would physically resemble Agent Jarrett in a few years.

"Does your department have any unsolved crimes presenting the same or a similar M.O.?" the Special Agent asked. A similar modus operandi often linked crimes together.

"Nothing like this," Yogi said. While he saw some weird shit in the last few years, this was off the scale. Yogi's worked files included cases where a jealous spouse hacked off body parts or left scars while her philandering husband slept, but the scale of savagery he found on the side of the road the night before was unusual.

"Then we may be correct in assuming this killer struck for the first time on that night and at the place you investigated, rather than as a serial killer who might leave a linked trail." Jarrett said. "If we start there, the cage is a strong indication that whatever was in that cage inflicted the injuries." Jarrett passed around some of the crime scene photos taken that night. "The mutilation of the white victim was a savage display. Whatever was in that cage was angry enough to kill and make a statement about his ferocity. That is not typical animal behavior."

Although Jarrett's voice was not quite as deep and melodic as Jonas's, his Adam's Apple bobbed as he spoke and commanded the attention of all the Rangers and Deputies who intently followed his every word. The gray at his temples combined with his known reputation, made him an authority worth listening to.

"While the killer could have been a man, the presence of the print and the slaughtered deer in the gorge the hikers found, make me think we are dealing with a big cat," Jarrett said. "If this is in the feline family, it is huge and dangerous."

Jarrett looked at Yogi and asked, "What do we know about the drivers or who they were working for?"

Yogi answered, "Just a couple of local boys. They did odd jobs for a lot of folks. I spoke with the Black victim's wife who said they occasionally picked up packages at the local airport on the Mountain and delivered them for people."

"We need to find out more about that. If that animal is an exotic cat, I'll bet he wasn't being imported or transported legally. Any of you guys know anyone in the area that has any exotic animals?" asked Jarrett.

Deputy Sparks said, "Only the guy who has all those funny looking cows?"

"Funny looking how?" Jarrett asked.

"Those black cows with the big white stripe around the middle," Sparks answered.

Jarrett looked over at Jonas with a question in his eyes. "He means the Belted Galloway cattle," Jonas said. "They don't look like anything else around here."

"Right," Jarrett said. "But, that's not what I mean. Anybody who keeps exotic birds or big animals is what I would be interested in." The others around the table just shook their heads.

"I'm planning to go back and visit with Lola Crockett this afternoon," Yogi said.

"Good. I'll be glad to go with you if you wish," Jarrett said.

"Fine with me," Yogi said.

Jarett looked past Yogi to the three dimensional topo map of the area that was displayed on the far wall. He stood and walked back to the map tracing a deep indention.

"Is something the matter?" Jonas asked as he rose and walked over to the map with him.

"We're here," Jarrett said pointing. "And what do you call this area?" Jarrett asked.

"That's the Sequatchie Valley. The headwaters of the Sequatchie River originate from a cave in an area known as Grassy Cove. When the water comes out the other side of the mountain, it forms the River and flows south towards the Tennessee River," Jonas said.

"That's a huge watershed," Jarrett said still studying the map and continued, "but I don't see many towns on this map. Pretty remote and agricultural?"

"Yep," the Ranger said.

"We had better hope we catch or contain that animal in Savage Gulf because if it escapes into that Valley it may never be caught," Jarrett said. He was clearly concerned that a man-killing predator could do a lot of damage in a remotely populated area. Jarrett asked about hikers and campers who had gone into the Gorge, and those who might still be down there. Jonas explained about the group from the Friends of the Gorge and the missing student, who was a top priority.

Jarrett said, "Jonas, we are going to need to go in after that missing student. I suggest one party go in the north side and another from the south side. Each team ought to have about four members. How much manpower have you got?"

Jonas looked at Yogi and asked, "Yogi can we count on three of you from the Sheriff's office?"

"Yes," Yogi answered, "the Sheriff has committed the three of us to this project."

"Ok," the Ranger said, "and I can commit three Rangers. I'll need the rest just to keep anyone else out of there. With you," he said to the USFWS Officer, "we are still one man short."

Yogi added, "I have a friend at the Tennessee Bureau of Investigation who helped us with a drug situation over a year ago. I may be able to get him here from Nashville."

"Good, that would be a help," Jarrett said. "This is probably going to mean spending a night down in that gorge so everybody come prepared. That also means scoped rifles. I have a couple of tranquilizer guns for each team which I will show you how to use. Our first priority will be to find anyone who's still in there, and secondly to apprehend that animal. I suggest we meet back here at first light in the morning." Everyone agreed as the meeting broke up. Jarrett watched as the young men left. They had no idea what they were up against. He wanted to hang around and discuss what was really bothering him with the old Ranger, but he needed to catch up with Deputy Baker and interview that woman.

CHAPTER SIX

Agent Jarrett followed Yogi off the Plateau and down Highway 56 back towards Northwoods and the area the Deputy called "Hard Bargain". Once again Yogi pulled up in front of the Crockett's modest home but this time Lola's two kids were playing in the front yard and she sat on the concrete porch steps smoking a cigarette. Yogi got out of his Department vehicle and waited until Agent Jarrett joined him. Together they strode toward the house as the kids stopped what they were doing and stared.

"Afternoon, Lola," Yogi said taking off his cap. Lola eyed him up and down and then looked over Agent Jarrett.

"What you need this time, Deputy?" she asked.

"Lola, this is Special Agent Jarrett of the U.S. Fish and Wildlife Service. We need to ask you a couple of follow up questions," Yogi explained.

Not thrilled with the additional interrogation, nonetheless she said,

"All right. Y'all come on in. Lucy, Tyrell you all come on inside now." The well-behaved kids rushed to the front door and inside, their eyes still wide at the sight of a police officer at their house. Seeing officers at other houses in Hard Bargain was not all that unusual considering there were few jobs, and idle men and teenagers often got into trouble. The officers took a seat in a couple of chairs and Lola went to the sofa.

"We are trying to finish up our investigation and need to ask you if Buster ever delivered any exotic animals for anybody?" Yogi asked.

"What do you mean by exotic?" Lola asked suspiciously.

Agent Jarrett spoke up, "You know, like animals that were coming in here from Africa or South America or some far off place. Animals you wouldn't find around these parts. Maybe some animals like you would see in a zoo, or brightly colored parrots."

Lola paused like she was thinking trying to recollect if her husband ever mentioned anything "exotic." From the kitchen area of her house a sound floated out that was throaty and gravely and clearly two similar but different voices were engaged.

"You kids stop that," Lola hollered.

"We ain't doing nothing Momma," came the response, yet the throaty call persisted. It was strange almost as if the two voices were struggling to speak to each other. As an experienced wildlife officer, Jarrett knew what he was hearing the instant it began.

"Do you mind if I see your birds, Mrs.

Crockett?" Jarrett asked, standing and not waiting for a reply. Before Lola could react, Jarrett crossed the small space leading into the kitchen area and said "Well, well."

Yogi and then Lola followed him into the small room. Jarrett stood before a large antique white metal cage that stood in one corner, its top coming to a graceful peak reminiscent of a Victorian cage that would adorn a fine parlor. Inside were perched two beautiful deep blue parrots still chattering to each other and wiping their beaks on the wooden branch.

"This Mrs. Crockett, is what I would call exotic," Jarrett said as he pointed at the blue birds with the yellow stripes around their eyes and beaks. "Deputy, these little jewels are Hyacinth Macaws, and they are not from around here, not even close. These birds live only in central South America. Each bird could be worth, say ten thousand dollars." Jarrett thought that would have approximated the value of Lola's entire house.

Yogi walked up to the cage where the display of color was unlike anything he had ever seen. The birds were such an iridescent blue Yogi wasn't sure they were real. More chatter demonstrated they were in fact alive. Lola held back, not knowing how to explain that Buster gave her those birds as an anniversary present.

"Mrs. Crockett, there is no way Buster could have bought those birds legally. What did he do? Tell somebody they escaped or died?" Jarrett asked. When Lola did not immediately respond, he said "Perhaps we should go back into the living room."

Lola was now at a loss for words but she led them back to the other room.

"Let's start over, Lola," Yogi said. "Buster and the other guy were transporting some exotic animals, weren't they?"

She looked up at the Deputy and nodded. Her hands were clenched tight in her lap.

"Mrs. Crockett, it is illegal to bring those rare birds into this country. The climate and food are not right for them. It is very unlikely they will survive. You know that don't you?" Officer Jarrett asked.

"But, they are so pretty, and Buster gave them to me for our anniversary," Lola pleaded. She loved those birds and the fact they reminded her of Buster.

"If you help us, I will find a way to help you," Jarrett said encouraging her. Lola raised her eyes and nodded. Something in the old Ranger's voice gave her the comfort he was honest and spoke the truth.

"Did Buster ever talk about what they were carrying, or who they were carrying them for?" Jarrett asked.

"He talked some about special packages that were birds, or monkeys or even cats," Lola said.

"Where did they get these special things?" Yogi asked.

Lola said, "Up at the airport. They always seemed to come in late at night when everything else was shut down." Yogi looked at Jarrett and then asked her,

"Do you know where they were taking these animals, Lola?"

She said, "All I know'd was he took some of them to Pierce's Farm. I ax'd him about it but he said he couldn't tell nobody. You're not gonna take my birds are you?" Tears started to well up in Lola's eyes and her lip trembled. Jarrett saw how attached she was to those birds, and however she had come to possess them, he knew she would be a good mother to them just like these two kids who now faced life with no father.

Jarrett spoke up, "You take care of those birds. I will get some information to you to help you know how to raise them and keep them well." Lola seemed relieved, but not completely certain she could trust the officers. She nodded and wiped her eyes.

Yogi and Jarrett stood up with the knowledge that they caught a lucky break and that the next link in the chain led on to Pierce's Farm and those Belted Galloways.

CHAPTER SEVEN

Yogi and Jarrett left Jarrett's official USFWS vehicle at the Sheriff's Department and rode together out to Pierce's Farm which occupied several hundred acres abutting the South Cumberland State Recreational Area. As the Collins River flowed out of Savage Gulf the terrain flattened creating pasture land and a much less rugged area. Jarrett saw that this route also provide a way out of the Gorge he did not anticipate. Yogi filled Jarrett in on what little he knew about Richard Pierce, who was somewhat of a mystery in Sequoyah County. It was rumored he was descended from some of the early Swiss inhabitants of the area, ran a prosperous business which he sold and then moved back to the county in the last five years to take up cattle ranching. The spectacle of the Belted Galloways set all the Co-op folks talking. Some offered that the meat was better than Angus, while others weren't sure if Pierce's Farm knew what they were doing. The field hands were not local and didn't mingle with the local cattlemen. All the locals belonged to the county Cattlemen's Association, but not a single person from Pierce's Farm ever joined the Association or participated in the local livestock shows or auctions or even the FFA events at the high school. Locals thought the Pierce men looked down on them and their dirty Carhartts. Real cattlemen, everyone knew, lived for the shows and the opportunity to display their breeds. Besides, how could you really be in the cattle business if you didn't go to the auctions? Pierce himself was reclusive and didn't associate with any of the county leaders. No one Yogi knew had even seen Pierce. The few locals who provided any goods or services to the Farm said the money was good and that Pierce paid in cash.

In a western style you might find in Texas or Wyoming, the gate to Pierce's Farm was an ornate wooden log structure with the name "Pierce" carved in recess into a chunk of thick wood supported on either side by a row of timbers decreasing in height as they curved away from the large opening. It was impressive, Yogi thought, imagining the crane it took to lift that log in place. Near the left side of the entrance to the ranch Yogi leaned out the window of his Explorer and pushed the buzzer next to the card reader. A husky voice said, "Can I help you?"

Yogi said, "I am Detective Yogi Baker from the Sequoyah County Sheriff's Department and we need to speak with someone about a couple of local guys who drove for this place."

"Which guys?" asked the voice from the speaker.

"Two local boys, Buster Crockett and Larry Glower," Yogi said.

"Never heard of them," the voice said and disconnected.

Yogi looked at Jarrett and said, "Looks like we are going to have to do it the hard way."

"I will get the FBI to do a complete background check on this guy Pierce," Jarrett said as Yogi backed out into the road and instead of turning back toward Northwoods, slowly crept past the entrance and along a very expensive span of wood fencing complimented on its inside facing with angled brackets supporting barbed wire. They could see the gravel road leading into the Farm proceed a few hundred yards before it forked. One branch to the right disappeared into a copse of trees while the other kept going as far as they could see. Yogi heard stories of a massive log home on the property but had never seen it. In the field adjacent to the highway at least one hundred fifty of the Belted cattle roamed and nipped at the grass. Against the backdrop of the high Plateau hills it all looked very pastoral and normal. The fence line went on beside the highway for at least a mile. Jarrett pointed out cameras positioned along the fence line at intervals and continuing until the fence itself turned back into the property and disappeared into a far stand of trees.

"He's got a fortune just in fencing out here," Yogi said.

Jarrett agreed and said, "and it's all electrified and watched by cameras."

"Do you think they're trying to keep something in, or somebody out?" Yogi asked having now stopped his Explorer at the end of the fencing.

"Wouldn't need electric fencing, a fancy wood fence and cameras to keep those cows in," Jarrett said raising a pair of binoculars to his eyes. "Is there any way to access the back of that property?"

"We'll just have to check the topo map back at the office. There's usually logging roads all over these hills," Yogi said.

"Ok, but for now we need to get ready for tomorrow. We have got to find anyone who's still down in the Gulf. I don't want to locate any hiker by the presence of vultures," Jarret said.

Yogi nodded understanding full well what that meant.

Back at the Department Yogi pulled out County topographical maps which Jarrett studied while Yogi called Special Agent Rockford Bradley of the Tennessee Bureau of Investigation. The two officers met at the training academy a few years earlier and S.A. Bradley took charge of the project to capture the drug runners during the Red Dagger events on the Mountain.

"Rockie, how ya doing?" Yogi said when Bradley picked up.

James W. Cameron III

"I am good, you?"

"Looks like we need your help again," Yogi said, then explained about the two murders, and the other incidents in the Savage Gulf area. "We are planning to go down into the gorge tomorrow from both Ranger stations and we could use some manpower."

Since Bradley was always sparking for action he agreed to meet them early the next morning at the Stone Door Ranger Station. While he couldn't bring any more personnel, there was some equipment he thought would be helpful. His awareness that Bradley was "queer for gear" was one of the reasons Yogi called him. Bradley was fond of East Tennessee and hunted down odometer tampering operations in several counties, but he was never been able to nail anyone in Sequoyah County despite constant rumors. Perhaps this was an opportunity to change his luck.

"Pack some food. We'll be spending the night down inside Savage Gulf," Yogi said.

"Roger that," Bradley said and hung up. He twitched with the excitement of a new adventure.

CHAPTER EIGHT

The *Sequoyah County Times* was the only newspaper of general circulation in the county and appeared twice weekly but only as an afternoon edition. Neither Yogi nor Jonas Rodgers was happy to see the headlines and lead story contained in the edition that lay on the desk of the Stone Door Ranger Station when Yogi arrived following the wasted trip to Pierce's Farm. The headline read:

Two Local Drivers Viciously Killed on Highway Outside Savage Gulf

"<u>Beersheba Springs, Tennessee</u>. Local authorities have confirmed the murder and mutilation of two local men last evening on Highway 56 outside the Savage Gulf area. Deputy Yogi Baker was first on the scene, and his preliminary report reviewed by this reporter indicates the cause of death was a laceration to the throat followed by the disembowelment of one of the victims. Names have been withheld and were not available at the time this story went to press. The official report does not speculate as to any motive, but implies a large animal may have been involved and may still be on the loose in the area. The *Times* will update this report as new information becomes available. In the meantime, the Sheriff's Department has asked all in the area to be on the lookout and to report any unusual sightings or activity."

"Well, shiiiit," Jonas said turning a four letter word into multiple syllables with his gravely baritone.

How in the hell had the paper latched onto that story so quickly? Yogi wondered. Getting the public all riled up would not assist in their investigation at all. As Yogi finished reading the article and looking for anything else in the paper that was noteworthy, his cell phone buzzed. The display said the caller was his friend, Jack Mathews.

"Yogi, are you guys planning to go back into the gorge tomorrow?" Jack asked.

"Yep. We need to find anyone still in there and get them out," Yogi replied.

"I need to go with you. That student is President Callicott's nephew and he has asked me to get personally involved, if that's ok with you," Jack said.

"Ok by me. We will spend the night down in there unless we get lucky and find them all right away," Yogi said.

"I understand. What time and where do we meet?" Jack asked.

"8am at the Stone Door Ranger Station. Is Emily coming?" Yogi asked, knowing Jack's wife was an experienced backpacker and hiker in the Gorge.

"Not sure. It's not been one of her better days. I will just play it by ear and see what tomorrow brings. See you in the morning," Jack said and hung up. Jack's wife, Emily, was still suffering the long term effects of post-traumatic stress brought on by shooting someone in Jack's house a year ago. Yogi said goodbye to Jonas and headed back towards Northwoods. It was now late afternoon but he needed to speak with the Sheriff and probably the County Attorney about a search warrant for Pierce's Farm. Jarrett went off to find a hotel room for the night and planned to meet him back at the Sheriff's Office later.

The tires of Yogi's Explorer crunched on the small gravel of the parking lot behind the Sheriff's Department as he pulled into his designated parking area. Boy, was he tired as he reflected back on all that had happened in the past 24 hours. The USFWS vehicle was in the lot indicating Jarret already found a hotel room and was waiting. Inside Headquarters Yogi found Jarrett reading email on his cell phone and Sheriff Mark Brown in his office. Yogi called the Sheriff "Cap" an abbreviation for "Captain" which was the Police Department rank in Chattanooga the Sheriff held before he retired and moved back to

Sequoyah County.

"Cap, we got the door slammed in our face at Pierce's Farm when we tried to ask about those drivers. I think we are going to need a search warrant and perhaps an order to bring in a couple of people out there for questioning," Yogi said.

"That won't be necessary, Deputy," the Sheriff said.

"I guess I don't understand," Yogi said. "We have cause to believe those two victims were working on a transport for Pierce's Farm last night when they were killed. There may be material witnesses at that place." While Pierce did not mingle in the community he was known to have made sizeable contributions to the local political campaigns including the campaign that got Sheriff Brown elected. Yogi thought he smelled a rat.

"Pierce has already called and will cooperate by talking with you tonight," the Sheriff said. "You have an appointment at 6:30 this evening."

"What caused the change of heart?" Yogi asked.

"Don't know, but you've just got enough time to get there if you leave now," said the Sheriff looking at his watch. Yogi nodded, turned and walked out of Sheriff Brown's office. In the waiting area he updated

Jarrett and the two of them pulled out of Northwoods in Yogi's SUV heading back out to Pierce's Farm. Jarrett was skeptical that it was a coincidence they had been denied entry but were now welcome guests at Pierce's Farm.

"Is your Sheriff clean?" he asked Yogi.

"Don't know," Yogi responded.

The gate to Pierce's Farm was still closed but Yogi saw a dark Hummer idling in the drive on the closed side of the fence. He punched the speaker button and a voice said,

"Deputy, please follow the Hummer up to the house. Mr. Pierce is expecting you." As the gate swung open Yogi passed through. The Hummer pulled away and Yogi followed. The oversized tires threw the fine gravel up against the inside of the wheel wells of his Explorer in a clatter. As expected the Hummer veered left at the split in the road. A half-mile and the road crept up into the trees to a magnificent log structure as big as an entire lodge. Yogi thought he was on the set of an HGTV special featuring vacation homes of the rich and famous. The post and beam construction reached at least three stories. Wide stone steps led up to the double wooden front door into which was carved a scene of an Elk standing proud in a mountain setting. As Yogi and Jarret got out of the Explorer, all four doors of the Hummer opened and fit young men all wearing black t-shirts and jeans exited. Each of these men were armed with semi-automatic weapons holstered on their hip. This group of six moved to the front door which was opened by another man dressed exactly like the other four, almost as if they were each in uniform. Something about these men disturbed Yogi and his senses were telling him something about this picture was wrong. Muscles bulged under tight t-shirts all around Yogi and Jarrett as they entered the foyer with its Elk-antler chandelier.

To the right past a large opening was a trophy room containing stuffed big game from all over the world. The centerpiece was an eight foot tall polar bear standing in attack mode with teeth bared as if it were protecting the other creatures as unfortunate as it was. It troubled Jarrett's heart to see all these beautiful but dead creatures on display representing many endangered species. He wondered what kind of man needed to prove his masculinity by killing another beautiful animal. One of the black attired men asked Yogi and Jarrett to follow him through the trophy room into a large study with paneled walls and artwork only seen in galleries in Santa Fe and Jackson Hole. Paintings depicting mountain scenes of trappers and Indians adorned the walls. The owner of this lodge obviously felt he was born in the wrong century and longed to test his skills as a true mountain man. Jarrett bristled at the idea and was prepared to take on this pseudo-cowboy if necessary.

Another well-muscled man in his fifties approached them with his hand out.

"Hello, I'm Dick Pierce," he said. The veins in his neck and on his arms were well exposed and his grip would have rivalled that of the polar bear. Pierce was dressed like a male model in *Cowboys & Indians* magazine. From the King's Ranch western shirt with its pearl snap closures, to the exquisite jeans held up by a large silver Vogt buckle to his Lucchese caiman boots, he look the part of a wealthy rancher. As much as he longed for it, he was not Ben Cartwright. Yogi couldn't tell if this man was all saddle and no horse, or ten gallons of bullshit. Something hung on a gold chain around his neck. It looked like a large claw or fang. The large man before him reminded Yogi of the actor, Jack Palance, in the way he smiled in an evil sort of way, more of a sneer than a smile. Part of you wanted to like this smiling man, but beneath the surface and behind the grin Yogi sensed a wild animal and viciousness.

Taking the man's hand deep into his palm so his fingers would not be crushed, Yogi said, "I'm Deputy Baker of the Sequoyah County Sheriff's Department and this is Agent John Jarrett of the Fish and Wildlife Service."

With the identification of Jarrett as an agent

with USFWS Pierce turned all his attention to Jarrett and extended his hand a second time. Jarrett met his broad smile coldly since he was still unnerved by the trophy room.

"Come, have a seat. How can I help you boys," Pierce said.

"Mr. Pierce, we are investigating the murder last night of two local men whom we think were driving for you," Yogi began.

"Murder? You must be kidding. I understand murder is rare in this area and that the major cause is hunting accidents," Pierce said.

"No, these men were murdered all right. Each man had his throat cut and one of the men had been disemboweled," Yogi said. Pierce did not seem at all disturbed by the violence. As a big game hunter he believed the game was kill or be killed.

"Let me ask you again, how can I help in your investigation?" Pierce asked.

"We have reliable information these men drove for you, and the truck they were using was registered to Pierce Farms, LLC," Yogi said. He looked over at Jarrett who had not yet uttered a word.

"What were their names?" asked Pierce.

"Buster Crockett and Larry Glower," Yogi

said.

"I remember those boys, but they haven't done anything for me in quite some time. You say the truck was registered to the Farm?" Pierce asked.

"The last registration for a 1985 Ford Panel Truck was to Pierce Farms, LLC," Yogi said.

"I believe we reported that truck stolen a few months back. Perhaps that's why I haven't heard from those boys," Pierce offered.

Jarrett, believing Pierce was lying to them, decided to take a harder line. Fuck the polite talk. He leaned forward and said, "Mr. Pierce, let's cut to the chase. We believe those local men were driving for you transporting illegal exotic animals. If we confirm that we will be back, you can count on it. Now we are faced with a potential dangerous animal loose in Savage Gulf. If you know anything about that you need to tell us. Whatever that animal does will be on your head."

Pierce stared over at Jarrett, clenching his jaw muscles that throbbed like writhing snakes and said, "Those are strong words, Agent. If you can prove what you say then have at it. If not, and for your own good, I suggest you mind your own business." Pierce stood, the smile now having completely vanished, and said,

"Gentlemen, this interview is over. Sorry I couldn't be of more assistance." One of the earlier black clad men re-entered the study.

"Please show our guests out if you would David," Pierce said and left the study via a door on the right wall.

Yogi and Jarrett were escorted back to the double front door. From this direction Yogi could see that if they had turned left upon entering the lodge they would have walked into a large living space anchored by a forty foot tall stone fireplace in which a couple of logs easily three feet long were burning. More Elk antler chandeliers illuminated the room in a warm and western way. This whole place just didn't fit in Sequoyah County, Yogi thought.

Back outside Yogi started to speak but Jarrett put his finger to his lips suggesting they talk after they were off the premises. This time the Hummer was nowhere to be seen. As Yogi pulled down the gravel drive toward the highway he once again started to say something, and once again Jarrett told him to remain quiet. Jarrett took a pad from his pocket and wrote "BUGS" on the sheet and showed it to Yogi who nodded and drove off in silence.

CHAPTER NINE

Jack Mathews was learning that a successful marriage took a lot of work. He imagined it like a chunk of fine wood from which could emerge an exquisite work of art but only if painstaking care was taken to carve away the unnecessary rough edges and you polished the grain carefully and with smooth even strokes. Naively, prior to his marriage to Emily he never considered the level of emotional commitment involved in loving one person the rest of your life to the exclusion of all others. Out of a field of flowers you got to choose only one. With all his heart he loved Emily and worked to assist her recovery from the mental injury she suffered after shooting Dr. Julian Browne in his living room the prior year when he was embroiled in representing the Cherokee Nation. Fragility still haunted Emily following the events of that day and there were times Jack couldn't reach her. He could not find the right words to say or the finesse to touch her in some way to bring her out of that distant place to which she retreated. The odd thing was that in that condition, Emily still painted at an astonishing pace creating gallery ready paintings as her creative energy exploded into light and color onto her canvas. She just couldn't interact with Jack, or as far as he knew, anyone else when she slipped into that nether world. Jack still held himself responsible for Emily's hospitalization when he was involved in the Cherokee litigation. He was absent in court at the precise moment she needed him most, and for Jack not being there was unforgiveable. On account of that, he did not accept Calvin Greathouse's offer to join him in the private law practice where even more of his time away from Emily would be demanded.

When depression came over Emily, she did not want to be alone and feared if Jack was absent. Unfortunately, the disappearance of President Callicott's nephew now forced Jack to join the search party and to leave Emily alone for at least a day, maybe two. He decided to leave his Golden Retriever, Rocket, with her rather than take his dog back into the Gorge, even though Rocket was an alert tracker and Jack could rely on her as an early warning signal if danger was near.

Emily stared blankly at the television when Jack arrived home from the University. He went over to the sofa and took her hands in his. As gently as was possible he broke the news to her that he needed to go back to Savage Gulf.

"Emily, I am going to have to go back to Savage Gulf tomorrow with Yogi and the Rangers to help find President Callicott's nephew. OK?"

She looked at him as if not comprehending what he was saying. "Emily, do you understand? I have to be away tomorrow and probably tomorrow night, but I will be back the next day. Rocket is going to stay here with you. You will be okay, and I will be back," Jack said.

When Emily looked as if she might cry, Jack took her in his arms and just held her rocking gently as if holding a child. They sat like that for some time, then Jack said, "I will have Rachel check on you, ok?"

Emily nodded. "Hungry?" Jack asked. When she nodded again, Jack went into the kitchen and fixed a broccoli and chicken stir fry. During dinner Emily became more conversational, more herself. These episodes of her depression passed more quickly now and Jack felt she would be through this fog within a short time. He hoped that soon it would all be behind them. Yet, in his mind, he was still choosing a promise to someone else, President Callicott, rather than what he owed his own wife. He would have to atone for this. After dinner he sat holding her for a while longer as they listened to the Bose machine sliding from one Andrea Bocelli song to the next until they went to bed. Jack hadn't even packed for the trip. He would worry about that in the morning.

CHAPTER TEN

After concluding the meeting with the two law enforcement officers, Richard Pierce left the study and entered a second and more private library. It was in this room that he conducted his primary operations. Two flat screen monitors on either side of the large carved oak desk watched the grounds with split screen displays as the default settings. Each screen split into four sections in real time. Although the oak book shelves held many volumes, none of the books in the library were read except for the travel and big game collection. From the desk Pierce switched cameras around his Farm and saw within a few seconds the entire grounds. Sometimes at night he would spend hours sipping single barrel scotch and just watching the screens. On the right side monitor the camera panned over the front of a low concrete block building with a two story attached warehouse. Both the building and the warehouse looking structure were painted in camouflage colors and from the air would appear almost invisible. The left side monitor displayed the front of a large cattle barn in one panel, the rear of the barn in a second panel, and shots of the inside where Pierce saw some of his hands tending to a few of the cattle in the third and fourth panels. With a flick he was able to change the view to many other perspectives around the property.

One click of the mouse then a password and

immediately he was into his scheduling software where he checked to confirm the next shipment was due to arrive that evening at the airport on the Mountain. The loss of the two drivers meant he would dispatch a couple of his regular hands for the receipt of the merchandise. Not willing to risk another incident Pierce decided he would also be present when the cargo was handed over. Picking up his cell phone he called David Ramparts, his chief of staff, to meet him in the study. David walking into the room when Pierce stepped out of the library closing the door behind him with a click as the magnetic locks engaged.

"What's up boss?" David asked.

"Did you get the bugs planted in the Deputy's vehicle?" Pierce asked.

"Yes, plus one GPS device," David responded. Pierce nodded.

"Our merchandise is apparently loose in the Savage Gulf area and we need to find or neutralize it. That one animal is worth at least one hundred thousand dollars and possibly more," Pierce noted, and then continued, "those two locals you were using got themselves killed and now the Sheriff's Office is making inquiries."

"I thought you had an understanding with the

Sheriff," David said.

"I do, but there is little he can do with the federal Fish and Wildlife officer involved. The Sheriff will keep us posted, but it's up to us to get this back under control. I want you to get into that wilderness area at first light tomorrow with two of your best men. Tranquilize that thing and bring it back here. If you cannot get close enough for the tranquilizer, then kill it and bury the body. It may have already killed two men which may be enough to get other law enforcement engaged. We came here to stay out of the public eye. If that thing is traced back to this farm, we're all in trouble," Pierce said.

"Yes, sir. What if we encounter the other law enforcement or a bunch of Rangers?" David asked.

"Do what you have to do, but do not let them see or identify you," Pierce said.

"OK," David said now considering which of his men he would bring with him.

"And, David," Pierce said, "have the pilot get the helicopter ready. I need to meet the next delivery. I will need two of your men and a truck at the airport by 10 pm."

When David left, Pierce went to his quarters where he put on his shoulder holster for the 9mm Glock he carried and threw on a leather jacket to conceal the weapon. Outside his Sikorsky S-76C warmed up. This thirteen million dollar aircraft was as sleek and plush as any private helicopter could be cruising at 178 miles per hour with a range of 473 miles. If things got too hot this helicopter was his back-up plan and ticket out of the sticks.

Animal trafficking was only the latest of Pierce's business ventures and came to him naturally since, as a big game hunter, he pursued these animals all over the world. Native guides and greedy businessmen were only too willing to cooperate for what Pierce considered to be peanuts. On the other end the demand seemed endless. Millionaires all over North America eagerly paid full retail for these animals as a symbol of their new found wealth. No one considered what they were doing to the animals or to the native habitat when an essential element was systematically removed. Whenever law enforcement got too close, Pierce merely transitioned into a new person in a new remote location. He morphed how many times now? Four? Five? Now there was a new concern: What would happen to the receiving habitat if one of the displaced animals escaped? And, what if that animal was an alpha predator like the Bengal Tiger? Could he find a place remote enough to hide from the damage such a beast could inflict? Part of him wanted to tell his pilot to forget the little airstrip on top of this plateau and keep on going, but he didn't.

CHAPTER ELEVEN

The sun was not yet above the eastern rim of Savage Gulf when Jonas, the Ranger in charge of the area put on a second pot of coffee, having dumped the first one into a large dispenser to keep it hot for the men who would be arriving soon. Jonas liked being the first one to the Ranger Station in the morning and the last to leave in the evening. It was a habit he picked up along the way of becoming a grizzled and veteran wildlife agent. When the youngsters could beat him into work, or outwork or outlast him, he would be ready to retire. So far, his current crew showed no such initiative, satisfied to follow his example with respect. The one good thing about his young crew of Rangers was that none were piss ants. Jonas hated piss ants, the kind who thought they were entitled to something and bristled insolently if he gave them a direct order. In this crew, each of his men carried his own load and worked as a team. Not piss ants by a long shot, but perhaps a little high strung, and so young.

Gradually, as the sky lightened his Rangers and other law enforcement began to arrive. Deputy Baker and John Jarrett were among the first. Before anyone else was there, each of them grabbed a mug of coffee and walked down the paved path to the overlook above the gorge. These mugs each bore the letters "FOG" and had been gifts of the local friends who helped support the wilderness area. On days when a blanket of white mist covered the Gorge, and Jonas stood on the observation deck with his mug, he smiled at the suggestion on his cup.

"It's just beautiful, isn't it," Jonas observed as he surveyed the expanse before him gesturing with his steaming cup. "Never get tired of it."

"That it is, Jonas," Jarrett said over the rim of his cup. The vastness of the gorge was almost overwhelming even if you had seen it daily for years. These two veterans had a lot in common born from their dedication to the work of wildlife officers. Each knew it took a special breed to handle this job and each made personal sacrifices along the way. So pervasive was their commitment, neither man made time for a wife or children. The wilderness and the job became the only family they knew.

"You planning to brief everyone before the parties go down in there?" Jonas asked Jarrett.

"I plan to scare the shit out of them, is what I plan to do," Jarrett said not intending any humor in his statement. He planned to pack these boys with a healthy dose of fear. Jonas looked over at him and grunted in agreement. Yogi, stunned by the brilliance of the first orange rays to creep over the rim, listened to the barely audible banter of the two old rangers.

Slowly, as the sunlight peaked over the rim and became a smear of pink, the three men turned and walked back to the Ranger Station. Rockie Bradley drove up and began lifting two bags out of his truck with a couple of the young Rangers. Soon Jack Mathews and the other Deputies arrived and everyone moved inside the Ranger Station where Jonas unfolded a topographical map of Savage Gulf and spread it out on top of the small desk. The men packed in tightly shoulder to shoulder listening to Jonas.

Placing his index finger over the Savage Ranger Station noted on the southeast rim, Jonas said, "Stephen, I want you, Tommy Yager, with Deputies Andrew Sparks and Aaron Burns to go in from this Ranger Station. We are looking for a solo student hiker, last name Callicott, and a foursome of Foggies who did not come out yesterday." Ranger Stephen Slydell nodded.

"From this side, Deputy Baker, Mr. Mathews, Agent Jarrett and Mr. Bradley will go in through the Stone Door," Jonas said having moved his finger to the opposite rim.

"Uh, that's Special Agent Bradley," Rockie said.

"Yes, you are correct. I apologize Agent Bradley," Jonas said not looking up. Being recognized by his official title was important to Bradley. Then

Jonas said, "Agent Jarrett wants to get everyone up to speed on what you might run into down there."

"Thank you, Jonas," Jarrett said straightening up and making eye contact with each of them in turn. His gravely baritone voice invoked respect. "We have reason to believe the animal loose down there is a Bengal Tiger weighing close to four hundred pounds from the size and depression of the print Mr. Mathews found. Both the US Fish and Wildlife Service and the Tennessee Wildlife Resources Agency concur with that finding." He paused to let it sink in. Some of the Deputies and Rangers exchanged worried and puzzled looks.

"An adult or near adult tiger like this is a very dangerous beast. With one swipe of its paw it can crush the skull of a bear, and we have seen what its claws can do to flesh," Jarrett said. Everyone's attention was riveted on him. One of the deputies gulped audibly.

"I want everyone to understand this is not a hunting party. Each team will have a dart gun but it's only accurate up to about 75 yards," Jarrett said as he lifted a case up onto the counter and removed a TeleDart RD 706 Injection Gun. He quickly assembled the stock, trigger mechanism and the barrel.

"See," Jarrett said, "this is very light. You will

each have two darts with 5 ccs of the recommended sedative. Keep your fingers away from the end of the darts. The drug is deadly to humans."

Deputy Sparks asked, "You mean if we see it we can't shoot it?"

"Chances are you will not know it is even there and you won't see it until it attacks. Shoot only in self-defense. If you have to shoot use the dart gun," Jarrett said. "Each of you will carry 2-way radios, but due to the distance between us when we start I doubt we will be able to communicate very well. The plan is to meet up at Sawmill Campground before dark. Do not get separated from your group. Stay together and don't worry about how much noise you make. Make as much as you can to keep this animal away. Our primary goal is to find those hikers."

Agent Bradley stepped up and put one of his bags on the counter.

As he started to unzip it, Yogi asked, "What ya got Rock?"

"A little something special from the TBI equipment room," Bradley said reaching into the bag and bringing out two sets of night vision goggles. "Military grade NVGs, but I've only got two per team." Bradley did a quick demonstration of how to wear the goggles and turn them on. Old queer for gear Bradley came through again, Yogi thought.

"You boys in Team 1 load up and head on back to the other Ranger Station. The Team here will start to climb down into the gorge in a few minutes," Jonas said.

"Any questions?" Jarrett asked. There being none everyone started to gear up and Team 1 left for the opposite entry point on the other side of the Gorge.

"What are you thinking, Jonas," Jarrett asked.

"These boys are mostly local kids. They've all been hunters and are pretty skilled outdoorsmen," Jonas said.

"That's good," Jarrett said. "But have they ever been hunted?"

CHAPTER TWELVE

Before daylight could reach the floor of the gorge the sun would have to climb high and clear the plateau that towered above the wilderness. The four members of the Friends of the Gorge who camped at the Stagecoach Road Campground the prior evening were in the process of climbing up and out of the Gulf when they heard it. Without warning the roar of a wild beast echoed off the walls of the Gorge sending shivers up the hikers' backs and causing the hair on their necks to stand and tingle. A second and then a third roar followed. No one could identify the direction of origin since the echoes mixed and ricocheted in all directions. The hikers stopped at once frozen by the sound and terror that paralyzed each of them. None of them trusted their senses to rationally explain what they had just heard. They were not in the jungle. How was this possible? One of the group finally came to her senses and said, "Let's get out of here." Quickening their pace the hikers soon ran into Team 1 who were coming down from the Ranger Station.

"Did you hear that?" One of the hikers asked.

"Yes. You folks need to get out of here as quickly as possible," Ranger Slydell said. He did not have to say that again or offer any further explanation. The worried hikers moved even faster up toward the Ranger Station a mile ahead. The roar gave the Ranger the shivers as well, but he had a job to do. Grimly, the four law enforcement officers pressed on into the Gorge with the apprehension of soldiers about to engage in jungle warfare where the enemy was likely unseen and ghost like and had all the advantages they lacked.

Slydell tried the two way radio to no avail. As Jarrett predicted there was too much distance between either rim for the com gear to work. Despite the instructions that this was not a hunting party, three of the four men carried rifles and the fourth bore the dart gun.

"Jesus!" Bradley said as Team 2 emerged from the Stone Door to the impact of the roar. "What in the hell was that? Has that thing just killed something else?"

"No, it's probably just looking for other tigers," Jarrett said. Team 2 stopped just outside the Stone Door taking their time climbing down the rock steps with packs and gear. Jarrett knew they would not be able to pinpoint the location of the tiger because such a roar could carry for miles. Compounding the problem was the reflective property of the walls of the Gorge which bounced the sound around in strange and changing patterns like a super ball launched randomly on a racket ball court. Jarrett and Jonas had not given any thought to having at least one Ranger on each Team. Now, it seemed to Jarrett, having a Ranger who was more familiar with the Gorge would have been an asset. As the most experienced Gulf hiker, it fell to Jack Mathews to act as scout.

"Let's move over toward Ranger Falls and then work our way back to the campground," Jack suggested.

"Copy that," Jarrett said. The men continued to sweep the trail and both sides of the path searching for any sign of the missing student, or for traces of the tiger or blood. The search was not productive since the trail was rocky and the forest floor uneven and knotty with vines. As quickly as the creek and river rose two days earlier, the water receded and was only ankle deep making it possible to ford and head in a southeasterly direction where Ranger Falls poured over a cliff and into the pool below. Yogi stopped often to examine prints and to look for signs. Since he had reconnected with his Cherokee heritage during the past year, Yogi became more and more a student of all things Indian. Jack had never seen Yogi so dedicated as he became in learning Indian ways. The sharp investigative skills Yogi mastered as a detective were amplified through his Cherokee lens. Suddenly, Yogi stopped and crouched low to the ground. He motioned to Jack.

"Jack," Yogi said, "come here." They approached Ranger Falls from the lower end where the pool collected and flowed out the creek bed.

As they arrived at the edge of a small clearing Ranger Falls stood at the other end with its pool spreading out below the wispy foam of the falls. Jarrett and Bradley moved laterally but Jack went straight to Yogi who pointed at scuff marks on the ground and said,

"Something's been dragged across here." Jack could see what he was referring to. There was an almost ten inch path where the rock and sand had been scraped by something.

"A body being dragged?" Jack asked.

"Or a foot," Yogi suggested. Jack and Yogi could see that the trail continued to where larger boulders were collected at the base of the mountain bluffs.

Rising, Yogi said, "Let's see where this goes." Both Jack and Yogi steeled themselves for what they were afraid they were going to find and walked slowly following the markings. The scrape marks were not universally straight but wobbled side to side which tended to obscure any other prints that might have preceded the scrape.

At the edge of the boulder field, Yogi motioned for them to stop and pointed to a crevice between two large rocks where a human foot protruded.

CHAPTER THIRTEEN

Pierce's team also heard the echo of the tiger's roar as they came into the Gorge on a four wheel drive track from the north. As with the Ranger's group a couple of days earlier they abandoned the truck when the boulders became impassable. Unlike the others, these men were thrilled to hear the big cat for that meant it was still in the Gorge. Reinforced with weaponry, night vision gear and communications equipment of their own, Pierce's men disappeared into the wilderness area like the precision hunt team they were. Pierce chose these men because each was special forces trained in one military branch or the other, were in splendid shape, and would do whatever he paid them to do. The names Pierce knew them by were undoubtedly false, but he didn't care, men like this were tools of the trade. Ruthless men used ruthless techniques. Larsen was the only member of the ops team Pierce had worked with previously.

David Ramparts, the leader, recognized he had the same problem as was being encountered by the Ranger's Teams. This place was friggin' huge. Locating one cat within twenty thousand acres was the proverbial needle in a haystack. His research on these animals said they were not entirely nocturnal, preferring to hunt before darkness set in. Their eyes were round, not slitted as with most felines, and although they had respectable night vision, much better than a human, some daylight worked to their advantage. Optimum hunting conditions to find the cat moving would be just before sunset and just before dawn.

Still, the Pierce Team moved to reconnoiter as much area as possible and find a good vantage point from which to watch for movement. After the initial sounds the cat was quiet. Pierce's men did not found scat or any sign of the cat by dusk so they located high ground that gave them a good viewing range over much of the Gorge and prepared to spend the night.

"Look," Larsen said pointing to the opposite wall of the Gorge where four men descended with packs. David took the binoculars from Larsen and examined the men in what was left of the dying daylight. He noted that each carried a rifle and looked very young. He decided this was a team from the Ranger Station because none other than law enforcement would carry weapons into a state park. Two of the group wore park ranger uniforms but the other two wore other law enforcement clothing. Ramparts figured them to be deputies from the county force. Studying his topo map David pinpointed the campground to which they were likely headed and marked it on his map.

"We will get closer after it gets dark," he told his men. Darkness indeed came soon and enveloped the forest in a dark shroud. Pierce's men strapped on their night vision goggles and moved down and toward the campground where they expected to find the Ranger group. Walking was treacherous anywhere in this park and at night even more so on account of the uneven rocks and tree roots that stretched toward each other like fingers forming a net. As they moved in closer they saw the flickering of the campfire the Rangers built and heard them talking huddled with their backs to the woods as the flames danced and threw witchy oblique shapes on the trees. From the nature of their conversation, it was clear to Ramparts that this group was nervous and disturbed that others they expected to meet at the campground were not there. David figured he could scare the shit out of these men, but decided to maintain the no contact policy. After motioning a signal to his group, he and his men pulled back a few hundred feet where they each took up a concealed position that still allowed surveillance with the night vision equipment.

The Team 1 members huddled around the fire pit using the light and warmth of the flames to bolster their sagging confidence. Their faces danced and swayed as the flames rose and flickered. They bantered many theories about the reasons the other team failed to show up, none of which instilled any comfort or security among the men. Some feared an encounter with the tiger, and others contemplated a fall or other injury. One option was for them to hike out that night, but most refused to leave the perceived safety of the watch fire. So, they hunkered down preparing to wait out the darkness, a firearm always within an arm's reach. A chilly wind rustled the leaves when they heard a rock dislodge and tumble into a collection of other rocks far down the face of the cliff.

"What was that?" one of the Deputies asked nervously.

"Sounds like something moving out there dislodged a rock," another one said in reply.

"I tell ya, if I see that thing I'm gonna shoot it, I don't care what anybody says," a third man said.

"From what that wildlife officer said, the chances of you seeing it before it jumps you are pretty slim," said one of the Rangers. "Can you imagine that thing jumping on your back and putting its jaws around your neck." A fearful shiver ran through them all. Amid the nervous banter exchanged by the Team 1 men, none of them noticed there was other movement in the woods around them.

Pierce's men heard the rock fall as well and trained their night vision equipment in the direction of the noise. David said in a whisper, "There." He pointed to a spot a couple of hundred yards above the campground where the distinct shape of a large cat climbed higher into the forest. It halted and turned to look back at David. In the night vision goggles the cat's eyes glared like two bright carbide torches. Pierce's men moved out of their cover and began the tedious journey toward the cat's last position.

The Rangers and Deputies were alone with no awareness of the drama about to play out around them.

CHAPTER FOURTEEN

Jack yelled for Jarrett and Bradley to come over as he and Yogi approached the rock crevice from which the foot emerged. At the end of the leg was a New Balance hiking boot similar to many Jack saw daily around the University campus where he served as Dean of the College. Prepared for the worst, Yogi trained his high beam military flashlight into the tight opening as he knelt down. There was a body inside that appeared to have crawled in rather than being dragged in since there wasn't enough clearance for the cat to have knocked the boy out and then pulled him into the hole. Lacking the room to go into the opening and when the body remained unresponsive even after they shook it, Yogi and Jack decided to slowly and carefully pull the young man out by his legs. The opening was just large enough to allow the body to clear. They were careful trying to protect his head and face from scraping the ground and gravel, but some wear and tear was inevitable. Yogi and Jack each thought it must have taken an ungodly effort for the boy to have pulled himself into that shelter.

Once the body cleared the rocks Yogi checked for a pulse while Jack searched for a wallet.

"He's alive. There's a weak pulse," Yogi said as he unwrapped a space blanket from his backpack and spread it over the figure.

"Callicott," Jack read from the driver's license in the wallet. "Thank, God."

"Do you see any injuries?" Yogi asked.

Neither of them wanted to look at the side of the boy's face that they dragged across the ground and which was now oozing blood. Jack felt for anything obvious then noticed how swollen the young man's left ankle was as well as a bruise that formed on one side of his face.

"He must have fallen or twisted his ankle. If he was knocked out it could explain why he didn't respond to his companion. Then, when he came to he must have pulled himself into that place for safety," Jack said.

"We are going to have to stretcher him out or rig up a travois," Yogi said looking around.

"Too rocky for a travois," Jack said, then turning to Bradley and Jarrett, "Can you guys go cut us a couple of poles? We will build a stretcher and carry him out." The student began to wake up as the two poles arrived. Through a groggy and disoriented haze he looked at Yogi and then Jack.

"Did you see it?" the student asked.

"See what? There, don't try to get up. You've hit your head," Yogi said.

"I think it was a tiger," the boy said and fell back exhausted. "But, how?" He was babbling at this point, a talking-in-tongues version of nonsense.

The Team 2 members looked at each other knowing the cat was nearby and that they were all at high risk of being attacked. While, under normal circumstances a tiger would only attack a single prey, this beast already demonstrated a lack of concern for the number of its adversaries. Jack took his tent's rain fly from his back pack and fashioned a stretcher around the poles Bradley and Jarrett had cut. His Boy Scout training kicked in automatically and in his mind he saw a page from the *Boy Scout Handbook* showing exactly how to rig up such a carry device. He practiced making a stretcher many times at camp. The difference now, it was for real.

"We are going to have to carry him out," Jack said. "If we hook back up to the Alum Gap trail back there, it's only three miles or so to the top, then a mile and a half back to the Ranger Station through the woods and along the rim. The top part is pretty flat, but getting there will test us." It was going to be a tough hike. Jack hoped the old wildlife agent was up for it. Heck, he hoped he and Yogi were up for it. The student's life would depend on it.

Bradley asked, "Shouldn't one of us go on to the campground to alert the others?"

"We are not splitting up. It's going to take all four of us to get this guy back to the top and there's no way we will get there before dark," Jarrett said. "Those guys will be ok. We'll come get them in the morning."

Jarrett spoke with confidence but the last thing he wanted was to leave those four young men in this Gorge overnight alone with a man-killer Bengal tiger, but what other option did he have?

CHAPTER FIFTEEN

Successfully hunting any game involves an element of surprise. If the object being hunted is aware of the hunter then the odds change and the contest becomes one of cunning and power. Will the hunted one double back, flip the odds and become the hunter once again? Such is the thrill with big game, hunters often placing themselves in danger to discover roles are quickly reversed. Pierce's men knew the odds of stalking this tiger in the dark in unfavorable forest conditions were not in their favor. Even in daylight the golden hues of fall camouflaged the tiger enabling him to move unseen while he pinpointed his prey if only by scent. David Ramparts hoped the four men from the Ranger Station would distract the beast and serve as the staked goat for their hunt. At least initially, that is exactly the situation they found as they followed the cat from a great distance. It moved not away from the four men, but in circle of them, sometimes climbing higher and at other times moving in much, much closer. When the cat stopped, Pierce's men stopped far enough behind the beast that it did not notice their odor.

At least once when one of the men around the fire walked off to piss in the woods, the cat intently focused on the man, hunkered down and twitched its tail back and forth in majestic arcs. If it was a few feet closer there was no doubt in David's mind it would have pounced, but it was too high up the side to make a clean jump even though it could easily clear twenty feet in a single leap. The man finished his business and turned back to the fire completely oblivious of the cat. That's when the cat roared for a second time, just once, just enough to send the men scrambling for their rifles. The tiger taunted the men. If they knew where to look they would have seen the campfire flickering in the big cat's terrible eyes. These were the eyes of death, yellow pools of liquid anger. But, as before, the roar echoed in many directions and the cat remained in concealment.

Pierce's men were fascinated watching the tiger play out the role of hunter and tormenter. The roar was unexpected and unsettled all of the humans, but David quickly recovered remembering that he too, was a predator in this play. Advancing slowly and quietly Pierce's men saw the big cat on top of a boulder not one hundred yards away facing the fire and away from the three hunters, its body in a prone position but low. Ahead not twenty yards was another group of boulders which if Pierce's men could reach that position, would provide a fine shooting position at the target. David took out a pad and wrote instructions to his men-to increase the CO_2 pressure in the injection guns-to shoot a little high-and to take up positions behind the low boulders. Each of them read the message with the night vision goggles and moved cautiously. When they were in position each man leveled his dart gun on the rock and took aim. This shot would stretch the limit of the gun's ability to accurately hit a target but it was the best chance they had and each of these men was a marksman. The noise from the campfire increased with the men's attempts to make as much noise as possible and not become a snack for the animal. This noise continued to distract the tiger as David said softly, "Now."

Three pops from the air rifles launched three full darts of sedative at the tiger. The first dart hit the boulder on which the tiger was standing and bounced off harmlessly, while the other two sailed away into the woods as the tiger instinctively jumped as soon as he became aware of the danger. Springing off the boulder to the forest floor ten feet below, the tiger moved fiercely deeper into the woods and for high ground. Pierce's men quickly reloaded and approached where they last saw the tiger but the phantom vanished leaving behind only the sound of the animal's crashing through the woods that echoed in many directions.

"Dammit," David muttered knowing the hard part began now because they pursued a beast who knew where they were and that he would have to be more cautious.

When the animal crashed to the forest floor the four men around the fire abandoned all hope or commitment of staying the night. Leaving all their gear but the goggles and their rifles they immediately bounded the campsite for the trail back up the Stone Door several miles away. The Rangers knew the trails even in the dark and the four men proceeded at a hasty pace away from the fire and whatever was lurking in the woods. Fear drove them faster and faster and they moved swiftly with the ghost of the big cat in pursuit. That they left the fire burning was not even a consideration. Each of the men shared the shame of having abandoned a post but that shame was no match for the primeval adrenaline that kicked in and forced them to flee. They couldn't stop or slow down. Each man's heart raced in synchronous time with the pounding of his feet. No one spoke or looked another in the eye such was the power of the force driving them. One controlling impulse dwarfed all others-to get out of that damn Gorge alive.

Pierce's men heard and watched the retreat knowing they were handed the opportunity to either continue the hunt without the rangers near or get out of there undetected. In the dark the advantage would certainly lie with the tiger and David preferred the odds in his favor. Ramparts opted to leave the Gorge, regroup and continue the hunt the following day. He and his men hustled back to their truck and got the hell out of there as well.

CHAPTER SIXTEEN

Yogi, Jack, Jarrett and Bradley were almost to the top of the rim on the Alum Gap Trail in the expiring daylight when they heard the second roar of the tiger faintly echoing in the distance. They were immediately concerned for the safety of the other Rangers and Deputies, as well as the Friends of the Gorge who were unaccounted for to their knowledge but there was not a single thing they could do. Each offered up a silent prayer for the safety of their companions. Carrying the student on the stretcher taxed them to the limit of exhaustion so they began taking more regular rest stops. As the daylight faded to gray, they were forced to use their halogen head lamps just to follow the trail. Yogi kept his eye on Jarrett since the Agent was breathing very hard for as he struggled with his share of the load. Yogi knew that once they reached the top of the rim, the trail flattened out and made it much easier to transport the injured student but they could not suffer the loss of Jarrett in the process. At one such stop before the top, Yogi asked Jack on a different subject,

"Did you work it out to be a part time lawyer?" Yogi and Jack spoke a couple of times about how much Jack really enjoyed the legal work he did for the Cherokee Nation the prior year when he and Calvin Greathouse established the ownership of Nickajack Lake for the Cherokee people before the United

States Supreme Court. Jack attended the University with Yogi and later went to law school at Vanderbilt in Nashville, but Jack pursued post graduate degrees and clerkships until he was called to return to the University as the Assistant Dean, a post he held until the official Dean opted to remain at the University of Georgia the prior year. While he held a law license, Jack was involved in only the one case on behalf of the Cherokee Nation and it turned out to be a biggie. He and Calvin Greathouse, a law school friend with a national practice representing people of color, were successful in defeating the claims of the States of Georgia and Tennessee to a portion of the Tennessee River Georgia tried to claim in order to find another source of water for the ever-expanding Atlanta area. The victory not only further bolstered Calvin's reputation but Jack also received praise for his work which left a taste in his mouth for the excitement of litigation that remained unresolved.

"Yeah. The President of the University has agreed that so long as my University work isn't compromised I can handle a few matters. Calvin has offered me an Of Counsel position with his firm. I would just work out of the house unless I'm needed to appear in Court somewhere," Jack answered. "Why do you ask?"

Yogi said, "Because Lola Crockett, the widow of one of the drivers, wants to talk to a lawyer about a wrongful death suit against Pierce's Farm over Buster's death, and I thought you and Calvin Greathouse might want to look into it."

"Let me call Calvin when we get back," Jack said, clearly interested in the project and excited by another chance to work with Calvin.

At some point the student woke up, and although still groggy he continued mumbling about the tiger. Jarrett tried to reach Team 1 for several hours but without any luck. Once his group achieved the rim he was able to contact Jonas at the Ranger Station who then called an ambulance that ready and waiting to transport when they brought the student back to the parking lot. Once the student was handed off to the EMT's, the Team 2 members collapsed onto the floor of the Ranger Station their backs resting against the metal filing cabinets. Jonas poured them coffee and listened to their account of finding the student and the haul up out of the Gorge. He and the team were still worried about the others but knew they did not have the strength to go back down that night. Their concern for the safety of Team 1 was allayed when the short wave radio crackled to the voice of Ranger Slydell saying they were on the way out and should be to the Stone Door within an hour.

By the time Team 1 reached the bottom of the Stone Door they were all exhausted with barely enough energy to commit to the climb up the stone steps to the peak of the rim. The forced march left them drained. Looking up, their headlamps illuminated the view up the narrow crevice to the top of the Stone Door which looked like a rock tunnel carved into the walls of a cave deep in the mountain, a place of honor for dwarves. The adrenaline rush that powered them away from the tiger evaporated leaving four young men leaning against the rocks, panting and trying to determine where the strength would come from to make that final climb. For the first time since bolting from the campground they began to look around at each other, although no one wanted to meet the others' eyes so heavy was their burden. A hearty dose of shame kicked each man in the ass.

Ranger Slydell took charge and said, "Guys, no one has anything to be ashamed of. We made the best decision under those circumstances to get ourselves out of the Gulf. Under better conditions and with more support we'll go back in there. Now, we just need to get up this passage. Strap it on, we can do this." He turned and started the climb even though his thighs burned with each step. The others followed him, a grim determination on the face of each man that was replaced with just a slight sense of relaxation as they reached the top and the paved path leading back to the Ranger Station. All they could do was to shuffle the mile back to the Ranger Station where light and coffee waited.

Jonas and Yogi greeted the men with big bear hugs at the door of the Station.

"Damn but it's good to see you boys," Jonas said.

Now that they were safe, Jarrett relaxed since he felt responsible for each of the younger Rangers and Officers. He saw that Ranger Slydell became the recognized leader so he encouraged him to lay out the events Team 1 encountered. Slydell recounted arriving at the campsite, lighting the fire and then being startled by the roar and later the crash in the woods. He did not elaborate on how quickly they abandoned the campsite or the gear.

Jonas confirmed the Friends of the Gorge came out earlier in the day so all the hikers were accounted for. He and Jarrett agreed the Gorge needed to be sealed off as much as possible and closed to hikers. Then they would need trained reinforcements to apprehend the tiger. The awareness they were fortunate to get everyone out safely began to sink in, but, this sense of relief was tempered by the knowledge they were facing a dangerous and deadly foe.

CHAPTER SEVENTEEN

Emily Mathews did not like the way she felt, as if she were floating in a dense fog unable to attach to anything. Her doctors said many times that they were confident she would recover from the trauma of having shot Julian Browne in Jack's living room, but maybe they were wrong. When images of Browne jerking and falling, when the sound of the gun's discharge and the smell of the cordite choked her senses the fog began creeping in again slowly until it filled the room. This panicked her and shut down her ability to function normally as she retreated into her painting releasing creative energy that replaced reason in an expression of her soul and what she considered beautiful. There were times when she emerged from the fog she looked at the easel and wondered where in the world that abstraction came from? There were times she did not recollect in what swirling image the content of her work was born. The painting was good, all right, and others commented on her innate talent, but whose hand wielded the brush that drew those images out of the canvas? What twisted psyche controlled her hand? For a while, all her paintings reflected sky and clouds and racing creatures. Then, the energy morphed into gossamer-like scantily clothed women who raced and danced across the canvas in pursuit of something unseen. In the midst of this frolic appeared a slash of red, almost blood like. At other times the canvass became more abstract, a blotch of color and unrecognizable shapes without form or reason. She strained and pushed herself to discover the object or goal towards which the women raced without success or what energy was being expressed in her art.

Going into one of these mysteries Emily usually felt slightly nauseous before succumbing to the fog. Coming out, the experience was a light headed glee, of escape and reward. Only two things seemed to anchor her back in the real world and tell her she was alive, Jack and making love.

Jack found Emily on one of these up swings when he finally arrived home early in the morning after helping carry the student out of Savage Gulf. It thrilled him to see her buoyant and bright like the old Emily who ran to him and kissed him deeply. His Golden Retriever Rocket was standing with her paws on his back demanding an equal serving of attention. Later, Emily sange in the kitchen preparing eggs benedict as Jack climbed into the shower letting the hot water blast away the prior night's trauma. By the time he dressed, breakfast ready so they sat on the back deck of their house enjoying the fresh new day and the splendor of early fall on the Mountain where the air was still warm but from time to time a cool breeze promised of the coldness to come. As he told her about their discovery in the Gorge, Emily's eyes grew large.

"A tiger? You actually heard a tiger down there?" she asked.

"Yep, and it gave me the shivers," Jack said as he cut into the poached eggs which did not run. She fixed them exactly as he liked.

"So, what's the next move?" Emily asked.

"With help from the Sheriff's Department, the Rangers are going to shut down access into the Gulf as much as possible. They can choke off access at the two Ranger stations and other known access points, but there are other ways into and out of that wilderness that are more difficult to patrol. That's where Yogi and his guys come in," Jack said.

"The Deputies are going to watch the logging roads and other entry points?" she asked.

"Yeah. There was a Special Agent from the Fish and Wildlife Service with us who is getting special teams from TWRA and the USF&WS to come in to catch that cat," Jack said.

"Some cat. Here kitty, kitty, kitty," Emily joshed.

"You should have heard it. Remember Special Agent Rock Bradley from the Tennessee Bureau of Investigation?" Jack asked.

"The guy who helped with the Red Dagger thing?" Emily asked, referring to their involvement with the exposure of a drug ring operating on the Mountain a couple of years prior.

"Yes. He was with us. You should have seen him jump when that cat roared the first time. I thought he messed in his pants." Jack explained. Both of them laughed.

"Were you scared?" Emily asked.

Jack honestly answered, "Of course. It's one thing to talk about this, but to be down there in the dark with that thing loose is something entirely different."

Holding the cup of tea to her lips, Emily said, "Jack, I want you to be careful." Her voice expressed the flavor of concern and fear.

"I'm ok. It will be the professionals next time. My task was to get the President's nephew out of there. What are you up to today?" he asked.

"I've got to meet with Henri this morning about a travelling exhibit he is trying to set up for next month," she said. Henri was Henri Jacques, the Art Curator the University hired to manage the school's art collection that not only hung in the school's art gallery but at various other places around campus. Emily was his assistant. Henri came to the University from a New York gallery with his wife, Rosalind, and cut a dashing figure around campus in his red beret amongst the button down shirt and khaki pants crowd so popular among the faculty and student body. He affected a French accent and wore European attire which gave him an exotic presence he cultivated. Almost all his clothes were black or gray and very tight. The ladies loved him. Rosalind taught French in the languages department and was quick to put Henri back in his place if he got too full of himself. Jack liked Rosalind but considered Henri to be a bit fruity. Emily was just the opposite.

Jack told Emily about Yogi's offer to introduce him to the wife of one of the deceased drivers for a wrongful death suit. She was completely supportive although she did not have any grasp of how challenging or dangerous such a case could be against something as powerful as Pierce's Farm, but with Jack and Calvin teamed up, Emily knew they were formidable. Calvin brought a great presence and the experience, while Jack presented a folksy down home Mayberry charm a jury would find irresistible.

Jack carried the dishes into the kitchen and looked out the window at Emily who finished her tea and sat gazing into the red and gold painted woods, a last respite before engaging in the business of the day. Her raven colored hair fell all around her shoulders shining in the morning sunlight. God, he loved her.

CHAPTER EIGHTEEN

Lola watched as the three men climbed out of the Jeep in front of her house. She recognized Deputy Baker from their earlier meetings, but not the other white man with him. The third man, she knew and her heart fluttered. By reputation and on national television this man was well known within the African American community for his courtroom victories and the power of his presence. When he spoke it was reminiscent of Dr. Martin Luther King, but better, because the voice also carried the qualities of James Earl Jones with a richness the density of dark molten chocolate. As this man stepped out of the vehicle his suit was not even wrinkled but shined in the afternoon sunlight like the sheen of a posturing raven. Lola knew, this was the Man and she was embarrassed the yard was littered with children's toys and that her house was not spotless. In her heart however, she knew such things would make no difference to a man such as Calvin Greathouse.

Calvin approached Lola and took her hand kissing the back of it in a gesture of humility and respect.

"Ms. Crockett, may I call you Lola?" Calvin said. Lola was speechless but nodded affirming his question. She thought Deputy Baker was joshing her when he said he would engage Mr. Greathouse and bring him to her home. But, here in her humble house was Calvin Greathouse! The Man.

"Good, and you must call me Calvin," he said. The cat had not yet dispatched Lola's tongue so she nodded again and opened the door for them to come in.

Yogi said, "Lola, this is my friend, Jack Mathews a local attorney, and I believe you have met Mr. Greathouse." Jack nodded and Calvin once again took her hand.

"Let's sit down. Ms. Crockett it is a terrible thing for us to meet under these circumstances but I want you to know that if you engage us, Mr. Mathews and I will be your lawyers and your champions to get you every dollar we can for the tragic loss you and your children have suffered," Calvin said. Lola smiled, her head bowed slightly.

As they sat down in Lola's living room, Jack and Yogi in arm chairs and Calvin on the sofa with Lola, they settled into a comfortable conversation about Lola, Buster, their kids and how life was in Hard Bargain. Like Lola, Calvin also came from humble origins in and around Greenville, Mississippi and fully understood Lola's situation. Lola knew Calvin understood her life and that he would fight for her. Just look at him, she thought, ain't he as good as any of those big shot lawyers? Lola opened up and began talking with Calvin as if the white boys were not even in the room. She explained how Buster drove for Pierce's Farm, how the pickups all seemed to come late at night and how everything was delivered to the Farm.

"Let me ask you, Lola, did Buster ever pick up anything and carry it away from the Farm?" Calvin asked.

Lola thought about that for a minute, and said, "Now that you mention it, I don't think they ever picked up anything at the Farm. It was always at the airport."

"How many times would you say Calvin made deliveries to the Farm," he asked.

"Lordy. Two or three times a week, sometimes more," Lola said.

"And over what period? How long had he been making these pickups and deliveries?" Calvin asked.

"About a year, I'm thinking," Lola said.

"I believe you told the Deputy earlier that some of these pickups involved exotic animals like birds, monkeys and things?" Calvin asked.

"Yes, and Buster saved two of the birds for me. Want to see them?" Lola asked.

"That would be very nice," Calvin said. The four of them rose and walked into Lola's kitchen area where the fancy cage with the two Hyacinth Macaws stood in a corner. The birds chewed on their perch and made that gravely sound down in the throat.

"Look at those birds," Calvin said admiringly, "Have you ever seen such a blue color? It just radiates."

Lola glowed at the praise, and responded, "They're something special alright. That nice fish and wildlife man sent me a book on how to take care of them and some food for them."

"Tell me, Lola, did Buster ever drive with anyone other than Larry Glower who was killed with him?" Calvin asked.

"Once or twice, I think. An old 'shiner named, Albert Mansker," Lola said.

"Is he still around?" Calvin asked.

"Might be. Deputy would know more about that than me," Lola added.

"We're quite familiar with Mr. Mansker at the Sheriff's Department," Yogi said. "He has issues with drinking too much of his own product."

"I see," Calvin said, then to Lola, "Lola if you want us to be your lawyers you need to sign the engagement letter Mr. Mathews brought, and we'll get started."

Lola eagerly signed the letter, and waived goodbye as the men drove off. On the way back up the Mountain after having dropped off Yogi at the Sheriff's Department, Calvin said,

"You see the obvious issue don't you?"

Jack thought about it, and said "Linking the Farm to the exotic animals and Buster's death?"

"Yes. Buster telling Lola he was driving for Pierce's Farm could be hearsay unless we can find some corroboration," Calvin said.

"And, that's where Mansker comes in?" Jack asked.

"He's part of it, although I'm afraid an old drunk moonshiner isn't the most credible or reliable witness," Calvin said.

"Then what," Jack asked.

"We're going to have to get closer to that operation," said Calvin. "Don't you think it interesting that Buster never carried anything away from that Farm? A smuggling operation only works if the product winds up in the hands of the end user who pays for it."

"So," Jack said, "there's pieces to this puzzle we still don't know."

Calvin said, "Exactly. Didn't Yogi say that he was conducting some surveillance of Pierce's Farm?"

"He said he was going to. You want me to go with him?" Jack asked.

"Only if you can be careful and discreet. No trespassing on Pierce's property and you can't get caught. It wouldn't look good in front of a jury that we were sneaking around, plus you could lose your law license," Calvin said. "But," he continued, "sometime you have to break a few eggs to bake a cake." Calvin grinned.

"It's not illegal or unethical for me to do some surveillance is it?" Jack asked.

"Not at all. How do you think plaintiff lawyers catch the illegal polluters, or miners, or timber thieves? If you are fighting the bad guys, sometimes you must engage in questionable tactics, as they say, fighting fire with fire. But out there somewhere is a line, and you'd best think through all the consequences of crossing that line, because there will be consequences," Calvin mused. Calvin wandered around that line his entire career occasionally straying far onto the dark side, but always on behalf of a good cause. He smiled at the thought that as his reputation grew he was able to kick that line further and further down the road. Big law firms and corporate defendants pursued him hoping one day to stake him on the wrong side and get him disbarred. They tried many times and continued raising the stakes, but so far, Calvin outsmarted the lot. Calvin knew Jack needed to recognize how the high risk-reward litigation game was played, because he worried Jack was far too naive and honest for his own good.

He looked over at Jack, when the Jeep was almost back to the top of the Mountain, and said, "those consequences will affect you and your family."

"How's Emily involved in this?" Jack asked coming to the stop sign as they joined the main highway from the narrow twisty road running from Northwoods up to the college.

"She's involved only through you. If we are really dealing with bad guys who are making a lot of money trafficking in illegal animals, they will not take kindly to those who start scratching around in their sandbox. They may retaliate in whatever they think is the most expedient way to back us off. Usually, going after someone's family will get the most immediate attention," Calvin said.

Before pulling out onto the highway, Jack looked over at Calvin and said, "I'm not sure I am ready to take that risk, Calvin."

"Then you better be careful, and don't get caught," Calvin said.

CHAPTER NINETEEN

Jack Mathews called Yogi on his cell phone to confirm they would engage in reconnaissance of Pierce's Farm that evening. Yogi told him to wear dark clothing and bring a pair of good binoculars. With the night vision equipment having returned to the TBI equipment room a couple of days earlier they would have to rely on ambient light and luck. By seven pm dusk set in and the line of darkness moved like a wave over the western side of the plateau gradually drowning Pierce's Farm in twilight. Yogi located an old logging road to the southeast of the Farm which on a topo map looked like it almost touched the eastern most boundary of Pierce's place. Since logging operations in that part of the county played out a decade earlier and waited for new growth to mature, Yogi knew the road would be rough if passable at all. That's why he arranged to borrow Leon Allgood's Dodge 4X4 Powerwagon. Leon's wife, Tammy, was Jack's assistant at the University, and Leon was intimately involved in the work for the Cherokee Nation the prior year. Even before that, Leon's truck carried a group to the University Forestry Cabin the night the Red Dagger case was resolved, so Yogi knew how tough and rugged a vehicle it was.

Jack met Yogi at Yogi's house in Northwoods

and from there they navigated the narrow country road to a point Yogi indicated must be the head of the logging road. Beginning at a broken fence line just off the paved road, the logging road was little more than a two-track trail whose ruts were deep and soft. At first the road lay at least a mile distant from the boundary of Pierce's Farm but as it neared the plateau and gained altitude the road curved back toward the Farm property. They bounced and bottomed out for more than a mile when the wash out of the logging road was too deep to go any further. Each man grabbed his back pack that was full of gear and Yogi spread the topo map out on the flatbed of the truck. Using a red beam Maglite he examined the map and said,

"If we are here, this road goes on quite a bit further up in elevation until it passes beneath this rock out-cropping and looks down into the back side of Pierce's Farm. I think we will need to get to this point to see what is going on at the back of the property."

"I understand," Jack said as he slung his backpack on.

"We need to remember that the front fencing of this property is electrified and covered with cameras," Yogi said, "So, when we near the boundary, we will need to stay under the canopy. I don't know, but I suspect there will be cameras on this side as well."

Yogi and Jack hiked the old logging trail in silence for most of a mile until it opened up into a small clearing. Behind them a bluff climbed up as it attempted to merge with the plateau. Below them lay a wire fence that appeared to be electrified with a single strand at the top. Two strands of razor wire angled back away from them crossing forty-five degree vertical support struts. Rather than approach the fence and trigger a sensor or a camera, Yogi and Jack stayed in the shadow of the bluff training their binoculars through the opening and into the field below. A cluster of trees was situated a few hundred yards from the fence line where a light flickered glowing softly in the darkness.

"There," Yogi whispered, gesturing toward the trees. "Do you see it?"

"I think so," Jack said. "It looks like a couple or three, even, small barns or warehouses."

"Yeah, I'm counting three, and there is a vehicle approaching on the left," Yogi said adjusting the focus to pick up the movement.

"I'm seeing a truck, like a local delivery vehicle. There's something painted on the side that I can't make out, some kind of a design," Jack said. The exterior doors to the barn like structure stood open revealing nothing beyond the cavernous opening itself.

"Dammit, we need a different angle," Yogi said as they followed the truck that backed into an opening at the end of one of the buildings. They could barely hear the back-up warning beeps as the truck pulled closer to the door. "Can you see anything?" he asked.

"No, the truck is blocking the opening," Jack said.

"Come on, we've got to get closer," Yogi said.

They crept to the edge of the fence, but were afforded no better view. Jack reached out to touch the fence but got popped by the current. "Damn", he said.

Yogi looked around for some opportunity to get over the fence, but the closest thing he saw was a large limb of a towering white oak extending out into the field like an arm.

"Wait a minute, Yogi," Jack warned. "You're not thinking about going over there are you?"

"Have you got a better way to see what's going on?" Yogi said. "If I can get out on that limb I could drop down, it's not more than about eight feet."

"And how are you going to get back?" Jack asked.

"I've got a rope. I will make a loop that I can

step in and swing back up," Yogi said already removing the rope from his pack. Jack did not like this idea. All he could think of was Calvin's admonition not to cross the line or get caught. They were about to do both.

"Yogi, there is no cover between this fence and that stand of trees. You will be completely exposed," Jack said. Yogi considered that, but with no moon he thought he could move undetected by staying low to the ground.

"Have you considered dogs?" Jack asked.

"Dogs?" Yogi replied.

"Look over there next to the barn door, isn't that a guard with a dog on a leash?" Jack asked.

Yogi used his binoculars to focus on the barn, and after a minute said, "Shit." Even from that distance the Doberman looked huge.

"Even if the guard doesn't see you, it's highly likely the dog will. That dog'll bite you," Jack said, quoting the punch line of an old paddling joke. Yogi wasn't laughing.

That's when two things happened to catch their attention. First, the barn door closed and the box truck began to pull away giving them a better view of the driver's side door on which was stenciled a design they could still not make out or place, but there was something familiar about it. The next thing they detected was a buzzing sound but they couldn't see where it was coming from.

"Up," Yogi said looking up into the night sky where the blinking red and white lights of an approaching drone were visible and they now heard the buzzing noise more dramatically. As the drone neared the fence it was still fifty feet off the ground when a spot light from the drone turned on bathing the ground in brightness. Jack and Yogi ducked but it was too late, the drone picked them up and was hovering just above them.

"Time to scram," Yogi said and took off running down the two track toward the cover of the trees with Jack right behind him. The drone lazily turned and followed like a mad hornet or a fighter plane about to strafe a barn sitting unprotected in a field. Once inside the tree cover Yogi and Jack continued to run back towards Leon's truck. They could see the beam from the drone playing on the leaf canopy above. Within ten minutes they were back at the truck and headed off the way they had come. For a while they continued to see the drone's lights on the trees moving back and forth, but it appeared to have lost them. Yogi bounced even more recklessly down the road to the highway still not having turned on his headlights.

Inside the Farm offices at one end of the barn, one man watched a large monitor while the other operated the controls of the drone.

"What are those motherfuckers up to?" one man asked.

"Don't know but Mr. Pierce ain't gonna be happy," said the other.

"Did you get it all recorded?" asked the first man.

"Yes. I think we got pretty good facials on both of them," the second man responded.

"Good. Take the disk on up to the house. I'll stay here and monitor the cameras."

CHAPTER TWENTY

Within two days Agent Jarrett of the US Fish and Wildlife Service in connection with the Tennessee Wildlife Resources Agency mustered ten field agents to go back into the Gulf for the tiger. These men were no young green recruits but seasoned field officers who dealt often with many difficult and dangerous situations in their line of work, whether the threat was presented by the animal kingdom or by a two legged varmit. Jarrett formulated a plan by laying out search grids in the park. Once each grid was searched and marked off, he thought they would be some certainty the noose tightened around the cat or it left the Gulf. He regretted having lost a couple of days but there was no way to mobilize the team any sooner. Hikers into the Gorge were effectively shut out of the area for two days so only the cat and his men should be in that canyon. What they did not know was that Pierce's men were already there and enjoyed a head start on them.

David Ramparts brought an extra one of Pierce's men with him this time and left him at the truck with a Polaris ATV. They planned call him with the walkie talkie to assist with retrieving the cat once it was neutralized. Other men were positioned at various points along the edge of the gorge with additional vehicles. The Polaris give them a little more mobility and even though it could not navigate many of the trails in the park, it was certainly preferable to carrying that heavy animal all the way out. Pierce's men would continue to practice stealth and remain hidden not only from the cat but also from the others who would undoubtedly be searching for the cat soon.

Meanwhile, the tiger killed another buck and felt pretty good as he cleaned the blood off his face and paws. He discovered a small creek that fell from the top of the northeast rim creating a break in the bluff that was more gradual to ascend. A fresh supply of water was important. This creek allowed him to come and go as he pleased. Bounding up the slope carved by the stream, he was at the top in minutes following a path it would be difficult for a human to duplicate. Lounging on a protruding rock high up on one side he perked up when he saw the glint of daylight off a metal object and recognized movement in the bottom from a group of men who came down from above and temporarily moved into a clearing. Soon they would pass beneath the tree canopy and he would lose them, but he knew from their presence the game was afoot again. Because he was in no hurry, and finished another fine meal, he simply continued to observe as the venison digested in his guts. From the rock perch the tiger reigned king over the sea of green, red and orange below. Soon he would be on the move.

Over the past couple of days the cat moved

silently along the rim and watched for humans. Those he encountered were not armed and he did not perceive them as threats. Still, he remained on guard. In the air he felt a coolness at night but because he found this area so strange and different from his home he did not know if the weather would change or not. At that moment with a generous food supply and water, he saw no need to relocate so he settled in at the top of the food chain in Savage Gulf.

David Ramparts and his two men remained concealed most of the day as high up on the bluffs as possible so as to watch for the movement of the other hunters, as well as to scan for the cat. Even from this perspective the density of the forest canopy obscured their surveillance efforts. The wildlife officers fanned out and using the preset grids covered the search areas very methodically but slowly, looking for signs or any trace of the cat. Occasionally, someone came across a print giving evidence that the cat passed that area, but no scat was found since the cat was careful to conceal its scent. Black vultures dispatched the carcass of the first deer, and the cat dragged the second deer up the crevice to a spot where it would not be seen by the birds or the men.

Each time a new print was discovered the men felt the hair bristle on their necks and they took extra caution to be vigilant. The parties were equipped with the dart guns and scoped rifles firing either .243,

30-.06 or .30-.30 caliber ammunition. At the end of the first day neither team learned much positive to report, and it was feared the animal had left the Gorge. Pierce's men were not so convinced and believed the big cat still lurked in the area.

The team that descended from the Savage Ranger Station arrived back at the campground where the two Rangers and Deputies camped only two days earlier. Evidence of a hastily evacuated site was abundant. Most of the pitched tents were still standing but holes chewed through the walls indicated chipmunks and squirrels detected food inside the coverings and effectively ruined the tents. Having read the report prepared by Agent Jarrett, the wildlife officers surveyed the campsite and spread out to search the immediate area. One of the Rangers described hearing a crashing sound less than a hundred yards from the campfire. The only rock formations were to the north east of the fire site so they concentrated in that area first. It took them only a few minutes to locate the rock where the cat must have stood and they saw from that position the cat had an excellent view of the campfire. Danger was very near the Rangers and Deputies that night. What most disturbed the team was the discovery of two tranquilizer darts near the rock.

The wildlife officer in charge of that team asked, "Any of you remember the Rangers or Deputies saying they fired the tranquilizer guns at the animal?" He carefully picked up, examined the darts and put them into a plastic bag.

"No," answered another officer, "they did not even see the cat, or discharge the dart guns."

"Then they had company down here," the leader said knowing that complicated matters even more and was something he needed to report as soon as possible. Who else would be looking for that thing?

Having been in this immediate area less than forty-eight hours previously, Pierce's men once again approached the campsite careful to remain concealed. They took up positions from which they monitored the searchers, but were too far away to pick up conversation. Comfortable with merely watching, David and his men settled in behind rock and forest cover. Two yellow eyes followed every movement of Pierce's men as the big cat maneuvered into position behind them.

Yellow sparks from the campfire sparkled up into the night sky as the oak and hickory wood caught fire. Pierce's men heard the muffled talk around the fire but not any of the specific words. After they watched like this for an hour one of David's men whispered, "David, I've got to go take a dump."

"What?" David asked.

"Sorry, but that breakfast burrito is tearing me up," the man said.

"Get way off over there and cover it up. I don't want to smell it, and I don't want that tiger to find it either," David said.

Unfortunately, this would be the man's last bowel movement. He moved off fifty yards behind another boulder and dropped his pants in a squat. Before nature took its course, the big cat was on him and snapped his neck before he could scream. This trained mercenary, man-for-hire, danced with death one final time. For good measure when the man ceased twitching, the cat took one swipe at the man's stomach and released his intestines onto the forest floor, breathing in the man's blood scent deeply before he lumbered back into the darkness.

CHAPTER TWENTY-ONE

Pierce was still working in his office when he received the call that one of the guards in the back was coming to the house with a disk from the surveillance drone that deployed when movement was detected at the rear of the property. The guard, dressed in the regulation all black clothing, came into the house and proceeded to Pierce's office where he found Pierce at his desk.

"Sir, this was stored in the last twenty minutes showing two potential intruders on the back side of the property near the barns," the man said handing the disk to Pierce. Pierce inserted the disk into his computer and pulled up the video.

"Do you know who they are or what they were looking for?" Pierce asked.

"No, sir. They did not breach the fencing or come onto the property as far as we could see," the man reported.

The brief video began to play and Pierce recognized one of the men as the Deputy who called on him earlier in the week.

"Dammit," Pierce said. "Thank you, I will keep this for now. Go ahead and let the dogs loose and let me know if you see any other activity. I will handle this."

When the guard left, Pierce picked up his cell phone and speed dialed the Sheriff.

"Sheriff, I thought you said your office was not actively investigating anything that implicated my cattle farm," Pierce said.

"I can assure you, Mr. Pierce, that we do not," the Sheriff said.

"Then why was your Deputy at the back fence line of my property not thirty minutes ago?" Pierce asked.

"My Deputy?" the Sheriff asked. "Which one?"

"The guy that came out here with that wildlife officer who threatened me," Pierce said. "Young guy with the funny name."

"Let me look into it. I will get back to you shortly," the Sheriff said as the line disconnected. What in the hell was Deputy Baker up to? Hadn't he given specific directions not to involve Pierce in the investigation? The Sheriff could not jeopardize his relationship with Pierce, the money was too good. Perhaps the Deputy should get the message a bit more directly.

The Sheriff picked up his cell phone and punched in a familiar number. It was the direct line to the man who brought Pierce into Sequoyah

County, and was its most influential citizen, County Mayor and car dealer William Cheatham, known to all as "Wild Bill."

"Wild Bill, here," said the jovial voice.

"Bill, it's Mark Brown. We have a problem," the Sheriff said.

"What kind of problem, Sheriff," Wild Bill Cheatham said, his voice becoming immediately more somber. "I thought things were running pretty smoothly for a change."

"One of my deputies has been snooping around Pierce's Farm. He was out there tonight with another guy they didn't recognize at the back fence area," the Sheriff said.

"I thought you told your guys to back off," Cheatham stated.

"Well, I did, but looks like he didn't take it seriously. This Deputy is good and when he gets on a trail, he doesn't give it up. I think he may need a little personal persuasion," said the Sheriff.

"It's your fucking problem so you need to clean it up. But, what I will do is to send a couple of my boys by his house for a little re-education as to how the cow ate the cabbage," said the car dealer. "Then we will see where the investigation goes."

Later, when Yogi and Jack pulled up to Yogi's house they saw Jack's Jeep and Rachel's car in the driveway, but surprisingly there were no lights on in the house and the side door from the carport was standing slightly open.

"I'm not liking this," Yogi said as he grabbed his flashlight in one hand and his service pistol in the other. The carport door opened into the kitchen which was dark. Following Yogi, Jack crept across the kitchen but didn't see anything unusual until they entered the small living room.

"Rachel, Rachel," Yogi called in a hushed voice. Their flashlights panned around the living room and immediately settled on the wall behind the sofa on which was written in red the following statement:

KEEP YOUR NOSE OUT OF PLACES IT DON'T BELONG

That's when Yogi reached over and flicked on the room lights. The message was written in block letters with a paint brush. The ink looked like blood as it oozed down the wall.

"Jesus Christ," Jack said

Noticing an acrid smell, Jack looked around behind an arm chair where he found Cherokee, Yogi's Labrador retriever, and his dog's, Rocket's, best friend. Cherokee was cut open, his guts all over the floor.

"Don't come over here, Yogi," Jack yelled. "Somebody's killed Cherokee. We need to find Rachel." Yogi stared in disbelief, but turned back and stumbled into the short hallway, calling "Rachel, Rachel."

They found Rachel in the bedroom lying across the bed, topless and unconscious. Yogi ran to her saying "Baby, baby, what has happened?"

Jack said, "I'm calling 911." He left the room for the phone he passed in the kitchen. Yogi found a pulse and confirmed that Rachel was alive although her face was swollen and bruised. He threw a shirt around her shoulders and sat on the bed holding her until the ambulance arrived. The EMT's allowed Yogi to ride in the back with Rachel. Before the doors closed, Yogi stuck his head out and said to Jack, "I'm going to get those motherfuckers." He tossed a pair of latex rubber gloves at Jack and said, "Watch what you touch."

Jack nodded and said, "I'll be there with you, partner. Let me take some pictures of the house and take care of Cherokee." Yogi nodded. Jack saw Yogi's jaw clenching and unclenching as anger coursed through his body. Always suppressing his temper just below the surface, when anger seized Yogi he became a single-minded weapon of revenge.

What had happened to his dog had not yet sunk in to Yogi. By inflicting violence on those he loved, the perpetrators crossed a line. Lawman or not, Yogi would not stop until he inflicted justice and his share of revenge on the wrongdoers.

CHAPTER TWENTY-TWO

Jonas and Jarrett sat in Jonas' office at the Stone Door Ranger Station sipping coffee into which Jonas occasionally splashed a little Jack Daniel's fine bourbon. The silky sweetness helped relax the men who were concerned about the other team still down in the Gorge and the safety of those few residents who built vacation cabins or houses along the rim of Savage Gulf. While most of the rim was protected within the Park, a few acres was developed affording spectacular vistas across the Gulf especially at sunrise and sunset. The county newspaper lay open on the desk displaying the lead story:

TIGER SEEN IN SAVAGE GULF AREA

Northwoods, Tennessee. At least one resident in the Savage Gulf wilderness area has reported seeing what appeared to be a tiger resting on a rock ledge looking over into the Gorge. The local Sheriff's office responded to the call but the animal disappeared before the Deputy arrived. Other neighbors have reported strange sounds and the loss of more than one dog. The Sheriff's Office had no comment other than to note that the resident, Mabel Porter, who reported the sighting, admitted to having had several drinks, and that she was the same person who reported UFO's in the area last year.

"The neighbors aren't panicking yet, are they," Jarrett asked.

"No. Most people discount what Mabel reports. She's a little touched, and a little too fond of Scotch whiskey," Jonas responded. "Have you seen anything like this before?"

"If you mean the tiger, I was assigned to the Denver Agent in Charge a few years back when a mountain lion went on a rampage up in Boulder. The no hunting ordinances in Boulder County meant the lion had a free rein to follow the game, mostly elk and mule deer, that came out of the mountains and straight onto the campus at the University of Colorado. The game was so numerous Elk lounged in grassy areas beneath trees outside the dormitories. The Boulderites thought it was all so serene they began to write poems about it and make documentary films. That all changed when the cougar moved into the neighborhoods behind the game. First, they cleaned out all the neighborhood dogs and cats. Then one of the cougars attacked and killed a cross country runner near his high school. People started to go nuts then."

"What happened?" Jonas asked.

"Some of us got dispatched up there, but that cat was smart. It managed to elude all efforts to track it down, but the activity forced it back up into the foothills. When it got hungry it came back and went after livestock in the valley. That's when the local cattlemen got involved and ordinance or no ordinance they tracked him and disposed of the cat."

"Think I heard about that," Jonas said. "Somebody wrote a book about it."

"Yep. Something called *The Beast in the Garden*, or something close to that. It was a wild time. If your question meant something like this animal trafficking thing, we've pursued these guys for years. They like fairly remote areas where there are not a lot of eyes watching them. There is way too much crazy money out there. A big cat like this one could fetch a hundred thousand dollars. Even stuffed it would be worth at least ten grand. Most of what we see however, is birds and monkeys. They are smaller and easier to handle. A good parrot could be worth five to ten thousand dollars, same for just a fertile egg. It's sad but most of the animals won't survive. Either the climate is not right or the food source is all wrong. Plus, they are kept in captivity and lose the natural ability to socialize with their own kind. Monkeys especially are susceptible to depression." Jarrett shook his head as he told the story.

"What's driving the trade?" Jonas asked.

"Clearly the money, but it's also power and standing, almost like owning a rare painting. When you've got everything else, money becomes unimportant, but being able to show a live Bengal Tiger to your friends and associates, now that's a testosterone shot," Jarrett said tipping the Jack Daniel's into the coffee cup once more. "Some of these assholes let them loose on large compounds so they can be hunted. You know, the same crowd that thinks shooting bears hibernating in their den is sport."

"This looks like a pretty sophisticated operation to be bringing in a tiger," Jarrett said continuing. "When the Deputy and I went out to that Farm, I was convinced there was way too much surveillance for a cattle operation. That guy Pierce also struck me as a little sleazy. He really bristled when I told him what I suspected."

"Pierce is well connected here, and spreads the money around. No way you can tell who is or is not on his payroll," Jonas said.

"I know how to watch my ass," Jarrett said. Jonas was thinking he was way too close to retirement to be sticking his neck out now, and that Jarrett ought to be thinking the same thing. A bond of brotherhood was forging between the two men.

"What's your best story as a wildlife officer?" Jonas asked.

Jarrett thought a minute and said, "The time we caught the animal traffickers with a man in a gorilla suit."

Jonas blew a mouthful of high octane coffee back into his mug, some of it right through his nose where it burned.

"What?" he said.

"Yep, we had these Mexicans trading in exotics out of Miami. Even though we knew what they were doing, we couldn't build enough evidence to nail them without money changing hands. They really wanted a gorilla and well, there just weren't any we could use as bait, so we dressed up one of our men, a Marine, in a gorilla outfit and stuck him in a cage in the back of a DC-3. The gorilla suit came with red flashing eyes so we had to take those out, but we put straw and real ape shit in the cage with him and gave him a two by four so he could bang against the cage. Our mark came onto the plane, saw the gorilla and paid us right there. Our code word was "Geronimo". If anyone said that, it was time to shut down the operation and make an arrest. Well, the gorilla said "Geronimo", opened the door and walked out of the cage. That's when the Mexican about killed me trying to get off the plane. He was that convinced a real gorilla was about to get him. Some Customs Agents we were working with helped me wrestle him down and handcuff him. We made that case. Hell, we heard from agencies all over the world after that story got around. I heard someone in Hollywood even stole the idea and put it into a Dan Akroyd movie."

"No shit," Jonas said in his south Alabama drawl.

Long into the night the two veterans shared war stories of years spent managing wildlife and wilderness areas. They both despised poachers and traffickers as subhuman. Meanwhile, their men crouched around campfires and listened for any sound that might announce the presence of the beast.

CHAPTER TWENTY-THREE

When fifteen minutes passed and his man did not come back from relieving himself, David Ramparts began to feel very uneasy. It was taking way too much time for a task that should have lasted only a couple of minutes. Afraid that his man could have slipped and hurt himself, David signaled to his partner, Larsen, that he was going to check. As the red lens of his flashlight moved back and forth across the rocks and roots beneath his feet, David carefully negotiated the difficult terrain so as not to dislodge a rock or give away his presence. He reached the rock where his man disappeared and stepped around it to find the dead mutilated body. Damn it, he thought. Now what to do? His man was dead and the scene was gruesome. Instinctively, David crouched low and looked for any signs of the tiger. There were none he saw only the savaged body in front of him. It would not be wise for him and Larsen to separate but they couldn't leave the body exposed. Instead, David elected to cover the body with stones and brush and come back for it later. He was coming to grips with the knowledge he was over his head trying to tranquilize this animal. It was too powerful and too smart. David was not a man to admit a failure and Mr. Pierce was not one to acknowledge failure either. He and Larsen would have to regroup in the daylight, retrieve the body and come up with a better plan. So that he could find the exact spot tomorrow, David left his cell phone beneath leaves where he covered the body and began the journey back to the truck with his associate.

Ten men camped in the Gorge that night at different campgrounds a few miles apart. None of these men were witnesses to the deaths inflicted by the tiger, but their imaginations ran wild with speculation anyway. Around two campfires the officers recited experiences of big game hunts and even man hunts in terrain even more rugged than Savage Gulf. Some of these field officers served in postings to the mountains in Wyoming, Montana and Arizona and were full of tall tales of adventure, most of which were true. Such stories of danger and survival were intended to bolster the groups' confidence, but it provided only marginal comfort. In the rustle of the breeze through the forest canopy each man perceived different sounds and nuances of sound and each man felt as though unseen eyes were watching him the way your entire body itches all over after you find a single tick crawling on your neck.

When they retired for the night, ten pairs of eyes stared up at the tops of their tents as each man rested but could not sleep. Abruptly, sometime during the night the men at the Stagecoach Road campground were startled by the yips and snarls of coyotes not a hundred yards from the campsite. Excited high pitched barks indicating a successful hunt were punctuated by snarls and aggressive snaps of teeth. At that point sleep was beyond hope and the men climbed out of their tents with guns and flashlights. Someone yelled, "Fuckers," while others grunted and stretched. As beams of bright halogen cruised the tree stands a dozen sets of red glowing eyes appeared constantly moving and challenging the campers from the rocks near the bluffs. These animals protected and fought over something, some food source. The officers began flailing their arms and yelling at the canines as they approached the area of disturbance only to find that the animals had dug up a body and were jerking and yanking flesh and entrails.

"Oh my God," one of the officers said as the others gathered having now chased back the coyotes. "Go get me one of the tarps or rain flies so we can wrap this up." He said to another of the officers. The gory scene unnerved them all. "Frank, get on the sat phone and call the other group to come on over here," the officer in charge said. "They can't be more than a mile or two up that path. We are going to need to regroup."

Within a short time both groups were together at the Stagecoach Road campground. It was clear to them that the grid search method did not produce the desired result and was not likely to since this animal was smart enough to double back and come at them from the rear. In the night the faint barks of the retreating coyotes reminded them what a survival challenge this wilderness presented. These men were professionals in wildlife management and hunting, but not skilled in counter-measures to protect themselves when they became the hunted.

CHAPTER TWENTY-FOUR

The medical staff treated and released Rachel having diagnosed a mild concussion with contusions. Whomever did this struck or slapped her hard in the face a couple of times and in falling she hit her head. Yogi was relieved to learn she had not been sexually assaulted so as to save her that trauma. Still, his fury burned with an intensity he rarely felt. That someone would do this to the girl he loved who was innocent of any offense was unforgiveable. There would be consequences for anyone involved, he vowed. Since his home was now a crime scene Yogi and Rachel couldn't stay there for a few days and he did not feel the place was safe for Rachel anyway. Jack invited them to stay with him and Emily whose schedule was flexible leaving her with time to help care for Rachel as Rachel cared Emily previously. Jack called Emily from the hospital when it was clear Rachel would be ok.

"Em, Yogi and Rachel need to stay with us a couple of days, you ok with that," Jack asked over the phone.

"You know I am, what's going on?" Emily asked.

"I'll explain when we get there, but Rachel's been beat up and someone trashed their house," Jack said.

"Beat up?" Emily asked. "What have you and

Yogi gotten into this time?"

"I'll explain more when we get there," Jack answered.

"Bet your ass you will," Emily said as he disconnected. Good, Jack thought, that was the old Emily talking.

After Jack and Emily married they moved to another faculty home on the Mountain, not unlike the one Jack leased before, but different enough that it did not evoke memories in Emily of the fateful night when she took on Dr. Julian Browne. No matter how much fresh paint he applied, Jack knew Emily would never make it in his old home. Some stains persevere and resist eradication. A large second bedroom on the second floor of this new home was used frequently by friends passing through so Emily kept it ready for the next visitor with clean sheets and towels. She was not ready, however, for how Rachel looked when they arrived. Emily thought Rachel to be one of the most exquisitely featured women she had ever known. High cheek bones supported her ocean blue eyes. Rachel could have been carved from ancient alabaster so smooth was her complexion and so finely chiseled was her face. But, tonight all that charm and beauty was disfigured by swelling and facial bruises. One of Rachel's eyes was almost swollen shut. Emily saw the worry on Yogi's face and his set jaw as they helped Rachel to the door and up to the guest bedroom.

Jack came back down to the living room as Yogi got Rachel settled in.

Emily asked him, "Where's Cherokee?" Cherokee and Jack's dog Rocket were best friends and Emily had gotten Rocket excited telling her that Cherokee was coming for a visit. Just the mention of Cherokee's name caused Rocket to take on a wiggling fit.

Jack looked up the stairs, then back to Emily, "Those animals killed him. Right now he's in the back of my Jeep." Emily gasped.

"What," she asked, "is going on?" Her voice was firm and not about to put up with any bullshit, so Jack leveled with her.

"The wrongful death case Calvin and I are working on parallels an investigation Yogi is involved in, so tonight he and I went out to check out the backside of Pierce's Farm," Jack said.

"Yeah," Emily asked, "what has that got to do with Rachel? Who would want to hurt her?"

"We didn't do anything, didn't even go on the Farm property. But, someone saw us before we could get away. I think Rachel was a message. There was a sign on Yogi's wall telling him to keep his nose out of other people's business," Jack said.

"You said you were with him. Did they see you, too?" she asked.

"I don't know, but we are going to have to be watchful," Jack said, understanding that Emily was now aware they might also be targets. She was not happy. Nosiree, she was not happy.

Yogi came to the bottom of the stairs and wished Jack and Emily "goodnight." Since it was almost one a.m. he said he would try to get a little sleep before things got rolling in the morning. He turned to climb back up the stairs then stopped and looked at Jack. He didn't have to say anything. Jack knew simply from the question on his face.

"I've taken care of him, Yogi. Get some sleep," Jack said not prepared to tell Yogi that he had not yet buried Cherokee on his property next to the sweat lodge but would do so tomorrow. Yogi slowly climbed the stairs with the weight of a five hundred pound gorilla on his back.

CHAPTER TWENTY-FIVE

At first light the ten wildlife officers broke camp and hiked back to the Ranger station sharing the weight of the remains of the unknown man on a stretcher. Jarrett and Jonas were up all night nursing the coffee and Jack Black. As soon as they received the first contact with their men over the radios, Jonas enlisted Jarrett in helping him fix a breakfast of sausage and biscuits on the hotplate and small convection oven at the station. The report of another body triggered Jarrett to call Deputy Baker who answered his cell on the second ring.

Rachel slept soundly so Yogi was up and left Jack's house as soon as he dressed. He scribbled out a note and left it by Jack's phone. On the way down the Mountain to the Ranger Station he hit the "play" button on his cd player and Clapton's *Layla* exploded out the speakers. The power of that riff rocked him. Rachel was his Layla, and by god, he was going to kick someone's ass for her. Someone was going to pay, and right now his money was on Richard Pierce. His Cherokee blood boiled over until the piano break took over and his emotions crashed like waves into Fingal's Cave. Then, Yogi broke down and cried all the way to the Ranger Station. Amid the fury of his anger Yogi reflected that some element of his nature previously kept him from asking Rachel to marry him. It certainly wasn't her fault. She was everything he ever hoped to find and he loved her. Maybe in his growing up, which had been tough at times, he somehow missed the gene that allowed him to make the kind of commitment it took for marriage. He knew it would kill him to lose Rachel, and he knew what he had to do.

For the second time that week the ambulance was called to the Stone Door Ranger Station. It was pulling away as Yogi arrived at the parking lot. Yogi's boots crunched the gravel as he determinedly strode across the lot to the Ranger's cabin where a crowd was gathered. Jarrett quickly introduced the wildlife officers and brought Yogi up to speed on the latest developments.

"Using a search grid was simply not my best idea," Jarrett said. "That cat is sharp enough to double back, making the grid more like handcuffs than a useful tool."

"So where do we take it from here?" one of the wildlife officers asked.

The Agent in Charge said, "We need a real tracker." Jarrett agreed.

"Yes. I think that's what it is going to take. Someone who can think like that cat, follow the spoor and find him," Jarrett said.

Yogi spoke up, "Sir, my cousin, Johnny Running

Bear was a combat tracker, Army Special Forces, trained at Fort McCoy in Wisconsin. He is nearly full blooded Cherokee and I hear he was one of the best."

"I've heard of the Bear," Jarrett said. "He was brought into the Boulder situation but the ranchers got there first."

"I'm sure he would help us," Yogi said.

A few miles away, Pierce gestured with his arms and yelled at David, "You incompetent fool. I obviously sent the wrong men to do the job. I should tell you to pack up your shit, you and that turd assistant of yours, and fire you. But this job's not over yet. Get out of here and see if you can help identify the second man on the drone film Carl has got at the back barn." David nodded and left.

Pacing his office like a caged lion Pierce went back and forth until he realized that he was dealing with a wild beast, and that it would take someone who thought like a wild beast and who had the experience to track such a beast. From his desk phone he called the black ops agency from whom he employed David Ramparts and the other guards at the Farm.

"Mr. Pierce, how can we help you today?" asked the proper young woman.

"Your men have been a serious disappointment

we will need to discuss at the appropriate time," Pierce said.

"I am sorry to hear that, Sir. Mr Ramparts came to us very highly recommended," the lady said.

"What do you mean "highly recommended?" I thought he had been associated with your organization for an extended period."

"Mr. Ramparts came to us only a few weeks before we deployed him to your area," the voice said. Pierce was not pleased with that revelation but filed it away for later consideration.

"What I need now is the best tracker you can find. When I hunted near the Sarengeti I met a tracker who was most special. He may be getting a little old now, but he was good. Man's name was Mingati Kakenya," Pierce said.

"As it happens, Mr. Pierce, Mr. Kakenya is known to us and has worked with us previously on a contract basis. He is one of the best in the world," said the woman.

"I want the best tracker in the world," Pierce bellowed.

"I understand. Mr. Kakenya's reputation is first class especially in large animals," she said.

"Is he the best?" Pierce demanded.

"If he's not the best, he's in the top two. You will not be disappointed. We can have him to you tomorrow. He is in the States' now. Usual delivery at the Mountain airfield, at noon tomorrow?" she asked.

"Perfect. I'll be there. Tell him to look for my helicopter," Pierce said. He was rubbed the tiger claw hanging from his neck and thought "no more Mr. Niceguy."

CHAPTER TWENTY-SIX

Johnny Running Bear traveled light. His knap
sack contained a rolled up space blanket, a water
bottle, some energy bars, a flashlight, a hunting knife
and a stick. It was not any old stick but one that
Johnny made after researching the size and stride of
an animal as big as this tiger. There were other
notches on the stick to mark important distances that
were significant only to Johnny or another tracker
who possessed the same skills and knew how to
calculate the subtle differences between a stride, a
lope or a flat out run. As a tracker Johnny mastered
the subtleties of following a wild animal over rugged
terrain. A depression here, or a clump of hair there
could be the only sign he was on the right path, the
only hint the animal passed this way. The stick fit into
a slot on the sack and was attached with Velcro tight
to the pack sticking up taller than Johnny's head. His
pickup truck pulled into the gravel lot by the Stone
Door Ranger Station at dawn where he was greeted
by his cousin, Yogi Baker. Yogi wanted to meet
Johnny at the start of the mission, but he had other
plans to follow up on that day. Inside the Ranger
Station, Johnny was introduced to Jonas, the Ranger
in Charge, as well as John Jarrett, and two other
wildlife officers from USFWS. Over the objection
and caution of Jonas, Jarrett committed to fill out the
team of four who would descend into the Gorge to
track the animal.

As the men studied the topo map Johnny ran his fingers along the rim lines where they were closer together and thus steeper points of demarcation. Johnny was dressed in buckskins with his jet black hair tied into a ponytail at the back. At six feet two and two hundred pounds he looked the Indian chief he was becoming. The Cherokee Nation recognized him as a natural leader who would one day sit on the Tribal Council. His cousin, Yogi, knew of Johnny's skills and was proud to be related.

"What are you looking for?" Jonas asked.

"Points of escape," Johnny said. "I would like to start at the place where the last body was found," he said to Jarrett who looked at one of the wildlife officers who was at the scene the day before. Johnny was a man of few words and preferred the direct approach. There were no shades of subtlety in his speech, no shades of gray. With Johnny what you saw was what you got.

"I can get us there, but I am afraid that sight is pretty messed up with our tracks and the coyote prints," the officer said.

"That won't matter," Johnny said. "It may make it a little harder to get started but that is a fixed point where we know the cat was present."

Grabbing their packs, the four men took the trail

down the Stone Door and then back into Savage Gulf following the switchbacks until they met up with another trail and turned north towards the place the last body was discovered. All the while Johnny's eyes scanned the path and woods for any evidence of animal tracks. For the most part the trail was packed hard by the feet of hundreds of visitors who made their way through the Gorge each day and left no signs that would help locate the animal. Johnny asked the officer to let him know when they were within a hundred yards of the site so, when they stopped, Johnny knew it was time for him to go to work.

"Please remain here until I call," Johnny said. The others nodded and watched as he carefully walked off into the woods his head down scouring the forest floor for signs. Before he passed out of sight they saw him drop on all fours his face only inches from the ground. From time to time they watched as he removed his moccasins and moved lightly around the area. Johnny was observing everything from the turn of a leaf, to a scrape on a tree, to depressions beneath the leaf cover his fingers feeling for warmth or coldness. After an hour he emerged from the forest and said,

"Please follow me, single file and make as little disturbance as you can."

Johnny led them along a circuitous route to the boulder where the body was found but stopped them several feet from the rock. They looked around and saw plenty of disturbance but nothing that spoke of a trail left by a marauding tiger.

Johnny spoke, "There has been much action of this area. The body was lying here. Surrounding the body are coyote tracks leading to and away from where the corpse was. The earth still bears the stench of death and blood stains."

Crouching low and using his stick as a pointer, Johnny continued, "Here and here, we see man prints, some of which may belong to our officers, but others that are different, at least two different sets with boots that are more military issue. Those would have been the compatriots of the victim."

Strain as they would none of the others in the group picked out anything but rustled leaves and scuffed up dirt, but they were impressed with Johnny's skills and the attention to details. Still in a crab walk Johnny scooted fifteen feet from the boulder to the high ground behind it.

He said, "And here, is where the cat stood when it jumped him. There are clear feline impressions in the soil."

Standing, Johnny walked back to the placement of the body. "The cat left in this direction," he said gesturing with his arm along the side of the bluff. Johnny knelt again and with his stick measured from one print in an arc until he located the next impression. He placed his hand on the ground and said, "the tracks left by this animal are generally nothing more than depressions in either the soil or the leaf cover, but I think we can track him."

Jarrett walked over to Johnny and said, "Ok, let's get started. Is there any sign he doubled back?"

"No. But, there is something disturbing," Johnny said.

"What?" asked Jarrett.

"We're not the only ones tracking that cat," Johnny said. "We've got company, and he's good."

"What are you talking about?" Jarrett asked.

"Here is a bare footprint," Johnny said pointing at a faint depression in the soil. "The second and third toes are longer than any of the other toes. I know that print."

"You know bare footprints?" one of the officers asked incredulously, clearly impressed by Johnny but not at all convinced he could identify a bare footprint in a 20,000 acre wilderness. He knew there was good, and there was also bullshit.

"I have tracked with this man before, but I thought he had retired. He is a Maasai named

Mingati Kakenya. We just called him Gati," Johnny said.

"What's a Maasai?" asked one of the officers.

"An African tribe known for its warriors and trackers. Gati was the best in the world at one time," Johnny said.

"So, who's best now?" the officer asked.

"Me."

CHAPTER TWENTY-SEVEN

Not being able to identify the image on the delivery truck's door really bugged Yogi. He knew if he could follow that lead it would open the investigation even wider and provide valuable avenues to run down. The vehicle was too far away and it was dark, but there was something vaguely familiar about the symbol. He knew the symbol on the truck's door was a familiar one. Yogi sat at the front table by the expansive plate glass window bearing the script identifying the store as The Dusty Donut, the local Northwoods coffee shop. In deep thought, Yogi's mind rolled the images of the delivery truck over and over when he heard the "beep-beep-beep" of a truck backing up outside the window. He was immediately jerked back to the present. It was a delivery van from the local Chevrolet dealership trying to back into a parking space next door. On the passenger side door was the Chevrolet "bow-tie" symbol. He squinted his eyes to make the door look smaller and wondered if that could be the image he saw at the Farm. Yogi watched as two blocky men got down from the cab and came into the shop for donuts and coffee. He covered his face with his hand as if he were reading something and made himself inconspicuous until they had left. Detective Yogi constructed a plan.

Yogi drove to town that morning in a borrowed pickup truck that belonged to a friend.

When the delivery truck drove away from the café, Yogi followed it to its destination, a typical glass and metal gray and blue Chevrolet dealership. Yogi was a Ford man himself and didn't believe in paying for all the unnecessary bells and whistles GM put into its vehicles to justify raising the price every year. Driven by his determination to bring justice to whomever hurt Rachel and to do his job, Yogi pulled into the "Customer" parking area of Wild Bill Cheatham's Chevrolet dealership. Driving his police unit on the lot would have ruined the mood. It was his intent to find out what he could about the parts delivery drivers, but he was not on the lot more than a minute when a cheery voice hailed him.

"Howdy, pardner. My name's Scotty, how can I help you today?" Salesman Scotty learned to sell cars the natural way. His grandfather taught him how to sell wagons. "Son, you get a man interested in a wagon and he asks you how much. You tell him $400 for the wagon. If he doesn't flinch you tell him the wheels are extra and you say they are $100. If he still doesn't flinch you tell him EACH." Salesmen were the same everywhere, friendly and packed with bullshit. That also meant they were the easiest to bullshit in return. The early morning breeze rustled the triangular red, white and blue flags running off the light poles and tied to the low fencing across the front of the lot. Each vehicle on the front row flew an American flag over its antenna. Wild Bill was a patriotic guy, and the Memorial Day Sale worked so why not leave up the tinsel for another six months?

"Looking for a new ride," Yogi said doubling down into his Appalachian accent where "nice", "white", and "rice" all rhymed. Although he and Jack graduated from the University together, Yogi naturally slipped into the local dialect he heard his entire life like changing pants.

"Here at Wild Bill's we are the walking man's friend," Scotty said. Yep, Yogi thought, the bullshit was about to get deep.

"Let's look at pickups. Gotta be four wheel drive," Yogi said.

"Wouldn't have nothing else would we?" the salesman said as they walked to a row of shiny new Silverados glistening in the early morning sun. This late in the season most of the selection were either white (although nothing was "white" but rather "arctic" this or that) or hang around brown. Yogi admired the chrome and pretended to examine the window stickers and let out a "Whew," scratching his head.

"Don't let that sticker bother you. Wild Bill wheels and deals on the price," Scotty said.

"What about parts and service. A good service department and plenty of parts is real important to me," Yogi said.

"Then this is the right place for you. All of our technicians are certified and Wild Bill has the largest wholesale parts operation in the mid-south. Our parts manager, Bobby D ships anywhere within a two hundred mile radius."

"All the way to Atlanta?" Yogi asked.

"Yep. We have regular runs to Hot 'lanta," the salesman said, now in full stride.

"How many trucks ya got?" Yogi asked.

"Just two but they keep rolling," Scotty said.

"I used to have a cousin who worked over here as a driver. Who's driving for you boys now," Yogi asked.

Salesman Scotty said, "Wild Bill uses a couple of guys, one's named George and the other, Potts. Why you asking all these questions? You going to buy a truck or not? You've been busting my nuts for a half hour." The salesman sensed his balloon was leaking badly and what he thought was an opportunity for a sale just went screaming up into thin air.

"Maybe not today," Yogi said. Having decided Yogi was a tire kicker and not a real pigeon, Scotty walked off having dumped Yogi like a bad habit. Scotty was much too busy to waste his time on this guy. Yogi wandered around to the back of the store where the two parts delivery trucks were parked and opened the door that was marked as "Parts Department." He stepped inside a small room with a counter that was bare except for a computer monitor and two of the beefiest arms he ever saw. The arms, somewhat resembling Popeye's, popped with extended veins reaching up to massive shoulders and a square head devoid of any semblance of a neck. Yogi knew there were some steroids in this boy's diet.

"What you need, pal?" said the man whose dark hair was close cropped military style his skull shining through the stiff black stalks of hair. There was so much meat on his face his deep set eyes were a permanent squint and made him look almost hog like. The man's nose was flat and flared and his chin was marked with the largest cleft Yogi had ever seen on a human.

Yogi stepped up to the counter and extended his hand, "Y'all hiring?" he asked.

The big man who had the name "Potts" sewn on a patch above his shirt pocket also reached out and shook Yogi's hand, his big paw completely swallowing Yogi's hand. It felt to Yogi like he was in the grip of a wild bear. Potts' squinty eyes looked Yogi up and down, thinking they met before somewhere, but not certain. A permanent grin, well maybe more of a sneer, was etched on the man's face.

It was the kind of face that invited you to insult him, after which he would destroy you. Potts was convinced he was bullet proof with such a low center of gravity he could face a charging wild boar and win. Yogi extracted his hand and assumed his best "aw shucks" posture. This guy was clearly the kind of muscle a kingpin would use to rough someone up. Was Wild Bill one of the bad guys? Yogi knew Cheatham was the County Mayor but had never interacted with him personally. Occasionally, Yogi would have to stand post at the County Commission meetings so he knew who the Mayor was. Potts on the other hand had thug tattooed all over him. Yogi noticed his right knuckles bore the ink stains of the word "HOGS" over the knuckles in a style Yogi observed on county inmates who went to state prison at least once and were on the way back.

"Wild Bill's pretty particular about who works back here. Don't think we need any help right now, but you stay in touch," Potts said looking back at his computer screen as he dismissed Yogi.

"You can count on it," Yogi said as he walked back toward the door. He reached for the door knob and looked back at Potts. Without speaking he gave Potts a glare that said you bet you will see me again. His instincts told Yogi, he was on the right track.

CHAPTER TWENTY-EIGHT

While watching Johnny work was fascinating, it also bored the shit out of the other team members. He missed nothing, he assumed nothing. Tracking both the tiger and another tracker he expected the unexpected. A couple of hours of this and they moved maybe a mile from the original position by the boulder. Overhead the wind continued its endless roar down the canyon. Early morning chill was being replaced by warmer air as the day wore on.

Johnny bent down and said, "Ah."

"What?" Jarrett asked.

"Cat paws," Johnny said.

"Yeah, well we are following a tiger, aren't we?" asked one of the USFWS Officers somewhat sarcastically.

Johnny gave him a quick look of disdain and explained, "The tracker has covered his feet to throw us off. Cat Paws cover shoes or bare feet and disguise the trail. He believes someone is out here behind him. He did not use much care concealing his trail and left just enough of a track that a following tracker would be thrown off." After surveying the area Johnny said, "I believe the tracker went off in that direction, but the tiger went this way," as he gestured back into the woods. "And, I believe this is misdirection by Gati, who suspects someone may be following him."

Johnny moved in the direction he thought the cat travelled and came to the edge of a creek. "Ah," he said again pointing to the other side of the creek. "Boot prints. The others did go this way." A smudge of water on a round river rock bore the tread of a boot. "We are on the right trail."

Ahead, Kakenya removed the coverings on his feet and rejoined the trail where Pierce's men followed in the general direction of the far bluff Gati pointed out before deviating onto a false trail. Gati knelt and felt a tiger imprint on the loose soil. It was still warm and they were getting close. The team leader came over and spoke with Gati then returned to his men and everyone steeled themselves against the final approach. Gati went ahead to the edge of the bluff surveying every stick and pebble then hurried back to his employers.

"The tiger has followed a narrow path up a gulley along a creek to the top of the rim. His tracks are very clear but it will be a difficult climb due to the wet soil from the rain a couple of days ago," Gati said in broken English, then holding up his hand for silence, looked toward the top of the bluff almost eight hundred feet straight up and then back in the direction from which they had come.

"Others follow," he said. "We have an advantage but not much. Your two best climbers with the dart guns need to go up as quietly as possible and take whatever shot presents itself. The tiger may have food up there so it will defend the area."

The team leader put his finger to his lips then motioned for two of his men with tranquilizer guns to begin the climb. One man lingered behind in case those who followed needed to be discouraged. Quietly, the former special forces soldiers began the climb up the gulley using the trees lining the creek to stop themselves from backsliding as much as possible since the area was sticky with mud from the earlier rain. For thousands of years water and wind eroded the rock formation until the rock melted into a gradual incline for most of the way to the lip of the rim. With weapons slung across their backs the men reached points where they free climbed up to a ledge and then up to another until they were within a few feet of the top. The tiger climbed quickly and the strength in its arms and legs propelled him effortlessly to the rim. Only a couple of feet from the top the two men paused side by side and braced against the rocks. One of the men pulled a periscope from his back pack and slid the lens just over the edge of the rim. There, not twenty feet away lay the tiger and nearby the carcass of a freshly killed deer. The cat's back undulated as he breathed deeply in and out. What a magnificent creature the hunter thought. He passed the scope to his partner who stared briefly at the same vision of the sleeping animal.

With the pace of a wooly worm each man inched upward until his head cleared the rim and he had a clear sight line to the tiger. Silently each man checked the rifle to confirm a dart was chambered. The soft click as the bolt closed on each gun was not unnoticed by the tiger who ears moved and rotated to the sound. As one of the men counted down, three-two-one the big cat sat up. The CO_2 cartridge in each gun spat a single dart with enough chemical to knock out a horse. As the first dart struck pay dirt and buried deep into the animal's flank, the tiger leapt up and roared, but there was nothing he could do about the dart embedded in his leg where he couldn't reach it. The beast shook his body side to side in an attempt to shake the dart off. Once again rage erupted in him and he lurched into action now facing the edge of the bluff. The tiger lunged at the two heads visible over the rim and swung his huge paw connecting powerfully with the head of one of his attackers. The blow knocked the man into his partner causing both men to lose their grip and fall back into the gorge. Few were present to hear the sound of the bodies landing with a dull thud and bouncing off the rock faces a hundred feet from the rim. As the drug overcame him, the tiger stumbled and collapsed but he did not pass out. He was lucky the second dart missed wide for the second dart would have been a knock-out punch.

From below the team leader and the others watched in horror as the men bounced like stuffed mannequins face first down the face of the bluff. When the bodies came to rest, the team leader scrambled up to his fallen men but it was clear the effort was hopeless. Both were dead. One man's head was crushed from the side which knocked out both his eyeballs and the other man's face collided with the rock walls multiple times on the way down rendering him almost unrecognizable as human. The team leader yanked out his satellite phone and called for the ATV transport for the top of the bluff. Not knowing where they would ultimately track down the animal four such ATV's were positioned on each rim out of sight. The team leader, the Maasai tracker and the last living member of the team scrambled back up the crevice but the tiger was nowhere to be seen. Gati pointed to the ground and followed tracks back into the woods.

"Come on Gati. We will circle back later. For now we need to move out," the Team Leader said.

A pair of ATVs arrived within fifteen minutes and five minutes later, they disappeared back into the forest and were gone.

Johnny's group heard the roar from the beast and hustled their pace, but they could not overcome the sizeable head start of the other group. By the time they located the creek gulley leading to the top, the ATVs and the tiger had already disappeared back into the forest at the top. The two mangled bodies of the nameless men bearing no identification lay jumbled against tree trunks like two heaps of broken straw many feet from the top.

CHAPTER TWENTY-NINE

Wild Bill Cheatham took the call on his cell phone before the second ring. The tune playing was *The Lion Sleeps Tonight* which, considering their current dilemma, was just a bit ironic but it identified the caller as Pierce.

Richard Pierce said, "Reporting that we have not secured the tiger."

"What happened this time?" Cheatham asked.

Pierce laid out the details of his men's report and that the tiger was wounded somewhere near the top of the Gorge.

"How long before you have the animal?"

"A couple of days should be fine," Pierce answered. "But, you need to know we lost another couple of men, who were left in the Gorge."

"Dammit. How'd that happen?" Cheatham asked.

"They got too close to the tiger," was all Pierce said and left the call.

Cheatham did not like leaving loose ends especially when those strands were dead bodies of hired guns who would be hard to trace. Too many questions could be asked, but nothing was traceable back to Cheatham or so he thought. In the past, when the TBI had got a little too close to his stolen car parts operation, he branched out into exotic animals. Stolen parts were easier. All you needed was a few local "chop shops". Parts didn't eat or run away and were always in demand by other chop shops throughout the rural south. He missed those good old days. Back then he rode shotgun on his delivery trucks with a buckshot loaded twelve gauge just for the hell of it. Nobody fucked with Wild Bill.

Finding Pierce was a stroke of luck, almost too lucky he thought on occasion, and until the incident with this damn tiger, their operation ran smooth as silk. Pierce came highly recommended as someone who could play the part of a gentleman farmer and kept his mouth shut. And yet, as impregnable as Cheatham thought his cover was, an uneasy feeling plagued him that something was beginning to unravel the way one loose fiber of a knitted sweater could set off a chain reaction destroying the entire fabric. For the first time Cheatham felt the uncomfortable angst of vulnerability. He considered the two million dollars a year they netted on the animals, and how the trade just grew and grew. Sure, he skimmed off the top of his car dealership. All his Finance and Insurance income and rebates hit his personal account. Insurance companies fell all over themselves paying him commissions so long as he could hook the unsuspecting customer. For years he stole from General Motors for years by adding unnecessary work to his warranty claims and reporting parts sold under warranty that never made it to the customer's car. Those parts disappeared into the black market stream of stolen and reassembled vehicles only to reappear in his bank account. One hundred per cent profit is what that was called. Create your own opportunities. Yippee Hiyay. Isn't that why they called him Wild Bill? Since he also owned the local bank, there was no scrutiny of what flowed into and out of his accounts.

Wild Bill didn't get where he was by taking unnecessary chances or not having back up plans so he concentrated on who was tugging on his web. He kept coming back to the Deputy who appeared on the scene of the wreck, then showed up at Pierce's front door, followed by an appearance at Pierce's back door. Despite barking at the Sheriff to keep his man in line, and despite having sent Potts and George to visit the guy's girlfriend, the Deputy hadn't backed off yet. But where was he? And, who was the second man at Pierce's that night?

Cheatham obtained a photo of the Deputy from the Sheriff's Department website and emailed it to Potts in the Parts Department with the tag *Be on the lookout for this guy*. Within minutes of hitting the SEND button, Potts had replied,

Looks like the guy who came in here today looking for a

driver's job.

God dammit, Cheatham thought, but typed *RU Sure?*

Pretty sure, was the reply.

Find out where he's staying. I don't think he's been back to his house since you last visited there, Cheatham typed.

OK. Potts responded. Before long Potts reported back that the Sheriff heard the Deputy and his girlfriend were staying with friends at the University, a Dean of the school whose name was Jack Mathews. Cheatham pulled up the University website on his computer and clicked on the "Administration" tab. BINGO. He recognized the second man at Pierce's farm from the video as soon as the photograph of Jack Mathews loaded. Wild Bill wetted his lips and prepared to call Potts.

CHAPTER THIRTY

From the top of the rock ledge above the gulley Johnny picked out the tracks of two ATVs, the boots of several men, the tiger's prints, and the distinctive footprint of the Maasai tracker. Trackers know a print is a word, but a set of prints is a story. This story told Johnny they were too late. The absence of drag marks in the gravel connected with random track and confirmed the cat walked off under its own power. Johnny picked up a few of the strands of orange and black hair and held out his palm for the others to see. He looked back over his shoulder at the beautiful expanse of Savage Gulf bathed in the golden glow of sunset. The dark line of sunset coursed like a slow wave across the Gorge throwing the forest into twilight. Using ropes the Wildlife Officers hoisted the two bodies up into trees at the bottom of the Gorge to protect them from coyotes. There was not near enough rope to pull them to the top and the gulley did not provide enough traction to complete the process. Rain jackets were duct taped around the head of each dead man to protect from the crows. It was all they could do. Once this gruesome job was finished Jarrett and the other officers joined Johnny. At the top, Jarrett's cell phone connected to the nearest Ranger Station who dispatched help and a vehicle to pull them out. Thank god they would not have to hike back down and back up the Stone Door today, they all thought.

The sun melted below the western rim as the team finally arrived back at the Stone Door Ranger Station. Jarrett briefed Jonas and the Sheriff's Department was called to retrieve the corpses. For the third time in a week the same EMTs showed up at the Ranger Station.

"What kind of party are you boys having over here Jonas?" one of the EMTs asked.

"You don't want to know," Jonas said. Nothing like this had ever happened on his watch. Jarrett thought the same thing, if you didn't count the high school runner the cougar killed in Boulder. With headlamps and climbing gear the EMTs and Rescue Squad went after the bodies.

Yogi responded to the call for the Department and completed the Incident Report. He saw how tired and disappointed Johnny Running Bear was for having arrived at the scene too late to catch the tiger and prevent the deaths of the two men so he suggested they stop at a local pub for a beer before calling it a day. The joint was known as "The Boot Scoot Lounge" and lay in a curve of the road on the way back down to Northwoods.

The Boot Scoot flourished with plenty of cold longnecks and the ambiance of a biker bar. Slightly larger than a double wide, the main room consisted of a half dozen round tables and a few booths along the left side wall. The other end was closed off for the small kitchen area and a couple of rough bathrooms, one bearing the picture of a rooster and the other, a hen. Food was handed through a pass-through to the bartender and the lone waitress who quickly took it to a table so the nachos didn't cool off. If it couldn't be reheated in a microwave, it wasn't on the menu. Along the back wall were shelves of hard liquor and a laminated bar top lined with a long row of bar stools in the form of saddles. Mirrors on the back wall made the place look larger than it really was and enabled the bar tender to watch over his shoulder for trouble. A portion of that wall held a sign that said "The Wall of Pain." Beneath the sign were photographs of legendary University of Tennessee football players including Reggie White and Derek Barnett, the most recent addition. There was nothing but Vol fans in these hills. Neon beer signs added a color palette to the otherwise grimy interior. Health inspectors didn't bother to stop.

Most of the regulars sported *Duck Dynasty* beards and wore Carhartts. Yogi wasn't a regular and was careful not to wear his uniform or go into the Boot Scoot packin'. Parnell, the owner, tolerated law men, but didn't want to make a habit of it, seeing how it would be bad for business. The sight of a uniform or a holstered pistol was too inviting a target for a drunk local boy to overlook. He would be glad to measure himself in a bar fight where all his buddies would swear the lawman swung first. The Cherokee DNA that ran through Johnny and Yogi made it impossible for either of them to grow a decent beard and Johnny's jet black hair pulled back in a short pony tail further broadcasted that these two were not typical regulars. The old joke about the taxidermist mounting dead animals was born in this place. "He's one of us, boys" the punchline went.

Experience taught Yogi to pick the nearest table to the door, and preferably with a good sight line to the only door into or out of the Boot Scoot. Regulars lived for bachelor parties at the Lounge which usually devolved into paid talent laying the groom on the floor while onlookers poured beer on both of them. To say the Boot Scoot was a classy place might be an overstatement. Yogi nodded at Parnell who returned it with a twitch of acknowledgment. The waitress, Lois, brought them over a couple of Budweisers. There were other brands in the cooler but nobody drank anything but Bud.

Yogi told Johnny about Rachel and how a couple of thugs knocked her around and left him a message on the wall. The bitterness and anger in his voice had not subsided.

Grimly, Johnny asked "Didn't they realize that was the wrong message?" Yogi never backed away from a fight and he always, always got even. Johnny saw a flash of something in Yogi's eyes, a look that told him Yogi was at the boiling point where his rage would overwhelm common sense and cause him to destroy anything in his way no matter the consequences. He had seen that look before. Hell, he had seen the same look in his own mirror.

"She ok?" Johnny asked.

"Emily's looking after her, and we're staying at their house for a while," Yogi said. Johnny knew and liked Jack and Emily from their adventure the prior year with the Cherokee Tapestry when Jack and Calvin Greathouse represented the Cherokee Nation in the lawsuit involving water rights to the Tennessee River and won. Afterward, the Cherokee Nation adopted Jack into the Long Hair Clan.

"Good people. Know who did it?" Johnny asked.

"I've got a couple of candidates in mind, in fact one of them is sitting over there right now," Yogi said as he gestured with the bottle to a massive back at a table at the other side of the room where Potts sat with a group. If that back belonged to a boar hog, he would have been named Hogzilla.

Johnny followed the direction of the bottle and said dryly, "Normal sized guy, huh?"

One of the men at the table with Potts saw Yogi pointing and said something to Potts who pushed his chair back and while twisting his torso stared at Yogi. Something else was said at that far table and several of the men laughed, probably at some comment directed at the somber Indian who sat stone faced nursing his Budweiser. Potts pushed himself up out of the chair and ambled like a Sumo wrestler over to Yogi and Johnny who watched as he approached without even acknowledging the big man stood in front of them.

"I figured out where I seen you," Potts said to Yogi who had not moved. "You're that Deputy ain't ya? The one that came snooping around Wild Bill's."

"I might be," Yogi said having locked eyes with Potts. Those eyes revealed no fear of the larger man.

"The one with that pretty blonde girlfriend, right?" Potts snickered. Yogi didn't respond. Potts let that sink in, then he said, "How you like living up at the University, pal?" Yogi remained mute.

"The pretty blonde with the nice rack," Potts taunted looking back at his pals all of whom were grinning encouragement. Yogi slowly rose and Johnny with him two bodies in perfect symmetry of motion. At six feet two Johnny towered over the fireplug shaped Potts.

"You stay out of it, Sitting Bull," Potts said. "This ain't your fight, unless you want to stick your nose where it don't belong, too."

"We are family," Johnny said.

"Funny, Deputy Dog there don't look Injun," Potts said, the words slobbering out of his mouth like spit grits.

Potts turned and squared up to Johnny sizing him up in his buckskins and moccasins. As that phrase about sticking his nose where "it don't belong" emitted from Potts' mouth, Yogi knew who had been in his home, who had assaulted Rachel. This was the retard who would pay.

Without moving his head Yogi looked over at Johnny who came to the same conclusion. Johnny gave the slightest nod. Although Yogi raged on the inside his discipline enabled him to bury the fury for the moment and assess the situation. He remembered "don't swing before the bell rings," a phrase he and Johnny quoted to each other many times growing up. They were been in scrapes before and never, ever lost. Now, Johnny faced off against a no neck, red neck. Advantage, Johnny. Three other Cro-Magnons stood in reserve each armed with at least one glass bottle. Advantage? Who knew?

"You are making a serious mistake," Johnny said. Yogi and Johnny were men of a different caliber than Potts had engaged before.

"Aren't you supposed to say kemo sabe, Injun? Yes, sir a real nice rack on that one." Potts intended to provoke Yogi at which point his three friends would join in and beat the shit out of these two. Everyone would swear the lawman or his Indian buddy threw the first punch. Potts forgot the old saying "Be careful what you wish for, you might get it."

Johnny faced Potts with his left hand cradled in his right elbow and his forearm slack, raised as if he were going to make the next argument in a political debate. A second passed and before Potts could launch another taunt, like a piston Johnny's arm cocked and two straight fingers slammed forward into Potts' solar plexus knocking him off balance and completely paralyzed. As Potts gasped for air and began to crumble Johnny brought his right elbow up slamming into Potts' jaw and dropping him like the sack of shit he was. Johnny was trained to throw the first disabling blow before the enemy had a chance to score any points. There was no need to spot your adversary any advantage. Potts lay unconscious as Yogi stood over him and poured the rest of his beer on that massive belly. Potts made a serious mistake tangling with a special forces Indian who exacted revenge on the ape who assaulted his cousin's girlfriend. Expecting the others to join the combat Yogi squared up preparing for the charge and set his feet, but it never came. Johnny moved so quickly and with such force against Potts the other three stood there dumbfounded. Nobody had ever demolished Potts like that and none of them were drunk enough to want any part of Johnny. Potts blubbered like a beached whale blood trickling from the side of his mouth where Johnny's forearm broke his jaw and married his bottom teeth to the top of his mouth. When the three men were not able to match the stare from Johnny and Yogi, they knew it was over.

"That's enough boys," Parnell said to the three guys who looked from Potts to Johnny to Yogi. "Get Potts out of here."

"Hey," Yogi yelled after the men who were struggling to drag the three hundred fifty pounds of limp Potts outside, "tell fat ass when he wakes up, we're not done with him yet."

"Tell him," Johnny said, "if he ever touches our women again I will find him and feed his nuts to a tiger."

CHAPTER THIRTY-ONE

Jack Mathews left the faculty meeting he conducted at the University boardroom where he outlined plans for new courses and additional cultural activities for students and faculty in Africa, Asia and South America. He managed to forge strategic alliances with NGO's on three continents who welcomed college students into their workforce. This was exactly the twenty-first century transition the President and Trustees envisioned when he was hired as assistant Dean of the College and then subsequently promoted to Dean when his predecessor never returned from a sabbatical. Jack was also well liked and respected among the faculty as the arbiter of inter-departmental squabbles and the omnipresent maneuvering over funding.

One of Jack's responsibilities was to supervise the annual faculty evaluations. There were always one or two of the faculty who either didn't quite measure up, or who were rumored to be a little too friendly with female students, or who were just so weird or unique they bore additional scrutiny. Emily's boss, Henri Jacques, fit into the latter category. As the Curator for the University's substantial collection of art, he taught at least one Art History course per semester and spent the balance of his time managing the collection and arranging for travelling exhibits to display at the University. Thus, he didn't interact with the other faculty except on a limited basis, and was perceived as "strange" by many. Physically, Henri was also different. He eschewed the black academic robe in favor of a beret and fashionable New York clothing one would see at any gallery in the Big Apple. His boyish good looks and piercing blue eyes also made Jack uncomfortable. The fact that Jack's wife, Emily, worked for Henri and spent a lot of time with him did not help ease the natural tension between the two of them. Subconsciously, Jack knew Henri bore watching.

Jack's predecessor in office arranged for Jacques to be hired, so Jack knew nothing of his background except that there was a year's delay while Jacques fulfilled his obligation to the New York Gallery before coming to the Mountain. There was something about the guy that just didn't ring true to Jack.

The first year of Jack and Emily's marriage was afflicted with Emily's trauma of having shot a visiting faculty member. Jack loved her more than anything and prayed daily she felt the same way. While Emily never gave him any reason to question her love or loyalty, when she disappeared into that dark place, she wasn't the same Emily. The past couple of days where she stood up to care for Rachel, as Rachel earlier cared for her, seemed to root Emily back in their world, and it felt good to Jack.

As Jack left the Administration Building and crossed the Quadrangle he felt his cell phone vibrate in his pocket. The image said Emily was calling.

"I was just thinking about you," he said cheerfully.

"You'd better be, lover boy," Emily said.

"What's up?" Jack asked.

"Yogi called. He needs you to come bail him and Johnny out of jail in Northwoods," Emily said.

"Jail? Are you sure he didn't say he was <u>at</u> the jail?" Jack came back.

"Oh, he's at the jail for sure, but on the wrong side of the bars," Emily answered. "He said he and Johnny got in a fight with a local guy at the Boot Scoot who decided to press charges."

"Jeez. Ok, I will head down there. My schedule is pretty open now that the Faculty Meeting is done," Jack said.

"Did Henri, talk with you?" Emily asked.

"Henri? About what?" Jack asked tentatively.

"He's looking for funding for an art trip to New York," Emily said, "And, he thinks I need to come too."

Jack's heart raced. A moment passed and he said, "No, he didn't mention it. We'll talk about it when I get home." Emily was beautiful in many ways. Her innocence of spirit fused with Jack's soul during the Sweat Lodge ceremony the previous year bonding them like the assemblage of light in a crystal spectrum, alternate colors coming together to form a single white beam. Physically, she was a beauty of much distraction with raven hair and turquois eyes like deep pools into which Jack fell when they first met. That all men found her irresistible and desirable stabbed Jack. He knew he was lucky and unlucky at the same time. Emily turned heads changing the energy level and temperature simply by walking into a room. The thing, Jack realized, was that Emily scarcely knew how or why she had such effect on men because it came to her so naturally. Sensuality was as much a part of her as the blood running through her veins.

"Let me go get Yogi," Jack said. "Love you."

"Love you too," Emily said, and she meant it.

CHAPTER THIRTY-TWO

For Jack, the ride to the Northwoods jail that day was very long. Professionalism demanded he compartmentalize his personal concerns and leave them to resolve at a later time while he focused on Yogi's situation. He was so focused on Yogi he forgot to turn on the radio in his Jeep. Down the plateau, he rode in silence which was only disturbed if he veered too close to the edge of the road where state crews left warning notches in the pavement to alert the driver he was leaving the roadway. Emily's revelation about a trip to New York with Jacques dropped kicked him off the edge as sure as if he had fallen off the observation rock above the Stone Door. Jack drew on his training as a white water paddler and long distance runner to suppress the pain by locking onto a different thought. That day the thought was the singular focus needed to navigate Quarter Mile rapid on the Nolichucky River in northeast Tennessee. A solid quarter mile of Class III-IV rapids tolerated no distractions as he and Yogi learned early on as whitewater canoeists. After that rapid kicked his ass once, he learned to shut everything out of his mind except for the moment his paddle executed the perfect move needed to drop from one series of rapids to the next one following below. For now, Emily would have to remain compartmentalized in his mind, safe and remote until he focused on her again.

Jack was admitted to the interview room by another deputy who was clearly disturbed that the Sheriff ordered that Yogi and Johnny be arrested.

"Ok, guys, tell me about it, from the top," Jack said. After they retold the story of The Boot Scoot Lounge confrontation with Potts and the others, Yogi said,

"We didn't even get through Northwoods before we were pulled over and arrested."

"Seems pretty quick to me," Jack nodded.

"The Sheriff could not have talked to a judge to get a warrant issued in that short time," Yogi said. "You need to know he also suspended me."

"Suspended? Without a hearing and when Johnny actually threw the punch?" Jack asked.

"Yep. No badge, no gun," Yogi said holding his hands out palms up. "Jack, Potts knew Rachel and I were staying with you and Emily."

Jack jumped up and said, "Oh Shit. Look, I will call the Judge and arrange for you to be released, but I've got to get back to Emily and Rachel quickly. Putting you two in here takes pieces off the chessboard, at least for awhile, and opens the door for these guys to do more harm. Do you trust one of these other deputies?"

Yogi said, "Ask Andrew Sparks to come in here. He's the one who escorted you back here."

When Sparks came in, Yogi said, "Sparky, I have reason to believe someone is going to try and hurt my girlfriend Rachel and Jack's wife. Will you go help him? Don't let the Sheriff know."

"You got it. Let's go," Sparks answered giving Yogi a questioning glare that meant "we need to talk about this."

Sparks took the lead and jammed the accelerator of his unit heading back up the country roads from Northwoods to the University. Jack followed in his Jeep as best he could. The square Jeep was no match for the sleek police cruiser. Jack gave Sparky the address as they left the station. On the way Jack used his cell phone to call the Circuit Court Clerk in Northwoods who patched in the Circuit Judge and arranged for a R.O.R. release for Yogi and Johnny. Releasing them on their own recognizance meant no cash bond would need to be posted and that they would be out of jail in a couple of hours. The fact that Yogi was a Deputy and Johnny had no prior record in addition to the fact that the prosecuting witness was a known local thug, along with the fact that the Circuit Judge was a fraternity brother of Jack's back in the day, helped to spring them sooner rather than later.

Pulling up to Jack's driveway both Sparks and Jack came to a screeching stop, their cars still rocking from the emergency braking as they jumped out. Jack ran to the front door which was partially open and yelled, "EMILY,...RACHEL" several times as he bounded from room to room. There was no response but as he passed through the living room, the wall separating the rest of the house was dripping with wet red paint and said: "You been warned."

Jack's feet couldn't keep up with the pace of his heart that was pounding against his chest and throbbing against his temples. There was no sign of either Emily or Rachel, or of Rocket's leash that always hung on a peg in the kitchen. Jack jumped the stairs two at a time to the upstairs bedrooms but again, there was no sign of either woman or his dog. It was a short leap for the image of Cherokee to flash before his eyes and Jack said under his breath over and over "NO, NO" willing his loved ones to be safe.

Sparks made a thorough search of downstairs and was taking photographs of the living room wall when Emily and Rachel came up the front walk led by Rocket who was straining against her leash.

"What's wrong?" Emily asked confused by all the commotion at her house. Rocket, now off her leash charged in through the front door, Emily and Rachel close behind, found Jack and started her full body wiggle as he acknowledged her. Emily's hand came up to her mouth and Rachel just stared at the living room wall.

"Thank god, you two are ok," Jack said putting his arms around Emily.

"Where's Yogi?" Rachel asked.

"He's on the way with Johnny. I got Judge White to release him on his own recognizance," Jack said.

Deputy Sparks said, "Mr. Mathews, I think I have enough to complete the report. You do want me to file a report don't you?"

"Absolutely. Let me know if I need to swing by the Department and sign anything, and thanks for your help," Jack said.

Deputy Sparks touched the brim of his hat and said, "Just my job, but I'd do anything to help a friend of Yogi's."

When the Deputy left, Jack suggested they sit on the back deck and wait for Yogi. Emily poured herself and Rachel a glass of wine as Jack grabbed a Rolling Rock, and they digested what happened that afternoon.

"It was such a nice day Rachel and I decided to stretch our legs so we took Rocket down to the Alley for a hike. There's not much blooming this time of year but the blue asters stand out against the trees," Emily said.

"We haven't been gone more than thirty minutes," Rachel said rubbing her temples. Her face still ached with the bruising from the beating she endured. She only snatched a glimpse of her attackers, but it was enough for her to describe one of the men as short, wide and thick necked with squinty eyes and huge shoulders. Yogi took all this down but did not put it in an official report just yet. The description matched that of Potts who swore out the complaint against Yogi and who Johnny had destroyed at the Boot Scoot.

"What have you gotten us into?" Emily asked Jack. "What?"

Jack pondered how much he could, or should tell her. He finally decided trying to bullshit his wife was the worst option.

"There are some bad guys who are involved in crimes that involve Yogi's office, and my client Lola. I know this places us all in a bad situation but you have to trust us," Jack said.

"Jack, I didn't buy into personal danger, and neither did Rachel," Emily declared. Rachel held her head in her hands leaning over her knees.

"Trust me," Jack said imploring Emily. "We will

not let you be hurt."

"Right," Emily said, "like you protected Rachel?"

There was little Jack could say in response to the scathing comment. "Trust us," felt hollow and not even Jack believed it. Yogi and Johnny arrived and walked out onto the deck. Yogi rushed over to Rachel and hugged her. Johnny stood and nodded acknowledging each of them in his own agnostic way.

"The good thing," Yogi said, "is that we have identified the enemy."

"And what does that mean?" Emily asked.

"We know who assaulted Rachel, and who they work for, and that there is a relationship between that person and the illegal trafficking operation," Yogi said. He did not yet realize Emily's wrath and thought he was presenting a most reasonable explanation.

"So. What does that mean?" Emily challenged. "How is that going to keep us safe?"

Yogi was flummoxed and looked over to Jack for support. Jack shrugged, but said, "I am not sure, but you have to believe we will keep you safe."

"Right." Emily announced. Jack looked over the precipice between him and Emily at that moment and calculated the vastness of the divide. As everyone checked out to their bedrooms Jack knew there was a problem when Emily chose simply to climb into bed and turn away from him instead of giving him a good night kiss. Could he be absolutely sure he could protect her? Was Emily's coldness a predicate for something else going on with her?

CHAPTER THIRTY-THREE

Limping, the tiger moved as quickly as possible away from the bluff where the men shot him following close to the rim but remaining within the cover of the forest. The dart now pained him with every step and blood dripped down his leg. Still, he continued to move driven by a sense of danger and the need to rest. His mind was still clouded by the chemicals in the dart and his limbs felt so heavy the back of his paws dragged along the ground as he labored over every step. From time to time he stumbled, caught himself and momentarily stretched as he fought the urge to lay down and sleep.

Jonas and Jarrett walked out to the rock overlook above the Stone Door and sat on the cool rock cross-legged with cups of coffee. Above them the fall sky stretched forever as stars sparkled like strings of tiny Christmas ornaments embedded in the clouds of the Milky Way. It was not necessary for either man to speak for each of them looked with awe into the history of the universe displayed before them. Many times each man at one posting or another had marveled at the splendor of the stellar display visible from a remote area where light pollution was minimal.

"Remember when you were a kid and your father took you outside at night to watch the dim light of a satellite pass overhead?" Jonas asked.

Jarrett chuckled softly. "Yeah, and we all wanted to be astronauts." In those days satellites were a novelty and the time of passage was reported by the evening news when Sputnik flew through the sky.

"Is it any wonder the ancients found so much mystical about the night sky?"

"You know what Native Americans believe?" Jarrett asked in a solemn tone of voice.

"About the Path of Souls?"

"Yes. They believe the constellation the Southern Cross, or Cygnus the Swan, marks that path and that all the stars are souls in process of wandering on that road."

"Makes about as much sense as anything else," Jonas said sipping his coffee.

"In the winter when Cygnus rises it is smack in the middle of the Milky Way and the stars are so dense they look like clouds."

"What's the bright star in the Southern Cross?" Jonas asked remembering something about astronomy but not recalling the star's name.

"Deneb," Jarrett said. "That, according to Indian theology is the entry point into the spirit world. All those souls are moving toward Deneb."

As the Ranger and the Special Agent stared with uplifted faces into the speckled sky that blinked back at them a chilly breeze blew out of the north. Each of the men felt suddenly uneasy as if they had disturbed something unnatural. An even colder shiver vibrated in each man setting off alarms.

"Did you feel that?"

"I felt something," Jonas replied looking back over his shoulder. In the density of the trees a pair of orange eyes glowed as the tiger sat motionless staring at the men on the rock.

"Don't move," Jonas said under his breath. "The tiger is back there in the trees."

Jarrett remained frozen having become one with the rock. Continuing to stare beyond the expanse of the Gorge, he realized the cat was likely wounded and therefore even more dangerous than before. This was not the night he chose to walk his personal path of souls so he would remain still barely breathing. Jarrett crossed paths with predators before, and knew not to provoke the beast.

"What is he doing?" Jarrett whispered.

"Just staring at us," Jonas said as his neck began to cramp from the awkward position. Soon he would be forced to move.

The tiger panted heavily with his head lowered as thirst tore at his parched throat since he had not passed a stream after leaving the one that he followed up to his outlook. Although his leg throbbed, the sharp stab of pain that each step inflicted ceased while he sat and watched. When his eyes locked on the eyes of the man who looked into the trees he knew the man saw him. That the man made no movement to escape or presented any immediate threat calmed the tiger so he remained motionless and watched. Perhaps it would not be necessary for him to kill these men after all.

CHAPTER THIRTY-FOUR

Early the next morning, Jack, Yogi and Johnny Running Bear sat on the back deck of Jack's house drinking coffee. It was just before sunrise, a quiet moment in the day when the sun is not over the horizon but light still trickles in small packages changing black to gray. They watched as house finches, nuthatches and titmice attacked Jack's bird feeder. Their significant women were sleeping in, while Rocket roamed back and forth chasing the scent of night creatures that crept through the yard leaving a track and a challenge. Chase me. Identify me. Catch me if you can. Each man was lost in thought, when Jack asked,

"You actually got suspended?"

Over the rim of his mug, Yogi said, "Yeah. Sheriff took my badge and gun and suspended me for a week without pay for tangling with that jerk at the Boot Scoot. It didn't seem to make any difference that I didn't touch anyone, and that Johnny nailed that sack of shit when he got in his face."

Without moving, Johnny just grunted. He was almost but not quite smiling.

"Doesn't sound like your boss is providing much cover for his only detective," Jack said.

"That bothers me too. I'm not getting a good

feeling about this," Yogi said, then he continued, "I plan to get with the other driver today that Lola mentioned."

"I thought you said the Sheriff told you to abort the investigation, and that you were suspended," Jack said.

"He did, but this is personal. He can't stop personal," Yogi replied, a grim determination on his face that Jack seldom saw but always respected.

"Maybe after you talk to Mr. Mansker we'll have enough that Calvin will greenlight me to file the wrongful death suit," Jack said.

"I wish you could hold off for a couple of days," Yogi said. " 'Cause that will start a shit storm, and drive them underground. We still don't know if the Mayor who owns the Chevrolet dealership is involved or whether Potts is on someone else's payroll. Agent Bradley is coming up today from Nashville with GPS tracking devices I want to put on those parts trucks and follow them to the end destination."

"When are you going to do that?" Jack asked.

"If I can get the trackers in place, Johnny and I plan to follow them tonight," Yogi said.

"I was hoping Johnny could hang around here

and watch out for Emily and Rachel," Jack said.

"I'll be glad to do that. We won't begin to follow those trucks until after dark and by then you will be home from work," Johnny said.

"Thanks. I know that will make Emily and Rachel feel a lot better."

"No worries," Johnny said.

"I also need to get back out to Pierce's Farm, and the Fish and Wildlife guy, Jarrett, wants to go also," Yogi said.

"Better count me out of that this time. Emily is ripped at me already," said Jack.

"I understand, but it's about time for us to go on the offensive. I like the way Jarrett thinks. He's a tough old bird and can mobilize federal help which is what we will need because I am afraid the Sheriff's Department is compromised once again," Yogi said. "You know I'm not letting this go, Jack."

Jack nodded. He understood Yogi's code of honor would not let him walk away from the guys who assaulted Rachel, and attempted to intimidate them with a second break-in at Jack and Emily's house. Jack looked over at the two Indians with the Cherokee blood pulsing in their veins. Jaws set, they did not intend to be kicked around anymore and would deal with it with their special skills and fixed determination. Jack would not want to be on the receiving end when they unleashed that hell. How far this personal issue of Yogi's would drag Jack into the fight, he just didn't know. Jack could feel the coming struggle between his duty to his wife and his loyalty to Yogi twist his guts into tangles of stress. He had completely forgotten the issues involving Mr. Henri Jacques he would need to address later today.

Yogi and Johnny left to go meet Special Agent Bradley of the TBI with Johnny promising to return in a couple of hours. Emily wandered out onto the deck with her green tea, cupping the mug in both hands.

"Morning," Jack said.

"Morning to you," she replied.

"About last night," Jack started to say.

"Jack, I'm just worried about our safety. Look, we are supposed to be working for a college, in a quiet college town. How does all this violent stuff keep happening?" she asked. "I just don't understand. All I want is for us to be safe and happy. I just want to live for my art and love you."

"I'm sorry, these things seem to have a way of finding us, and neither Yogi nor I will turn away if someone needs help or there are bad people involved," Jack said.

"You and Yogi. You and Yogi," Emily said. "What about you and me?"

"I don't understand. I love you Emily," Jack said.

"Getting us in trouble is no way to show it," she said. "I can't live, always worried and waiting for the next time when something bad is going to happen." She paused, "I need to get away for a couple of days and this trip to New York may just be what the doctor ordered."

"Okay, if that's what you think is best," Jack said struggling not to express his true concerns.

"You trust me don't you?" Emily asked intuitively sensing that perhaps Jack was not being totally honest and was simply agreeing with her.

"You know I do, but I'm not sure about Henri to be honest," said Jack. He could tell she really wanted this trip, whether for work, or to get away from Jack and the current unrest, or to be with Henri, he couldn't decide. The dispute over getting them into trouble could be merely the distraction that would justify the trip, and the question about trust the final argument that put him into the inescapable box. Because he loved her, he had to admit to trust, and kissed her trying to impress that he was doubt free but that was far from the truth.

"Henri's harmless," she scoffed turning to go back into the house for more tea.

Jack prayed she was right, but he feared worse.

CHAPTER THIRTY-FIVE

The cat was more patient than Jonas' neck would allow him to remain locked on the animal's eyes. So, when Jonas slowly turned his head back to the Gorge to relieve his cramping neck, the cat noticed. Jarrett and Jonas tensed as they heard the leaves rustle with the cat's movement. The rock transmitted each ponderous step as the cat emerged from the woods stopping only twenty feet behind them. Neither dared to turn and stare into the eyes that almost glowed in the dark. If the cat struck they would probably be killed, or even worse. Looming only a few feet in front of them, the edge fell off a hundred feet below. If the cat didn't get them the fall offered no relief. The pain Jonas felt in his neck was negligible compared to the stiffness he now felt from sitting cross-legged for so long. Even with plenty of warning neither Jonas nor Jarrett would be able to move with any swiftness. So, there they were, completely at the mercy of the animal.

Suddenly, the cat sensed the presence of additional men, turned and vanished once more into the trees. At first the men twitched involuntarily but when it was clear the tiger was gone, Jonas and Jarrett stood and made their way off the rock with as much dispatch as their stiff old joints would allow. They found the paved path leading back to the Ranger Station and hustled back without speaking.

A short distance away Pierce's men tracked the cat from the GPS device built into the dart. They watched the display screen of the computer as the cat stopped for several minutes then abruptly followed the trail back in the direction of Alum Gap. This time Pierce employed twice the number of men and they waited for the cat to move back in their direction. All of them wore night vision goggles which lit up the forest and gave them an advantage.

Painfully, the tiger moved deeper into the woods keen to pick up any scent of the men although the pain in his leg dulled his senses. He did not see the man rise from behind the fallen timber and fire a second dart into his shoulder. The tiger stumbled on his front legs and his chin struck the ground. He wrestled in vain to stand but lost control of his limbs and rolled to his side. As his eyes began to close he saw many men with weapons emerging from the forest. Then everything went dark.

CHAPTER THIRTY-SIX

"Watch out for that one," the lanky man said pointing at the six by ten cage that contained the tiger. He carried a plastic coca-cola bottle into which he spit tobacco juice every few minutes. The round Copenhagen tin was a fixture in the rear pocket of his jeans. His associate, an older skinny man named Lester, stood staring at the cage transfixed in the presence of an actual wild beast this large and fierce. The tiger lay patiently watching their every movement as he panted, breathing in the aroma of all the other animals in the room. He could and would be patient. He could tell his presence caused fear to crackle like lightening through all the other animals whose cages were moved away from him and he sat alone in one corner of the barn within a barn structure. Where they kept these animals was climate controlled and yet, while the air circulated, the smell of urine and feces permeated everything. The tops of the larger cages were outfitted with heavy straps so that a tow motor could lift the cage out of way for the daily spray and wash cleaning. The tiger considered this procedure very demeaning.

Lincoln said, "He's a man-killer," gesturing in the direction of the tiger. "When you pick up that cage with the tow-motor careful he don't reach through the bars and getcha." With those last words Lincoln jumped at Lester who jerked back in alarm.

SAVAGE

"Don't do that," Lester pleaded. The tiger scared him and Lester treated the cage with respect. Its bars were too far apart for Lester. Earlier, he witnessed the tiger reach through the bars and bat a turd across the floor back at the monkeys. If that tiger got its arm out of the bars just enough Lester knew the cat would knock him across the floor just like that turd.

Lincoln just laughed. He enjoyed scaring the new guys and this was one large scary tiger. They both heard the stories of how many men he killed. Around the cavernous area other cages were stacked and arranged. Some held brightly colored parrots and other exotic birds Lester saw once on cable television. In another area were the monkeys of all shapes and sizes. There were no great apes, just the smaller ones with their big eyes and long tails. Lester and Lincoln were in the process of the morning chores of providing food and water to the animals. The monkeys always grabbed the water hose when it entered their cage so it became a game of tug-a-war. Lester learned to squirt the monkeys first to drive them back, but they were wily little critters who ducked and anticipated the spray. Each time the hose slid into the cage monkeys jumped and tried to grab the hose. If they were successful, the monkeys turned the hose back on the men to great delight among the monkey population.

When the monkey cages were near the tiger they didn't make any noise at all. Now that they were on the other side of the room they chattered and hurled insults back at the panting tiger. Some even threw feces across the room at the tiger who was not troubled by the antics. He was patient and waited until someone slipped up, then he would show the monkeys. It seemed to Lester that the birds never stopped chattering.

A loud "bong" sounded announcing the door at the far end was engaged and about to open. Lester and Lincoln turned to see Mr. Pierce come into the room. Pierce walked a dozen feet or so and stopped. He never came too far into the room since he didn't appreciate the smell and didn't want the animal poop they were spraying toward the floor drains to get on his expensive boots.

"Boys, come over here," Pierce ordered. Two men dressed in black tee shirts and pants were with him as always. Lester shut off the water and with Lincoln walked over to Pierce and the others.

"Morning, Mr. Pierce," Lincoln said.

"Yeah, you too Lincoln. I want you guys to get all those birds ready to transport tonight," Pierce said.

"All of them?" Lincoln asked. That would involve fifty cages to prep and clean for transport.

"Yes," Pierce said.

"Yes, sir. What about the tiger?" Lincoln asked.

"Not yet. We've run into a snag with his buyer that needs to get worked out. A couple more days yet on that one," Pierce said.

"Okay, Mr. Pierce," Lincoln said nodding.

"I want that tiger and the monkeys moved into Building B this afternoon. When you move the rest of the birds out after dark, I want this place empty. Let me know if you all see any strangers hanging around the place. We've had some unwanted visitors lately," said Pierce as he walked away. The door emitted the loud "bong" again as Pierce placed his palm on the recognition pad and the door opened.

Special Agent Rockford Bradley of the Tennessee Bureau of Investigation met Yogi and Johnny at the Dusty Donut in Northwoods. He brought with him the GPS tracking devices that were magnetized so they would stick onto any metal. It was early and as Yogi drove past Wild Bill Cheatham's Chevrolet dealership on the way to the café he saw that the two delivery trucks were parked at the rear.

"What about cameras?" Bradley asked wiping the powdered sugar off the end of his nose.

"Far as I can tell, they cover the front lot, and the rear doors, not the area where the trucks are parked," Yogi said.

"Where should we put them?" Johnny asked referring to the GPS trackers.

"Top of the cab for the best signal," Bradley said.

"Let's roll," Yogi said.

It was still early, way too early for even the service department of the dealership to be open. A slight breeze fanned the leaves that lay helter skelter along the city sidewalks while squirrels searched for acorns among the leaves. They parked down the street and hustled back to the edge of the dealership property far enough away that they could not be seen from any camera scanning the front of the lot where the new cars were displayed. Johnny and Yogi each took one of the small round devices and ran over to the trucks. In a smooth single motion they jumped onto the running board of the cab and slapped the device down on the top of the cab near the back where it stuck tightly and was out of sight. Johnny took Yogi's truck and headed back to Jack's while Yogi and Bradley located Albert Mansker's home on the county map and prepared to go talk with him.

CHAPTER THIRTY-SIX

Bill Cheatham and Richard Pierce met at the Cracker Barrel restaurant just off Interstate 24 at Manchester. It was well outside Sequoyah County and it was not likely they would run into anyone that recognized either one of them.

"How's your man?" Pierce asked referring to Potts after the devastating encounter with Johnny Running Bear.

"That fucking Indian almost cracked his chest open," Pierce allowed.

"You just going to take that?" Pierce asked.

"It's getting more complicated. I figure there's five or six who suspect about the animals right now including that Deputy, his Indian friend, that college guy, their women and God knows who else," Cheatham said. "Plus, there's a rumor that son of a bitch lawyer, what's his name, Greathouse, was snooping around in Hard Bargain a couple of days ago. We think he met with the widow of your driver, the one the tiger killed."

"Shit," Pierce said scratching the back of his neck.

"Don't worry about her. My boys are going to visit her and she won't be suing nobody," Cheatham noted.

"What about the rest of them?" Pierce asked. "We can't neutralize all of them can we?"

"If they all happen to be at the same place, at the wrong time, and have an accident, we can't help that, can we?" Wild Bill asked.

"What do you have in mind?"

Wild Bill said, "a little breaking and entering, a little gas explosion. You know, an accident that leaves no witnesses."

"Tomorrow night?" Pierce asked.

"Works for me." Cheatham said as he rose and picked up the ticket the waitress left for them. He tossed a Jackson on the table and walked to the check out desk prepared to pay in cash leaving no record they were in the place.

CHAPTER THIRTY-SEVEN

By the time Yogi and Bradley arrived at Albert Mansker's place at 9am, he was already drunk. Mansker's house was essentially a one room shack with the outside walls made of cherry wood planks scavenged from an old barn that had weathered gray. People said Mansker had a woman living with him at one time, but she left long ago. The rusted tin roof provided only a minimal covering for the shelter. Inside here and there a leak appeared during a hard rain. Four hounds that lounged on the front porch announced their arrival and charged up to Yogi's truck. Yogi rolled his window down but did not step out until Mansker came out on the porch in his red long johns and yelled at the dogs to shut up. His command was so fierce the dogs tucked tail and went quickly toward the back yard.

Yogi said, "Albert, remember me? I'm Deputy Baker from the Sequoyah County Sheriff's Department. Can we talk for a couple of minutes?"

Mansker scratched his nuts and eyed Yogi. "I guess so, come on up on the porch. Got any Red Man?" In fact, Yogi did have a pouch of Red Man chewing tobacco left over from the last time Mansker was a guest at the jail. Yogi remembered it was Albert's favorite. Albert turned toward one of the rusted metal chairs on the porch and Yogi noticed the back flap to his long johns was not buttoned and hung open giving everyone a framed view of his cheesy ass. Bradley gave him a look as they stepped out of the truck that communicated "Are you kidding me?"

Yogi introduced Bradley as his cousin since he wasn't in uniform and Yogi didn't want to spook the old drunk. When they settled in and Yogi passed the Red Man to Albert, Mansker announced, "I quit making the hooch, Deputy. Just want you to know in case that's what you're here about."

"Albert, me believing you have quit moonshining is like saying the President doesn't have orange hair," Yogi said. "But that's not why we are here."

Albert's breath and blood shot eyes said that while there was an outside chance he had quit making moonshine liquor, he certainly hadn't quit drinking it. Mansker wobbled just trying to stay upright in the chair.

"I hear you started doing some driving work," Yogi said.

"Yeah, what about it?" Mansker asked.

"Wouldn't want to run into you out on the road some night after you've tasted a bit of the 'shine, would we Albert?" Yogi asked.

"I promise, I'm clean when I'm driving," Albert

offered.

"Your nose is growing, Albert," Yogi said.

"My nose is what?" Albert asked reaching up to feel his nose. It felt like it always did, and as far as he could remember he had never misplaced it. Albert held two fingers up to his mouth and spit a brown stream an impressive distance out into the dirt.

"Helps me aim," Albert said winking at them. "The fingers. They help me aim better."

"What I hear, Albert, is that you are doing some driving for Pierce's Farm. You know, pick ups at the University airport and drop offs at the Farm," Yogi said.

"Where'd you hear that?" Mansker asked. His metal chair was now rocking back and forth as if it helped Albert maintain his equilibrium. Yogi hoped Albert wasn't preparing to launch himself into the yard like so much tobacco juice.

"Lola Crockett said you filled in sometimes for Buster," Yogi said.

Mansker thought about it a minute and said, "Too bad what happened to her."

"Yeah," Yogi said, "Losing your husband like that with two small kids, a real sad story."

"Naw, that ain't what I meant," Albert said rocking forward and launching another spit stream at one of the hounds who wandered back around front. The dog jumped out of the way at the last minute. It wasn't the first time he'd been spit at. "I'm talking about her house."

"Her house?" Yogi asked looking over at Rock Bradley who sat quietly taking in the scene.

"Burned down last night," Mansker said.

Yogi and Bradley stood and Yogi said, "Albert we'll come back and finish this conversation. We need to get over and see if we can help Lola."

"Won't do any good," Albert said.

"Why not?" Yogi asked.

"She's gone."

CHAPTER THIRTY-EIGHT

Although the folks who inhabited Hard Bargain lived in no better economic circumstances than did the white trash like Albert Mansker, their homes in the neighborhood were well maintained with pride since they worked hard to get what they had. When everyone took a step up so did they all. Yogi and Rock could see the smoke still rising from where Lola's modest home stood the prior morning. There was nothing left but a heap of soggy smoking ash. Wisps of what was Lola's home rose tentatively toward the sky until the breeze caught the trail and carried it off invisibly into the morning leaving only a memory of the laughter and sorrow the home had known.

"She gone," came the voice from next door. An old white haired Black woman stood on the front stoop of the house looking at the two policemen. She leaned hard on the metal pipe that served as her handrail as she descended the steps.

"What happened, Mrs. Crockett?" Yogi said as he strode over to the woman who called out to them remembering this was Buster's mother. Two white hairs grew randomly out of the old lady's face as she made her way down the concrete steps and Yogi held out his hand to assist her.

"She got burned out. Like the old days," the

grizzled woman said as she collapsed into a porch chair that was at the moment sitting in her front yard. Not unlike the metal backed chair he saw at Mansker's, the chair began to rock as she sat down.

"Is Lola ok? How about the kids?" Yogi asked.

"She's ok, the chillren too," said the old lady.

"Where have they gone?" Yogi asked.

"Can't say." Yogi saw this woman was not a talker, at least not to white boys asking about her family, and especially since white men were the ones who probably started the fire.

"Did anyone see what happened?" Bradley asked. Mrs. Crockett eyed him carefully.

"Nobody seen nothing," she said and began to sob. "Ain't it always the same?"

"Mrs. Crockett, we're going to find out who did this but we may need your and Lola's help," Yogi said as he reached out to hold the old woman's leathery hand.

"I wish'd you would, I really do," she said giving his hand a little squeeze. Yogi realized this was a major setback for him and for Jack.

Yogi and Bradley took their leave and climbed back into Yogi's truck.

"Two dead ends in a row," Bradley said staring straight out the front window of the truck. "Now, what?"

"I don't know, Rock, I just don't know, but these guys are pissing me off. I think we stick to the game plan. Have the trucks followed tonight and then we go in."

Just as he got ready to put the truck in gear and leave, he slammed the shifter into park and opened the door.

"I'll be right back. Just thought of something," Yogi said as he hurried back to the old lady in the metal chair.

"Mrs. Crockett, I forgot to ask, was Lola able to save the birds?" Yogi asked.

"Oh, yes. Those pretty blue ones." She said.

"Great. Lola showed them to me once. They are beautiful birds. Say hello to Lola for me," Yogi said and left. Mrs. Crockett just stared after him.

Back in the truck Bradley asked, "What was that all about?"

"Lola's birds. She saved them and that means they will have to eat. She can't get all their diet locally so I suspect she will mail order in things like palm nuts, macadamia nuts, and vitamin supplements. She will take care of those birds like her children. While they eat orange vegetables like sweet potatoes and carrots, their diet needs variety according to Jarrett at the Wildlife Service. He gave her a book on how to care for them. Lola almost had them talking the last time I saw her."

Bradley asked, "Ok, Crocodile Dundee, how does that help us?"

"Wrong. Dundee was Australia," Yogi laughed.

"Well, that Jane person, you know with the apes," Bradley protested.

"Wrong again, she was Africa," Yogi still amused at Bradley's futile attempt at humor.

"How about, Juan Valdez, smart ass?"

"Closer. My idea is that we can trace her if she mail orders those items, or even orders them off Amazon, because the Post Office delivers for Amazon up here," Yogi said.

"And that helps us how?" Bradley asked.

"My cousin, Randy McIntosh, is the assistant postmaster," Yogi said.

"Is everybody over here related?" Bradley asked.

"Pretty much, except for the folks in Hard

Bargain, and even then the lines get blurry," Yogi said.

In a couple of minutes they pulled up in front of the Northwoods Post Office. Yogi stepped out as did Bradley and they walked in. Bradley was shocked how much the Northwoods P.O. reminded him of the *Men in Black* scene where Tommy Lee Jones ran the rural postal service. Bradley prayed none of the workers were aliens.

"How's it hangin' Cuz," came the booming voice from behind the counter. Six feet tall with blazing red hair, the man looked like he stepped out of a lumberjack camp.

"Randy, I need to ask a favor," Yogi said.

"Anything you need, Cuz," Randy McIntosh said.

"I'm trying to find a local woman whom I believe is in trouble, and the only way I can think to track her is that I suspect she will be ordering food for a couple of exotic birds that may come through the post office. Might even be an Amazon order. Packages will likely contain macadamia nuts or palm nuts and be marked as perishable," Yogi said. "If you see something like that just note the address and give me a call."

"Not sure I can do that Yogi," Randy said. "Privacy and all that."

"It's police business, Randy," Yogi insisted.

"Ok, but I thought you got suspended," Randy jabbed.

"Just a misunderstanding. Let me know, ok?"

"Sure, if it's police business."

On the way back to Yogi's truck, Bradley said, "I don't get it."

"What?" Yogi asked.

"You say McIntosh is your cousin, and so is Johnny Running Bear, but none of the three of you look anything alike," Rock said.

"Like my family tree, in Randy's branch, Cherokee mingled with Scottish traders. Same with Johnny. It's just that the Scottish genes are more pronounced in Randy, like the Cherokee genes are in Johnny. Me, I'm just more of a mongrel and I don't look like anything," Yogi said.

CHAPTER THIRTY-NINE

Emily explained to Jack that the New York trip involved attending a special showing of paintings by Gino Severini, an Italian artist who was a member of the group of Futurists that painted in Rome and Paris in the early 20th century. The University owned four of his works in its permanent collection, one of the principal reasons, according to Emily, that Henri Jacques was hired as the school's art curator. Severini's work exhibited some of the same features that Emily unknowingly captured in her own abstract paintings images that appeared to Emily and which she brought to life on her canvas.

Jack trusted Emily and yet watching her get into Henri's Audi for the trip to the Chattanooga airport was the hardest thing Jack had ever done. Not even the long kiss and embrace Emily parted with stemmed the pain stabbing at his heart. He recalled the sensation of being caught underwater in the hole at Lesser Wesser on the Nantahala River, his lungs screaming for air and his vision obscured. Bubbles and water everywhere but no terra firma. If he trusted her, it would be alright wouldn't it? Yet, his confidence waned, not at a lack of trust, but in knowing Emily was vulnerable if she relapsed or something pushed her into that dark place.

Back in his office, Jack's mind wandered from the intra-faculty emails that sought his approval of various projects, to the ones that reported on what were becoming inane academic matters to him. It all seemed boring and insignificant. Using the secure password granted him as Dean with administrative authority he entered the human resources files on the University server and pulled up the file on Henri Jacques. If the resume were to be believed, a constant threat in today's world, Jacques worked at the Museum of Modern Art as an assistant curator immediately prior to his position at the University. Jack recalled that one of his classmates, Levi Solomon, was currently at the MoMA. He retrieved Levi's contact information from the Alumni records and dialed the Manhattan exchange.

"Levi Solomon, please," Jack asked when the line was answered.

"Just a moment sir, can I tell him who is calling?" said the professional voice of the receptionist.

"Jack Mathews, an old college friend."

A few seconds later, a voice said, "Jack, how in the world are you?"

"Levi, it's good to hear your voice," Jack said. "How is Chiara?"

"Wonderful. She's pregnant with child number two. How about you? I heard you and Emily Sellars got married. That girl was a looker," Levi said.

"Yes, things are great," Jack lied.

"So, you went back to the University. Didn't have you pictured for that. I thought you would be up here with a big time law firm," Levi said.

"I don't think I am cut out for the big firm experience, Levi, but I did get involved in a pretty big case for the Cherokee Nation last year," Jack said.

"That was you? I thought a guy named Calvin Greathouse handled that," Levi said.

"I worked with Calvin. Got myself adopted into the Cherokee Nation before it was over," Jack said.

"How about that. Pretty impressive. How can I help you?" Levi asked.

"I'm calling to get some background information on a new art curator who said his last job was as an assistant curator there," Jack offered.

"Who would that be?" Levi asked.

"Guy named Henri Jacques," Jack said.

"Curator? Are you kidding me?" Levi said, a touch of anxiousness in his voice.

"That's what his resume said."

"I'm not sure how much I can tell you since there is an ongoing investigation by the NYPD, but

Mr. Henri Jacques was not a curator at all. He was an assistant art restorer. No one from there called to check on him or we would have blackballed him. Not only did we have sexual harassment issues with him, but there are a couple of missing pieces of art, with a counterfeit piece hanging in the same frame. So far we have not been able to prove anything definitive but he is the primary person of interest."

Jack wanted, but at the same time did not want to hear this. "You said sexual harassment charges?" he asked.

"The guy is a real swinging dick. Thinks no woman can resist his faux French charm," Levi said. That's the part Jack did not want to hear.

"The missing paintings wouldn't involve an Italian artist named Severini would they?" Jack asked.

"How did you know that?"

"Lucky guess. We have some of his work in our permanent collection, and that may have been what lured him here," Jack said. "How would I check to see if anything we've got is fake?"

"You really need a professional to look at the piece. Sometimes you can look at the brushwork and see if it is consistent with how the color spreads across the painting. We've seen forgers use a print and go over the print with what looks like raised brush strokes but which is really a clear gel like solution. You might look from the back of the painting through to the front and see if you can see the different layers the artist used to achieve his color. Sometimes the color itself is a dead giveaway because we have so many colors today that may not have existed a hundred or three hundred years ago," Levi said. "I recall that Emily paints, have her look at it."

"Thanks, I'll do that. You take care Levi and say hello to Chiara for us. I'll keep you posted on what we find out," Jack said.

"Good to hear from you Jack."

The anxiety Jack felt a few hours earlier when Emily left with Henri now chewed at his soul like a badger with its teeth bared. He would need concrete proof to show her when she returned or she would not take him seriously thinking he was just being a jealous husband. What was Jacques up to, he wondered.

CHAPTER FORTY

Yogi wasn't listening to Bradley who chattered without pause and without the expectation that Yogi was actually listening to him. Bradley was good at one sided conversations, the kind of person who liked to hear himself talk. It was not that he was a narcissist or egomaniac, he possessed an overabundance of the talking gene. He droned on and on like a room full of birds. Yogi suspected Bradley didn't even realize what he was doing. The good thing was the chatter was so constant, Yogi was able to push it all into a side compartment where it became white noise and did not interfere with his analysis of their current situation. If Lola was missing, and Albert Mansker drunk and not cooperating, who else could possibly link Pierce's Farm to the animal trade? Yogi was attempting to build a case and realized he was running out of options. He wished his friend, Jack Mathews, a licensed attorney, was near so they could compare notes. Jack was trying to build a civil case against the same outfit for a wrongful death case to help Lola Crockett and her children. Out of the white noise draining out of Bradley the word "crazy" floated like a smoke signal.

His mind latched onto the word. Such a word was often used to describe Mabel Porter who lived within a couple of miles of where they were at that moment. Many in Sequoyah County thought Mabel's picture was featured in the dictionary next to the definition "unsound, crooked, askew". Mabel's cabin abutted the Gorge, and Yogi wondered, hadn't she reported having seen the tiger? Yes, it was in that newspaper article. It wasn't much but Yogi was running out of strings to pull and that's when he decided they needed to visit Mabel.

The snakelike road twisted and turned back up the plateau cutting between majestic oaks and hardwoods that showed the first colors of early autumn. It wasn't hard to find Mabel's place since the turn off to her house was marked by a bottle tree that was once a blooming dogwood, but now with its limbs chopped and decorated with blue and green wine bottles, it resembled something from the county fair marking the entrance to the palm reader's tent. Mabel also erected a second mailbox ten feet in the air with a sign that said "airmail" which made perfect sense to her but no one younger than Mabel even got the reference to "air mail". Now in her mid-sixties Mabel Porter served as the neighborhood nut for several decades. Some attributed her craziness to having been dropped on her head as a child, others said Mabel grew and smoked way too much pot, while most people just said she was "touched." As a child, Yogi and other kids who saw her around town were warned not to let Mabel touch them since they too could become infected with the same crazy affliction as Mabel, as if her touch radiated crazy zombie cooties.

Mabel was in fact harmless. Eccentric, yes, but without an ounce evil in her bones. For Mabel few brain cells connected her with her past life or with reality in general, since almost every day for Mabel was like the opening scene of a John Ford western where the door opened fresh onto a new vast panorama. Her only visible means of support was the small change local politicians gave her to hand out their political campaign buttons, pencils and bumper stickers. During campaign season Mabel was seen wandering the sidewalks of downtown Northwoods in her bib overalls, buttons pinned everywhere, pencils protruding from her pockets like weeds, and a handful of bumper stickers in either hand. She became as much a local fixture as the Confederate soldier standing on the pedestal at the town square and meant no one any harm. The county newspaper recognized that Mabel was always available for a good quote on current events. Public statements from Mabel often approached the topic out of left field, but once the quote was printed, it almost made sense leading some to think old Mabel was not as touched as they all thought. The local paper even floated a short lived column called *Moments with Mabel* until all she could talk about was UFOs.

As he aged, Yogi grew to like Mabel and carried

her fresh vegetables during the summer and now and then pork chops he purchased locally at a vertically integrated hog farm. It was beyond Mabel's ability to lie. She reported exactly what her world revealed to her. Mabel didn't drive and counted on others to pick her up and carry her into town. Locals would have picked up Mabel a lot more often had she bathed more regularly. If a Saturday night bath was good enough for Jed Clampet, Mabel reasoned it was good enough for her. Mabel watched a lot of television and old movies, and Yogi was an expert on movies himself creating a connection between the two that did not exist with Mabel and anyone else on the planet.

Yogi proceeded slowly down the chert road leading up to Mabel's cabin explaining to Bradley that he should listen and not speak unless he wanted to be pulled into the swirl of unreality in which Mabel existed. At the same time, Yogi reasoned that maybe Bradley deserved a good dose of conversation with Mabel. It might do him some good. They proceeded slowly because Yogi knew Mabel often shot at strangers with the side by side twelve gauge loaded with buckshot she kept near the front door.

As they pulled up, Mabel rocked on the porch in the same style of metal chair they saw at both Albert's and Mrs. Crockett's. Perhaps a chair salesman made his way through Northwoods once upon a time, like the paint salesman who passed through town and within a few weeks most of the houses on a street would all be painted the same color of blue-green or yellow. Yogi wasn't sure if the chair was a status symbol or not. "We're just as good as the Browns, ain't we? Got the same fancy chair in our yard as them."

"Mabel, how's my girl," Yogi said stepping out of his truck.

"Oh, my, if it's not my special deputy," Mabel said waiving her hand at Yogi. "You boys want some tea?"

"That would be very nice, thank you ma'm," Bradley said. That was his first mistake. Yogi capitalized on the comment and told Mabel he would go in and fix it for all of them. As the screen door slammed shut behind him, Yogi heard Mabel start in with her life story which Yogi had heard several times over and was still not sure which parts he could believe or not. He was pretty sure the part about being raised by wolves was a figment of Mabel's imagination. In the kitchen two Mourning Doves sat on Mabel's kitchen table bobbing their heads as Yogi came in. Mabel introduced him to Miss Emily and Miss Mamie years earlier and explained they were named after the Baldwin sisters on *The Waltons*. A saucer sat in front of them empty prompting Yogi to reach into the seed jar and sprinkle a little bird seed for them as the tea cooled and he added ice to the glasses. The birds appreciated the seed which they began to peck at, while at the same time pooping on the table.

Yogi balanced the three plastic glasses of tea in the crook of one arm and pulled the screen back open catching it with his shoe as he angled through. Bradley rocked in time with Mabel but the look he shot Yogi was clearly a deer in the headlights vision.

"The girls have pooped on the table again, Mabel," Yogi said. Mabel just waived it off. He handed around the tea and as Mabel sipped on hers, Yogi seized the opportunity to get back to Mabel's story about the tiger.

"Now, Mabel, I need to ask you about the tiger you saw the other day," Yogi began. Mabel rocked and thought over the question before speaking.

"He was right out on that rock, just over there," Mabel pointed back toward the rim of the Gorge. "Just lying there, sunning himself. The big kitty was licking his paws and bathing just like a housecat," Mabel said. "I thought Augustus was going to walk out there with me, but he hightailed it back to the house," she said.

"Augustus?" Bradley asked. That was his second mistake as they then had to endure Mabel's tale of

Augustus the French bulldog, who wandered up to her door, having been deposited by a spaceship piloted by Tommy Lee Jones and Will Smith. Bradley's eyes got big again. Augustus eyed him apprehensively from the corner of Mabel's chair.

At the next sip of tea, Yogi returned the conversation to questions about the tiger Mabel met.

"He didn't bother you?" Yogi asked.

"Oh, no, and he had the kindest voice," she said. Bradley choked on the tea he tried to gulp and about wet his pants. Augustus walked up and stared at him cocking his head to one side and then the other watching the strange human. Bradley returned the stare from Augustus and would certainly have screamed and run for the car if Augustus opened his mouth and asked, "How's it hangin'?" Yogi knew better than to ask the next question, but he did anyway.

"What did the tiger say to you, Mabel?"

"That I should call him Harvey."

"I think Harvey was a rabbit, Mabel," Yogi said. "Did he say anything else?"

"Mmm," Mabel said pensively as an old memory flew into her mind like a bat, circled and then vanished. Yogi rotated his hand to indicate she should continue with the story.

"That he missed his home, and he wished the bad men would leave him alone, and about how he was developing a taste for white tail deer," she said in a completely calm matter of fact voice.

"You weren't scared?" Yogi asked.

"Oh, no. He said he wouldn't eat me. I was too old and tough," Mabel giggled. Realizing this story was about to enter the realm of fairy tales, if it was not already there, Yogi asked,

"Was that the only time you saw him?"

"Until the men came and carried him away," Mabel's voice now sad. "I hope they didn't hurt him."

"What men?" Yogi asked.

"The men on the four wheelers. They had the poor tiger laid in the back and then they loaded him in the farm truck," she said.

"And you saw all this?" Yogi asked.

"Yes, they came out right over there," said Mable gesturing toward a tree line in the general direction of the bluffs.

"How did you know it was a farm truck?" Yogi

asked.

"It said Farm on the side of it. Pierce's Farm," Mabel said. "But, I thought you would have known all that since the police car was with them."

Yogi looked at Bradley who was still red faced from the coughing and not believing what he had just heard. As Mabel began referring to Harvey the Tiger again, Yogi realized she had slipped into the Twilight Zone so he stood up and motioned for Bradley to do the same.

"Mabel, we've got to run. You be careful and I'll bring you some chops next time I stop by," Yogi said giving Mabel a hug. Bradley wasn't sure he should touch her in case Mabel's crazy got on him or she gave him the Stink Eye, the most dreaded of curses. Mabel smiled and waived, the Queen Elizabeth wave, where her hand simply moved side to side at the wrist.

CHAPTER FORTY-ONE

Jack descended the stairs from the second floor of the Administration Building and crossed to the connecting building that was originally a large meeting hall and library but which now served as more of a lounge area. The walls of the room were replete with bookshelves, artwork, and historical photographs from the original founding of the University until the early twentieth century. If the room had been equipped with long dining tables it could have been used as a *Harry Potter* set. At the end of the far wall the door to the University Art Gallery stood open. Security was virtually non-existent except that the University's more valuable pieces were on display only in the Gallery which was locked in the evening and manned by student volunteers during the day. This was where the four Severini works were displayed.

Jack acknowledged the student at the entrance desk and wandered to the Severinis. They dominated one wall of the gallery making a grand display of color and movement. Jack could see the hint of similarities in theme between these works and paintings Emily brought to life. To his eye there was nothing to suggest any of the four works were fakes. The brushwork and colors seemed consistent and "moved the colors across the canvass" as Levi had instructed. Cautiously, he reached out and touched the surface of the canvas. In each case he could not detect a flaw. It would take someone more experienced and with a keener eye than him to investigate these paintings.

Just then his cell phone buzzed and Yogi called to say he was headed back to the house. Johnny stood on guard there all day watching out for Rachel so Jack decided to join them. One full day since Emily left on the New York trip and she had not called. Don't be silly, he told himself. She's just busy. On the way out of the Gallery he asked the student when she thought Henri would return from the trip to New York. The student looked at him oddly and said, "I thought Mr. Jacques said the trip was to the coast of Maine." Jack stopped, confirmed what she said, and left the Gallery for his car that was parked along University Boulevard. He could not get his arms around what he heard. It was as if a mule just kicked him in the guts. His breath came in spurts as fear consumed him.

Jack's mind wandered back to his college summer years when he worked as a deckhand on towboats on the inland waterways, staring over the stern into the churn of water kicked up by the powerful diesels that drove the boat and its tow. The brown green water exploded up from the depths and broke the surface in raging curls as the river was cut into bits and pieces by the metal screws. So was Jack's life roiling at that moment, except that he was being chopped and diced into slivers only to disappear as the next wave came on. There was no expectation he would survive and his hope and dreams disappeared into the depths of that murky waterway. If he leaned forward he would be sucked into the turbulence. A terrible thought twisted in his mind. Had Emily intentionally lied to him, or was she innocently walking into Henri's secret plot? What did it say about Jack that he would even think Emily would what? *Betray him?* Weren't those the exact words Emily had used in the sweat lodge that night? But, if Emily was in danger, how did he warn her?

Blindly, he somehow made it back to his Jeep and slowly pulled out onto University Boulevard on the way back to his house where Johnny and Rachel waited and Yogi would soon arrive. He wasn't certain that it was a good thing for them to be there or not. They were his friends and if he needed support it would come from this group. Something else screamed at him to be alone and retreat into himself to solve this distress. He twisted between these two alternate realities. Which one was real? New York or Maine? He couldn't reconcile this discrepancy or that Emily would have intentionally misled him. How was a man supposed to behave if he believed his wife was cheating on him? Did he know Emily, really? Did she have another life, another set of urges and desires he was blind to? How could he act as if it didn't matter, or that he could deal with it internally with no external support? Jack's reality was stretched to the breaking point as he stared disoriented at the road a few feet in front of his Jeep. Miraculously, he pulled into his own driveway having been guided home by some unseen hand. Recalling that journey later, it would scare the hell out of him that he did not recall a single foot of that trip as if his eyes were closed. For a few unsettled minutes he sat in the Jeep without relaxing his hands from the steering wheel. Rachel appeared on the front porch and motioned for him to come in. He obeyed walking through a fog. Rachel looked at him strangely.

His friends on the back deck all became distorted apparitions. Not really human, more the shape of humans but with accented flaws. Yogi's hair was too upright, Rachel was too willowy, Johnny was too much an Indian, and the other guy, the round one, Bradley, yeah, that was his name, was too happy. Someone pressed a beer into his hand and someone was talking, but the words didn't connect into sentences in his head. Jack saw mouths moving and heard words, disconnected words bouncing off the deck, the house and the yard. The words flew around like arrows but hit no targets and disappeared into the ether. A dog came up to him and placed its head in his lap. He knew this dog but what was her name. The deep brown eyes stared into him trying to will him back into her world, a world where he was her master, responsible for her care and feeding and where she provided a quantum of love and solace. This beautiful dog whom he loved so much, almost as much as who?

Rachel was beside him holding his hand, telling him it would be all right, that he needed to believe, he needed to trust. Jack wasn't sure he had spoken at all. Had he called Emily's name? What were these people talking about? What did some damn farm have to do with anything? Rachel, still holding his hand and occasionally kissing his forehead. Yogi, he remembered this guy, his brother, Yogi gripping his shoulder and saying they would have to leave soon. And Jack just looked at them. Uncertain what the plan was, and uncertain why everyone was on his deck. Another beer then another, and Jack began to relax. Rachel was still there and so was Johnny and the round one. But someone was missing. Jack's head swiveled and he thought he saw a dark haired woman shimmering on the edge of his vision, someone beautiful beyond description. Someone he called Emily.

Rachel was leading him down a hallway to a bedroom. She opened the door and helped undress him, then he collapsed on the bed and fell into a pool of nothingness.

CHAPTER FORTY-TWO

"That was fucking weird," Bradley said.

Yogi looked over at him without speaking. From the back seat of the crew cab truck Johnny said, "His soul is troubled. It wanders alone in a wilderness."

"Are we still on?" Yogi asked.

"Yes," Johnny affirmed. "We are to meet Jarrett at the Truck Stop."

Twenty minutes later they pulled up into the gravel parking lot of the Truck Stop Café on the perimeter of I-24 on the top of the plateau before the road descended in the east to Chattanooga and to the west toward Nashville. The three men walked toward the café, the gravel crunching beneath their feet. This was the final meeting before they executed the plan. Jarrett waited inside nursing a white coffee cup already stained by drops of the brown liquid from the waitresses' ever flowing pot.

"We need to go in tonight and confirm what we suspect," Jarrett said.

"I can get us in by a back logging road to the rear edge of the property but the fence is still in place, electrified and there's cameras, dogs and drones," Yogi said.

"I have a scoped camera that can take a long

distance shot," Bradley offered. "We may be able to get what we need from outside the property."

"No time like now," Johnny said his eyes finding the resolve in his compatriots. Once again Yogi borrowed Leon Allgood's Dodge Powerwagon. With the gear, it was a squeeze for the four men even in a "crew cab" chassis. They made it, bouncing up the logging road as far as Yogi and Jack travelled on the first visit earlier in the week, unloaded and started to hike up the two track trail. Yogi reminded each of the men that drones were deployed the last time he was there and that the point was to confirm transfers involving the Chevrolet parts vans.

After a mile the men arrived at the spot near the bluff overhang that was just above the fence and tree line. Johnny was the only man in the group who did not have a legal carry permit if you ignored the fact that Yogi had been suspended, so he had the job of carrying the long lens camera. The others packed weapons on the hip. As they crept among the rocks and perimeter trees to the fence line activity was bustling at the nearest barn, the large one Yogi saw on the first visit. Without speaking the men deployed along the fence, Johnny attaching the lens and preparing to record the events taking place at the nearest barn. He moved the lens from barn to barn adjusting to the distance and focusing on the barn doors. Box like trucks pulled up to the doors of two of the barns and a tow motor scurried between the trucks and the barn. Something was obviously being loaded onto the trucks but what could not be defined at that distance.

"We need to be closer," Johnny whispered.

Without thinking Yogi reached out and touched the wire of the fence. It was cold and did not present the electric charge he had been expecting.

"That's odd," Yogi whispered and motioned to the others that he touched the fence without being shocked by electric current. One by one each of them also touched the fence and shrugged.

They continued watching as one of the Chevrolet parts trucks pulled away from the smaller barn and waited at the larger barn while the first truck was being loaded.

They heard the "click" from Johnny's camera as he took picture after picture of the men loading the truck with what looked like crates or cages. Then the tow motor stopped and the doors to the first truck closed. It pulled slowly away from the barn and up the gravel path toward the front of the property. The second truck took its place and backed up to the barn doors. The tow motor sprang to life and more crates and cages were moved into the second truck. Once the process was completed, it too drove slowly away from the barn and disappeared in the stand of trees into which the first truck had gone. Yogi's men were in place out on the highway to follow each truck to its destination.

When, after twenty minutes Yogi and his squad could see no more movement around the large barn, Yogi asked, "Anybody see any sign of the dogs?"

"Nope," Johnny said moving the long lens in a ninety degree arc from one side to the other of the barn. "I don't get a good feeling about this."

"Almost like it's too good to be true?" Jarrett asked.

"Like someone is inviting us to look closer," Bradley said.

"Or someone is closing up shop and leaving," Yogi suggested.

"Could be that, or a trap," Johnny said.

Yogi rolled the options over in his head and came back to the same conclusion each time: they had to go check it out.

"Come on. We don't have a choice. There may not be another chance to see what's in that barn," Yogi said. Silently, the four men ran in a crouch across the open ground to the back side of the barn careful not to step on or crunch the gravel. Two large sliding doors typical of a barn structure hung on rollers. The floodlight at the top of the gable dark but the sliver of a new moon provided all the light Yogi needed. He pushed the barn door enough for a man to pass through and stepped into the darkness of another passage. Painting the walls with the beam from his flashlight Yogi noticed the entire inner wall was metal. To his touch it was cold and hard. In the middle of that wall another set of double doors appeared with a latch handle much like a commercial freezer and to the right of that a square pad with a green light flashing. Yogi grabbed the handle and the lever moved with a soft "bong" as the door swung out and open.

First Yogi, then Bradley and followed by Jarrett walked ten feet into the huge dark cavern and stood shoulder to shoulder. The only visible light was the green glow from the pad on the inside wall behind them and a similar green glow at the other end where Yogi suspected there was likely another set of doors. Johnny stood at the door propping it open with his foot. The floor was an unbroken sea of concrete that was still damp in places. Periodically, drains were cut into the floor every ten feet or so. The smell of animal excrement and urine mixed with bleach was present even though someone made an effort to clean up the place. The walls and roof which was flat and not arched like the arch of the barn itself seemed to be made of the same hard metal as the door.

Flashlight beams like searchlights over a large city panned around the room which appeared to be empty save for hose pipes connected to a spigot at the front and back of the walls. Beams of light struck one wall then bent and followed an oblique angle. Yogi thought he could have been standing in a long room inside Cumberland Caverns. The only sound came from the men's shoes sliding against the concrete and a distant drip-drip-drip. The room had not been empty for long.

"Spread out and let me know if you find anything," Yogi said to Bradley and Jarrett who moved off toward the side walls. After a moment Yogi heard Bradley say,

"Yogi, over here. I've got something."

Moving over to Bradley Yogi could see that a square of cardboard about two feet by two feet was taped to one wall. On the top of the cardboard was written: "FOR THE BEAR".

Yogi projected in a hushed voice, "Johnny better get over hear. There's a message for you."

Having no way to keep the door open any longer, Johnny, too, stepped into the room and toward the wall where three men and three flash lights were staring. Behind him the door latched as metal rods slid into cylinders and locked into place.

Johnny did not feel good about that sound, or his decision to enter the barn.

"Look," Yogi said pointing at the cardboard. Johnny saw beneath the "FOR THE BEAR" markings the imprint of a muddy foot. He immediately recognized the print with its second and third toes longer than the rest as belonging to Mingati Kakenya, the Maasai tracker. Beneath the print was the word "TAPALIKIEKI". Johnny stared at the word searching his memory for the Maasai meaning of such a word. Then it hit him. He said "Oh shit" and stared back at the door where the light by the pad had changed from green to red. At the other end the light glowed red as well.

"Well?" Bradley asked.

"It means "sorry"," Johnny said. "Do you smell that?" He scrambled back to the door but as hard as he could pull the door would not unlatch or open. Frantically, he placed his hand on the recognition screen but it was useless.

"Propane," Yogi said.

"We are inside a bomb," Johnny said. Each man was banging and banging on the doors without having the slightest effect. Their steel coffin was secure and quickly filling with gas. In seconds the men coughed and gagged as they withered to the floor no longer trying to beat their way out. Johnny was disoriented and nauseous at the same time fearing he would pass out when he heard a soft "bong" and the door began to open. Strong arms reached in and began to drag them out one by one until all of the men cleared the door.

"Stay down," someone yelled into the blast that blew through the steel doors shattering the outer barn doors and launching the five men several feet out into the yard. Yogi was sure he was deaf because all he heard was the tinty drone in his ears as if cicadas had taken up residence there and were conducting a symphony. From his hands and knees he saw the others trying to stand, each wobbly, coughing and disoriented. A fire crackled along the ground where the barn doors were blown into a heap and smoke rushed out of the barn.

Yogi thought he saw a man dressed in black helping Bradley to his feet and motioning for them to head back to the fence and off the property. Yogi, Johnny, Bradley and Jarrett stumbled like zombies in the direction of the fence as the man in black disappeared back into the shadows. As they climbed back over the fence pain shot through Yogi's hand as electric current ran up his arm and knocked him down fortunately off the property of Pierce's Farm. The electric charge now coursed back through the fence. The fresh autumn night air was replaced with the odor of the explosion and chaos. Without speaking the four men struggled back up the rise to the logging road and drug themselves back to Leon's truck that was waiting for them below the canopy of the forest. No one spoke as Yogi put the big diesel in gear and lumbered off down the ditch of a road careening into and out of deep ruts. The men smelled burnt and looked worse. Yogi looked over at Jarrett whose eyes were closed and his head fell back onto the glass of the passenger door. With every bump his head banged against the glass.

Out onto the highway, they passed the volunteer firemen headed toward Pierce's Farm but didn't slow up. Yogi headed straight to the Northwoods hospital emergency room. He worked out in his head a plausible story of a camping trip with a leaky propane tank valve that exploded. It was his story and he would stick with it.

CHAPTER FORTY-THREE

"Are you okay? How about some coffee?" Rachel asked from his kitchen where she perched on a bar stool. She wore jeans and a sweatshirt that said "Tigers" on the front.

"Yeah, sure, that would be great," Jack said rubbing his eyes and trying to remember the night before that was as sketchy as a charcoal etching of a desert scene someone had intentionally rubbed over to confuse and distort the image. When he awoke that morning he threw on a bathrobe and stumbled into the kitchen when he saw Rachel.

"Rachel, this is going to sound strange, but the last thing I remember was leaving the Art Gallery up at the University, then nothing else," Jack said as he sipped the black liquid.

"By the time you got here, you seemed dazed and confused, almost as if you didn't know who we were or why we were here," Rachel said. "Is Emily okay? You kept saying her name over and over."

Although his head was still fuzzy, he did have one clear thought, that somehow the coast of Maine was involved so he told her.

"Maine? What has that got to do with anything?" Rachel asked, now as befuddled as him.

"That's, that's where the girl at the gallery told me Henri had gone, not New York," Jack blurted out, a wave of pain flushing over him again. Once more his gut wrenched tight and he couldn't breathe.

"Oh," Rachel said gathering the import that Emily was with the art professor wherever he was. "I forgot to tell you something last night. Emily called and said she was coming back a day early."

"Really?" Jack asked. Now he was really confused.

"You don't know what Emily prayed for at our Sweat Lodge ceremony, do you Rachel?" Jack asked. Jack, Emily, Yogi, Johnny and some of their Cherokee cousins conducted a sweat lodge ceremony last year after erecting the structure on the forest property Jack owned out by the edge of the Mountain.

"No, she and I have never discussed it," Rachel said putting her cup down on the counter. Rachel was a good friend and struggled to listen to Jack's story without judgment.

"She said, "Don't let me betray him, the man I love"," Jack whispered now taking a long breath. "Later, she told me that prayer was solely for me, but at that time she did not want to tell me any more about why it was important for her to say that." Jack paused, then said, "Rachel, I'm worried, and scared. Her prayer was as if she had betrayed someone before me."

"She told you about her first husband and the Navy Seal, didn't she?" Rachel asked. Emily told Jack she was married previously which ended in a divorce involving her affair with a SEAL. Jack now knew she had also told Rachel.

"Yes, but there was more to it than that."

Rachel took his hands in hers and looked deeply into his eyes that were filled with pain. Then she said, "Jack, things are not always what they seem to be. You need to trust her. I don't think Emily would do anything to hurt you, and I believe you are the man she loves."

Jack squeezed her hands, looked down and then back up into Rachel's eyes, "I will try. I hope I have the strength."

Her phone that was sitting on the counter buzzed. She reached for it and saw the caller was Yogi. She listed for a couple of minutes and then said, "See you soon. Love you too."

She turned to Jack and said, "Yogi and the guys went back to Pierce's Farm last night but got into some trouble. They are mostly ok but a barn exploded at that Farm with them inside it. Yogi took everyone to the ER in Northwoods where they were treated for scrapes and burns. All of them except Mr. Jarrett were released. They are keeping him in the intensive care unit for now. Yogi called me earlier when they got to the hospital so I wouldn't worry. Right, like I wouldn't worry when he gets blown up in a barn. I can't understand how this violence keeps happening to us. Last night was a close call."

Jack wasn't sure he could process this new information about Yogi and wasn't in good enough shape to debate the whole "do the right thing" issue. "You sound like Emily," Jack said. "She got all over me about that before she left."

"Well, it's true. I know Yogi is law enforcement and we have to expect he may be put in danger's way, but you, Jack, you are a university dean for Christ sake. How dangerous is that supposed to be?" It didn't look like Rachel was going to cut him any slack either.

"All that evil needs…" he started.

"Is for good men to do nothing," Rachel finished. "I know, I know. But why you guys, and why us?"

"Maybe there's a shortage of good guys right now." Jack said.

CHAPTER FORTY-FOUR

Deputy Sparks followed the first truck to leave the Farm through Northwoods and up the mountain to its peak where Interstate 24 crested and fell off toward the Tennessee River. So far he did not need the GPS assistance because he could follow the boxy truck from a safe distance on the interstate all night long. The truck melded into traffic along I-24 past Moccasin Bend on the Tennessee River up Missionary Ridge and then onto I-75 South toward Atlanta. It was still dark three hours later when the truck left the interstate for a warehouse area. Sparks hung back as the truck pulled into a gated lot, watched as the gate slid open, and when the gate closed behind the Chevrolet parts truck, Sparks parked out of sight and ran from tree to tree until he was positioned behind one that afforded cover but also a decent view of the loading dock. Sparks pulled out his binoculars and watched as crate after crate of birds were unloaded one at a time and carried into the warehouse. He noted the address as 1101 Peach View Park and texted that back to Yogi. After a couple of minutes Yogi texted back *Good Job. Take photos and come home.*

Deputy Aaron Burns similarly pursued the second truck. It too, left the Farm, travelled through Northwoods and got onto Interstate 24 in the direction of Chattanooga. However, this truck did not stay on I-24 very long and took the Interstate 59 exit toward Birmingham. Burns stayed back at a safe distance occasionally looking over at the laptop on the passenger seat to confirm his target was dead ahead. Past the Birmingham International Airport the parts truck left the interstate and pulled into a commercial district where it too, proceeded to a small warehouse and pulled up to the padded loading dock. Just as with the other truck, the cargo was download quickly by hand. Crouching next to a dumpster Burns watched the entire operation. Punching the address of 307 Airport Complex into his cell phone he sent the text back to Yogi. A few moments later Yogi responded, *Good Job, Take photos and come home.*

Leaving Jarrett behind in the ICU at the hospital was hard on Yogi, Johnny and Bradley, but it was the best thing for him. The doctors explained it looked as if Jarrett took the brunt of the force so he must have been closer to the exploding tank. He was also decades older than the young men and less able to survive such trauma. Broken ribs, a punctured lung, one broken leg and a fractured arm were bad enough but the concussion was the most worrisome injury. The odds were not in his favor the doctors said.

The ride from the ER back up the mountain was spent in silence as each man gathered what he remembered of the prior twelve hours. They agreed not to go back to the Sheriff's Department over their fear that the Sheriff was somehow complicit in this affair. Why else would a police vehicle have been spotted by Mabel? The logical move was to set up operations at Jack's which would also let them keep an eye on Jack who behaved oddly the prior night.

Jack and Rachel were still talking on the back deck when Yogi and the others returned. While Rachel was dressed, Jack was still in his bathrobe and still nursed a mug of coffee. After hugging Yogi, Rachel went into the kitchen and brought out mugs for each of the men. Fatigue engraved wearied lines on each of their faces along with smudges of dirt and bandages. Each man's hair showed signs of the scorching following the explosion.

"Okay, Rock, tell us what's going on. Either the hand of God pulled us out of that barn or we had a guardian angel," Yogi said as each of them fell into Jack's Adirondack chairs on the deck.

Special Agent Bradley, whose normally short hair now exposed scalp burns in random patterns on his head, leaned back and said in a matter of fact voice devoid of its normal humor, "We have a man on the inside of this deal."

"The TBI has been investigating Pierce's Farm? And, you didn't tell us?" Yogi asked.

Now looking sheepish under the glare of Yogi

and Johnny, Rock Bradley said, "Couldn't until my commander gave the ok. The attempt to blow us all up was all he needed to bring you guys under the tent. There has been some concern in my office about working with the locals. If you remember we had that issue previously in the Red Dagger situation."

"So, who is it?" Johnny asked.

"I'm not at liberty to break his cover just yet, but I can assure you he is close to the flame," Bradley said.

"Did you find out anything interesting regarding the delivery of the cargo last night?" Yogi asked.

"I received an email a few minutes ago. Both warehouses are leased to an entity known as ACME Investments, LLC with its principal office located in Memphis," Bradley reported.

"Is that supposed to mean something to us?" Yogi asked.

"Not ACME itself but its members are other LLCs we have been able to trace back to a certain notorious Congressman from Shelby County," Bradley said relishing that he knew things they didn't. Bradley always liked playing the mysterious secret agent. Intrigue was sauce for his soul and right now his gravy boat was overflowing.

"Don't say anything else," Jack said suddenly. The others looked at him since he came out of his stupor to finally join the conversation, and in a very dramatic way. He continued, "Rock, you may not know it but I am associated with Calvin Greathouse's firm in Shelby County, and if your information touches the Congressman, Calvin may know him. What I know, Calvin knows. I cannot withhold information from my partner."

"Know him? Hell, our information is that Calvin's firm set up all these limited liability companies," Bradley spurt out. "He is also a person of interest."

"Holy shit," Rachel said.

"Guess this isn't going to be command central, is it?" Yogi said.

CHAPTER FORTY-FIVE

After everyone left, Jack walked into the spare bedroom Emily used as her studio. As with most artists the studio was littered with completed work intermingled with pieces that were still in process. The most prominent easel contained an abstract piece that looked vaguely familiar to Jack, but he couldn't quite place it until his eyes fell on a picture taped to the wall behind the easel. It was a photograph of one of the Severini's in the University gallery. What in the hell? He thought. Why would Emily be duplicating one of the school's paintings? Her work was good, indistinguishable from the original. As Jack stared at the unfinished painting, alarm built in his mind. If Henri was an art thief as Levi had hinted, was Emily somehow complicit? Glancing at his watch Jack realized there was just enough time to shower, dress and meet Emily's flight in Chattanooga.

"Stay here, girl," Jack told Rocket as he grabbed his keys to drive to the Chattanooga airport to meet Emily's plane. Rocket wagged her tail and climbed into the most comfortable chair in the living room.

"Calvin, we need to talk," Jack said into his cell phone once he was on I-24 descending the Mountain.

"Good morning to you too, my man," Calvin said his rich voice booming over the line.

"Do you represent Congressman Dodge?" Jack asked.

Calvin laughed and said, "Jack, you know I represent every Black man in Shelby County with ten bucks in his pocket, and some with a lot less than that."

"Are you familiar with ACME Investments?"

"Sure, I set them up, or one of my associates did. What's this about?"

"You know the exotic animal case over here?" Jack asked.

"Of course, we are representing Lola. Are you going to tell me what's up or do I have to reach through this phone and yank it out of you?"

"Lola's gone, Calvin. Somebody spooked her enough to take her kids and leave. The TBI has evidence ACME is involved in the distribution chain, and on account of your work for ACME, you have become a person of interest." Jack let the last sentence hang. Calvin was quiet for a moment.

"Let me get back to you."

"Did you hear me, Calvin? They suspect you are involved. Is there something I need to know?" Jack asked.

"Later, I said." Then the line disconnected.

Jack struggled to organize and compartmentalize what he needed to deal with. First, all the issues with his wife, and now his law partner? Had the world tilted on its axis, or was he trapped in some bizarre dream? He reached over and pinched the back of his hand. It hurt all right, and he certainly thought he was awake. Unfortunately, he couldn't remember anything about the last twenty miles he travelled and that by itself was scary. He focused on the road as he pulled into the Arrival area of the Chattanooga airport. Emily and her bags stood by the curb. She waived at him and he pulled over. Emily threw her bag in to the back seat and jumped into his Jeep. Before pulling on her seat belt she leaned over and kissed him.

"I missed you," she whispered.

"Me, too," Jack said smiling back at her, at those turquois pupils that peered at him from within her liquid eyes. "How was your trip," he asked.

"The Severini show at the Brooklyn was spectacular, and I ran into Levi and Chiara, who said to tell you hello," Emily said.

Jack decided to ease into the topic of the painting. "I chased Rocket out of your studio this morning and noticed it looked like you were working on making a copy of one of the Severinis we have at the gallery."

"Henri asked me to see how close I could get to the original, just for fun."

"We need to talk about Henri, Emily," Jack said deciding to raise the issues Levi referred to. Emily, however, was on another angle of the story.

"What about him?" she asked defensively.

"I also spoke with Levi," Jack said and watched the puzzlement come over Emily's face. "Were you aware that Henri is under investigation by the New York police for art theft? More specifically, the theft of a Severini from the MoMA?"

"I can't believe that," Emily countered.

Keeping his eyes on the Interstate Jack responded, "Levi told me and said it was highly confidential. Did you know that no one from the University contacted MoMA? I guess he fell through the cracks when my predecessor went on sabbatical. Henri was not even an assistant curator as he put on his resume, he was a restorer."

"A restorer? He didn't tell me that," Emily said. "Henri told me he is not an artist, but a restorer has to have the skills of an artist."

"When we get back, I would like you to look at

the Severini paintings hanging in the Gallery and see if you can confirm they are all four originals."

"Surely, you don't think…" Emily's voice trailed off.

"What I think is that if Henri is planning something, the switch has not occurred yet and that he plans to use your painting in place of the original. Will you help me?"

"Of course. What do I need to do?"

"I want you to complete the painting but mark it in some way only you will know it is not the original. Then let's see where it leads. We will either be wrong about Henri, or we will catch a thief in action."

"Okay," Emily said not sure where all of this would lead.

By the furrows on Emily's brow Jack could tell she was struggling with the information. "Why did you come home early?" Jack asked.

Emily looked over at him and said, "There was a side trip planned he didn't tell me about."

CHAPTER FORTY-SIX

As Calvin Greathouse hung up the call with Jack Mathews, he knew what he had to do. It had been a long time coming. Calvin worked too long and too hard to watch his career blow up like this. The nights and weekends he spent building his practice and taking care of his clients were one of the sacrifices he made in pursuit of his dreams. He and Robin put off starting a family, perhaps forever, as he fought the system to champion the cause of those less fortunate. He couldn't let that same system now grind him up like so much sausage which it would do if given half a chance. The system sought to yank at anyone who rose above the norm, at anyone who dared take off like a rocket in a trajectory that out shown the system itself. Calvin experienced this his entire life, almost as if the system dared him to excel and paused to see if it could shoot him down once it could draw a bead on his flight path. Big firms were been only too quick to file ethical complaints against him when he beat them at trial on the facts and the law. None of those complaints ever scratched the hard polished metal of his armor.

Calvin's father also spoken with him about a man's reputation and how you never got a second chance. Once you were placed on the wrong side of the reputation equation you couldn't ever crawl back. When he began to practice older lawyers told him how his reputation would be made during his first five years at the bar. He would be perceived quickly as either, honest and trustworthy or a shady character who would bend the rules when it served his own financial interests. Some called it situational ethics. Calvin's father was a musician in a razzle dazzle world involving money, drugs, women and back stabbing. Somehow he maintained an immaculate reputation over a fifty year career. No one ever questioned Gabriel Greathouse's integrity or honesty. Calvin grew up listening to the silky jazz Gabriel released from his horn and guitar like opening your palms and releasing a flurry of excited fireflies into the warm summer night. When Gabriel's trumpet sounded, the walls fell and the smoky room filled with transformational emotion. If only Gabriel were still alive, Calvin would seek his wisdom. He remembered his father in his sixties, tall, proud and a face framed with the whitest whiskers. His hands were magic. Now that his father passed, Calvin's anchor was the memory of Gabriel and his own inner strength. While he liked and respected Jack Mathews, Jack was too new to the private legal world to understand all the nuances of Calvin's present dilemma.

Calvin knew, or should have known about the ACME connection and he was going to act decisively. His father always told him to find something he liked to do and do it better than anyone else. There was so much mediocrity in the world,

Calvin always knew he would be the one to shine because he wouldn't settle for average. As a Black man he always worked harder and longer. With no avenues into the power structure he built his own reputation, and that meant bloodying a few noses and kicking some ass. There weren't many Black faces at the Cotton Ball in Memphis. In the fight against old money, however, temptations were omnipresent. The lure of easy money, as the song said, could make a man do strange things.

Demographically, there were more African American voters in Shelby County than whites, and once they realized that fact, electing Blacks to Congress became the norm. Even a Black United States Congressman knew power and opportunities that opened doors and filled the bank accounts. The firm of Greathouse and Williams hitched its star to the young Congressman Dodge from Memphis and he to them. The "brothers" knew if they didn't hang together they would all hang separately. The strategy and structure behind ACME Investments had Greathouse and Williams stamped all over it.

Calvin scratched the side of his jaw and prepared for a meeting too long in the making. A meeting that would define the rest of his career. He picked up the phone and speed dialed the number he knew by heart.

Meanwhile, the cell phone on Pierce's desk buzzed twice before he picked it up. "Yeah," he said.

"Pick me up in the helicopter at the airport on the Mountain in an hour. We need to discuss where we are and what happens next. I have arranged for the hunting camp to be made ready. We will pick up our man in Memphis on the way down. Well, not exactly our man, but his man will meet with us," Wild Bill Cheatham said.

"Do I need to bring any of the men?' Pierce asked.

"Your call," Cheatham said, "it's up to you. We have men on site, but if it makes you feel better, go ahead. The Committee has asked for this meeting."

"The Committee?" Pierce asked. Pierce heard of the Committee but never met any of its members, like he had heard of the hunting camp that served as the proposed meeting site but was never been invited there. The camp was located at a place known as Greenville, Mississippi somewhere along the Mississippi River south of Memphis. For the Committee to have called for a meeting was unusual. He thought it might be wise to have Larsen and Ramparts go with him, just in case.

CHAPTER FORTY-SEVEN

Yogi sat across from Rock Bradley in a corner booth at the Truck Stop Café on top of the Mountain finishing a three egg ham and cheese omelet. Bradley wiped the maple syrup off his lip as he finished a large bite of a double stack of pecan waffles. Bradley asked Yogi to meet him without Johnny since he was technically not law enforcement which freed up Johnny to travel back to Cherokee, North Carolina for a couple of days.

"So, where does the investigation stand?" Yogi asked.

Not able to answer a direct question without a bit of a dramatic flair, Rock leaned back and stretched his arms over his head and began,

"Interestingly, the parts trucks have not been back to the Farm."

"You are still tracking them?"

"Yeah. The only trips have been to other dealerships and body shops within a one hour drive," Bradley said.

"Did those last runs move all the animals?" Yogi asked.

"We don't think so. Those looked like bird runs only. None of the crates or cages looked large enough."

"So, where's the tiger?"

"For all we know, he's still out there at the Farm somewhere." The TBI took over responsibility for monitoring the GPS devices planted on the delivery trucks.

"Are you planning a raid on the Farm?" Yogi asked.

"Not yet. We are still running down the Memphis Congressman angle and those Memphis lawyers. We can't spring the trap without having a better handle on the entire operation. Closing one transportation point only means the distribution will run to another remote location. Our goal is to nab all the bad guys at once," said Bradley. Yogi nodded as he added cream to the fresh cup of coffee the waitress left.

"I am really concerned about the involvement of Calvin Greathouse, and how that impacts Jack Mathews," Bradley said. "You need to know we are focusing on Calvin as a primary target. The fallout could hang every lawyer in that firm. There are those at the TBI who think Greathouse would be a nice catch."

"Holy shit."

"Right. We are already securing all the banking records of that firm, and for the Congressman," Bradley said. "How about your end?"

"Not much has changed. The Sheriff officially shut me down. Lola is still missing, Mansker is still drunk, and Mabel is on another planet," Yogi reported.

"I would like to catch Meacham and Pierce acting together. Those drivers are so dumb, if Meacham denied knowing what they were doing, we might have a difficult time tying him in. Pierce not so much since his Farm has evidence all over it."

They paid the tab and walked outside onto the gravel parking lot which was empty save for a handful of long haulers in big rigs that were lined up in the lot. As Yogi began to open the door to his Explorer he looked up in time to see a shiny sleek helicopter flash overhead headed in the direction of the Sequoyah County airport.

Yogi looked at Bradley and said, "I believe that is Pierce's copter."

"Nice. Wonder where he is off to?" Bradley said.

Just then Bradley's cell phone buzzed. He answered the call and said tersely, "Roger that." Bradley put the phone back in his pocket and pumped his fist.

Yogi stared at him and said, "What was that all about?"

The international man of mystery said, "We have a delivery truck headed west. This is breaking the pattern of the recent local deliveries."

"So, you think they are moving something?" Yogi asked.

"Looks like it."

"What do we do?"

"We are following the delivery truck, but the helicopter could be a more difficult target," Bradley said.

"Can't you just pull its flight plan?" asked Yogi.

"It's not that easy with a rotary aircraft. They are not obligated to file flight plans unless they are going into a densely populated area. My office is checking on that now."

Yogi looked up to see the helicopter once again airborne but this time pulling away west. Bradley's phone buzzed. "Thanks," he said into the phone.

"We've caught a little luck. The pilot filed a flight plan. He's on the way to Memphis," Bradley said.

"What's in Memphis?" Yogi asked, then answered his own question. "Congressman Dodge."

"And, Calvin Greathouse."

"Whew," Yogi exhaled. He wanted to call Jack but knew he couldn't.

"Did you pack some clothes?" Bradley asked.

"Yeah, as you suggested."

"Then lock your vehicle and hop into mine," Bradley said.

"Where are we going?"

"Sounds like Beale Street, my good man."

"Johnny?"

"He's already on the way."

CHAPTER FORTY-EIGHT

Emily finished the Severini and was quite proud of the work as she compared it to the photograph of the original taped to the wall. Jack walked up behind her and put his arms around her kissing her neck.

"Emily, that's really, really good," he said untaping the photo and holding it up next to hers. "How will we know which one is yours?"

"You see this area?" she pointed to the lower right of the painting that was bathed in a red slash. "Right in the center, the red swirl is one shade darker than the original. That's how we will know."

Jack looked where she was pointing and frowned. Even hoping he could tell the subtle difference when the time came was futile.

"Are you taking it in to work today?" Jack asked.

"Yes. Henri and I are to meet at eleven. He said he had something to show me."

"Like what?"

"Don't know. Did you know there was a tunnel beneath the cathedral that leads away from the campus?" Emily asked.

Jack was glancing around the room at some of her other recent work. "Did you say a tunnel?" he asked doubting he heard correctly and wondering why Emily raised that at this time.

"Yep, Henri says it was dug back in the sixties as an escape route for faculty if student unrest couldn't be controlled," she said.

"That's amazing. It is hard to believe this place was ever threatened by student unrest or that the school would feel so vulnerable it had to construct a secret passage to ferret away the teachers. I guess you had to be there."

"Remember Kent State? Wasn't it at Yale where students seized the admin buildings? Old student newspapers from the day were full of anti-war letters to the editor. Peace symbols were all over cars and even the academic gowns worn by the Honor Society."

"I assume the Red Dagger Society was around back then. I bet the sixties drove some of them nuts."

"Don't you know it. So, am I supposed to give this painting to Henri?" Emily asked as she lifted the painting off the easel.

"Yes. Then the next move is his. Do you know if he has any out of town trips planned soon?"

"As a matter of fact I think he was visiting a gallery in Louisville in a couple of days," Emily said.

"My money says that is when he will make his move."

"What do you plan to do if he makes the swap?"

"I'm not sure. I can't let him leave with the Severini, but I checked with Yogi and Johnny and they have something going on in Memphis or Mississippi the next few days."

"So," Emily said, "it's just the two of us." It was more of a statement than a question. Jack remembered that she wanted it to be Jack and Emily, not Jack and Yogi, he thought, so here goes.

"Can I borrow your gun?" Emily still had the semi-automatic service pistol, a 9mm Beretta. It was the gun she had shot Dr. Julian Browne with.

She gave him a quizzical look and said, "Sure, I guess."

CHAPTER FORTY-NINE

When his cell phone buzzed the third most famous Black man in Memphis began talking to the second most famous Black man in Memphis. The first being U.S. Congressman Dodge who was their client.

"Damascus, we have got to meet and I mean now." Damascus Williams came from a large family that sharecropped cotton in west Tennessee for four generations. When the opportunity presented for him to get off that sun beat farm he took it without looking back. All along the way he was praised and rewarded for the ingenuity he applied to businesses he helped structure, and the deals he was able to forge between those that had money and wanted more, or those just tasting the sweet fruit of the dollar for the first time. Where Calvin Greathouse was flamboyant and aggressive, Damascus was intense and back roomy. He preferred to have the knife between his adversary's ribs before the man knew he was even in a knife fight. Calvin would call out his enemy and then pommel him in broad daylight before the largest audience the venue would permit. With Damascus there was no public display. The other side was simply out maneuvered and out of the game before the bell rang.

Damascus often structured transactions with a

series of trusts to protect the identity of the real party in interest. This drove bank lawyers crazy as they tried to find out the nature and identity of the borrower or his assets. When they looked at a Damascus deal only hard obsidian trusts were discernable that sheltered the true owner from scrutiny and liability. In dealing with Damascus, lenders knew the race card was only a flicker away, so they learned to accept what they saw, and rationalize away all those picky questions their lawyers continued to ask about. It had been a perfect arrangement that obscured the nature of the underlying transaction and made it look all so legitimate. When the money began to flow into and swell his client's bank accounts even the lenders stopped asking questions.

Somehow Congressman Dodge had been introduced to someone who knew someone who was able to install ACME Investments as one of the final links on the chain of distribution for some very desirable items. Damascus provided the legal documentation and the only person who even knew the Congressman was involved was Damascus. ACME took off like a Space-X rocket, without anyone legitimate knowing what its true business even was. Money ran like a river into ACME's accounts at Cotton Bank which was then used to acquire real estate and warehouses across the mid-South. Almost overnight ACME was worth millions and produced the collateral to support real loans. Meanwhile,

Congressman Dodge sponsored and pursued legislation that was whispered to him by Damascus. One good turn deserving another, and so on.

Calvin Greathouse was impressed with the ability of Damascus Williams to attract and satisfy clients. As Calvin pursued his socially correct cases, the profits of Greathouse & Williams continued to rise, and everyone was happy. Until, that is, something began nagging at Calvin. It was the constant buzz of the easy button. "That was easy" he would hear in his mind, knowing that nothing was easy, at least not in his experience. There were too many details, too many unknowns to be batting 1000 all the time. Where was the curve ball, the slider? Damascus never had a deal go bad, never got rejected on a business deal, and always appeared to be in absolute control of all the levers. Even Calvin lost one now and then, but not Damascus.

Then it was the clients themselves. The people who came to the office to meet with Damascus looked slippery to Calvin. Having won the best dressed man three years in a row at Vanderbilt Law School, Calvin appreciated fine clothes and ties that matched. That was not it. The people who called on Damascus looked too fancy, too made for television, too greasy. That was the word, greasy. Calvin felt he needed a bath after passing in the hall or sharing the men's room with them. He was also committed to his wife, Robin, where it was not a secret that Damascus had many women in his life including his secretary, Collette. Roxanne, Damascus' wife, hardly darkened the door any longer. Calvin's father taught him that a man who would cheat on his wife would cheat you in business.

Calvin's sin was that he looked the other way until the fear began to crush him. That fear would no longer allow him to avoid confronting Damascus, so he called him.

"Damascus, we have got to meet and I mean now."

"Ok, brother, whatever you say. How about Monday at lunch? I've got to be away for a couple of days," Damascus said in his calmest voice.

"I need to know what the deal is with ACME, the Congressman, and probably most of what you have been involved in for the past couple of years," Calvin said.

"All in good time. Why all the alarm?" Damascus queried.

"Yesterday my contact at Cotton Bank said they had an inquiry about our accounts, and last night Jack Mathews informed me the TBI is looking into our firm's activities. You have got to tell me what's going on."

"Are you absolutely sure you want to know?" asked Damascus in a threatening voice Calvin had never heard. Calvin was stunned.

"Hell yes, I want to know. What do you mean by even asking that question and where are you going?"

"I have a business meeting down in Greenville. As soon as I get back we can talk. Everything's going to be just fine. No worries."

"Damascus, if you are into some kind of illegal activity, you are on your own," Calvin threatened.

"It may not be that easy, Calvin. Aren't you the one who says ain't nothing easy?"

"Jesus Christ," Calvin said and hung up the phone.

CHAPTER FIFTY

The Sikorsky S-76C jet helicopter touched down long enough at the Memphis FBO of Knight Air for Damascus Williams to climb aboard, its rotary blade slowing but never stopping. Damascus looked around but recognized only Bill Cheatham. The others nodded, but no names were exchanged as the luxury craft lifted up and powered south. Damascus leaned back in the leather seat, closed his eyes and dreamed.

Greenville, Mississippi is as sleepy a Mississippi River town as there ever was. So near the River, downtown Greenville is protected by a giant levee which has not broken since the great flood of 1927. River boats pull off the main channel of the Mississippi into a lagoon or lake where deckhands tie the boats off and walk from the docks up and over the levee into the old streets of downtown Greenville. There they are greeted by stately buildings and tree lined residential streets. The Chamber of Commerce promotes it this way:

"We are the land of cotton and the Delta Blues where the stories are bigger than catfish and as powerful as the waters of Old Man River. We have been shelled, invaded, burned, flooded and plagued. And we still capture imaginations and treat our visitors warmly like long lost friends." (From the official Greenville website.)

Southern charm runs through this town like the sweet aroma of jasmine flowers. Although completely burned out by the Yankees on the way to Vicksburg during the War of Northern Aggression, Greenville stands proud as a rebellious southern village where Blacks and whites found paths to coexist, and where the economy is still mostly agrarian but also filled with literature and music. Why this place was chosen by the Committee was only guessed at by Damascus. Surrounding the town were hundreds of thousands of acres of cypress groves and cane brakes rolling down to the edge of Old Man River. Along the River itself at night hundreds of white tail deer collect and socialize their mournful eyes aglow while the dark Mississippi River ebbs by. The placid river flow is only occasionally disturbed by a river boat with its lights and laughter or a tow boat pushing commerce up or downstream. It was here Walker Percy wrote *Lanterns on the Levee* and Holt Collier guided Theodore Roosevelt on the Mississippi Bear Hunt that resulted in the creation of the Teddy Bear.

Damascus recalled a few of these things as the helicopter touched down on the grass landing strip of the Wolf Creek Hunting Club, but he was not sentimental like Calvin. Calvin, having grown up in Greenville, lived with a host of other memories about the place. His father, Gabriel Greathouse knew and played with jazz and blues luminaries like Tyrone Davis, one of the early performers on the Chitlin'

Circuit, and Walter Turnbull, Sam Chatman, Roosevelt "Booba" Barnes, Mamie "Galore" Davis, and Eddie Cusic. Gabriel used to tease Calvin that Mary Wilson of the Supremes was almost his momma. Where Calvin's eyes would have glistened, Damascus' eyes only hardened as he stepped from the flying machine.

ATV's carrying the guests jumbled along the trail through the woods to the Lodge which was a two story restoration of a 19th century hunting camp. The five thousand acres of the club was flush with doves, bear, deer and wild boar and snakes the size of a man's leg. No one wandered into the Reserve, as they called it, unarmed unless they were man enough to face down a boar with a bowie knife. The lodge itself was a wooden structure with a wrap-around screen porch on the first floor. A series of barracks beyond the main lodge housed the men who patrolled and protected the compound. Day workers were imported from Greenville to cook and keep the place clean. A side entrance was gated and with a guard house that screened all those laborers going in and coming out each day. Damascus took it all in as he stepped out of the ATV and grabbed his overnight bag. Having dropped Pierce, Cheatham, Larsen, Ramparts and Damascus, the ATV's throttled up and away as other men dressed in camo outfits greeted them at the steps leading up to the porch. A man who identified himself as Bailey patted down and then removed handguns and cell phones from everyone except Damascus who was not armed.

"They will be returned to you upon departure," Bailey said in a matter of fact voice. Larsen and Ramparts felt naked, but also knew their bags were not searched. A small security lapse but a mistake just the same.

Other men guided each of the new arrivals to his room and announced that a meeting would be held at 3pm followed by dinner. Larsen and Ramparts shared a room. After throwing his bags on the double beds, Ramparts announced he was going to take a shower. Larsen fell back on the bed and said he thought he would catch a short nap. David Ramparts nodded and kicked off his boots, grabbed a towel and his overnight bag and went to the communal bathroom down the hall. As soon as the door to the room closed and Larsen heard the footsteps proceeding down the hall, he leaned over and picked up Ramparts' boots. Turning them upside down he pried up the soles with his knife but found nothing. He then turned the boots upright and reached in to remove the interior sole of the right boot. Beneath the padding was the circular tracking device he was afraid he would find. From the way the device created a bump in the sole, he knew if he removed it Ramparts would immediately recognize the difference so he left the device intact. Larsen found what he expected and would duly report it to Pierce.

When Ramparts returned Larsen appeared to be sleeping. However, Ramparts noticed his boots were moved ever so slightly from the position in which he had deliberately left them. He smiled at Larsen's back then reached into his day bag and withdrew a four inch titanium sheath knife which he strapped onto his calf.

Damascus paced around his room. It was nice enough but rustic. The single window looked out onto a green wall of pine trees so dense it would be difficult to walk through. He wondered why they were brought to this place, and what he was going to tell Calvin when he returned.

Cheatham visited the camp on other occasions and knew that a summons from the Committee could not be ignored. He believed his position with the group was secure, but still his stomach twisted and gurgled as gas raced around his intestines.

Pierce didn't like anything about this place. On many big game hunts where he stayed in lodgings similar to this or even more primitive, but for the very first time, he felt the sensation of confinement and loss of tactical advantage. Well, not entirely. From his bag he removed the .38 caliber throw down handgun and locked it down into the holster on his right ankle.

CHAPTER FIFTY-ONE

Having joined the conspiracy to expose Henri Jacques, Emily carried her duplicate of the Severini painting into the working studio at the rear of the University Art Gallery and placed it on a spare easel. The room was well lit with natural light pouring in through the beveled glass windows. It also served as a studio for art students and for the storage of work yet to be displayed around the University. She took three steps back and admired the work. It was good. Hearing steps behind her she turned her head as Henri came up and placed his hand on her neck.

"Well done, my dear," he said and squeezed her tenderly before moving his hand down to the middle of her back which he began rubbing in a soft way. His hand lingered as he took in the painting. Although Emily made no move to remove his hand, she wasn't pleased that he thought he could touch her whenever he pleased. Apparently, he did not read the message carefully when she refused to travel to the Maine coastal cabin with him.

"I am most impressed with the way you have captured the spirit of the Severini, the way the brush strokes rise from the canvas. I am not sure I could tell it from the original," Henri said. They stood like this for another five minutes facing the painting before the Westminster Chimes outside announced it was noon. Henri patted her back and said he must leave for a meeting. Emily nodded as he scurried away relieved he was gone. Jack told Emily to make the painting a gift to Henri and then remain watchful to see what he would do next. All this intrigue made Emily uncomfortable but she promised Jack she would help. She grabbed her shoulder bag and made a pass through the Gallery glancing at the group of hanging Severinis. Hmm, she wondered. How long before Henri would make the switch? And, if he didn't what would that say?

Special Agent Bradley's SUV rolled down I-40 toward Memphis through middle Tennessee and across the Tennessee River clicking off the miles as pastures gave way to cultivated fields and bottom land nourished by the river. Along the way he explained to Yogi that Johnny Running Bear was meeting them at the Memphis office of the TBI along with other TBI agents who would assist in following the trail of the helicopter. Bradley consented to allow Johnny join the group since he was tribal police. Involving non-law enforcement was where Bradley drew the line. He learned from the Red Dagger events and wouldn't put civilians in harm's way any longer. Yogi understood this and didn't even ask for Jack Mathews to be included. Besides, Yogi recalled, Jack seemed to be distracted about something to do with the Director of the Art Department at the University and Emily.

"You should know that we have located the

delivery truck," Bradley said.

"Where abouts?"

"Outside Greenville, Mississippi. A hunting camp. The truck arrived last night and has not moved."

"So, the GPS is still working?"

"Yep."

"Who owns the camp?"

"Some company with a bunch of initials. We haven't had time to drill into that yet."

"Is that where we're going?" Yogi asked.

"As soon as we can confirm the helicopter has gone to the same location. We would like to recover the tiger, for sure, but it's the two legged savages we want."

"How are you going to track the helicopter? Surely you don't have a tracking device on that machine?"

"Even better. Our device is inside the 'copter with our man."

"Interesting," Yogi mused. Working with law enforcement that had the resources of the Tennessee Bureau of Investigation was a lot more fun than the

Sequoyah County Sheriff's Department. The miles blew by and Yogi spoke again.

"But, you do realize we are all outside our respective jurisdictions and we couldn't arrest Jesse James in Mississippi," Yogi said.

"I believe those boys just drove Mr. Tiger across a state line, which violates federal law. I believe we will have FBI support when we arrive," Bradley said having already lined up FBI involvement. This wouldn't be the first time the TBI and FBI worked together. They almost nailed Wild Bill Cheatham a few years back on the stolen auto parts investigation but failed in that mission when some source within the TBI leaked the investigation. Before they could recover, Cheatham's operation closed down and once again the slippery car salesman skated. Although the source of the leak was never discovered, Bradley still felt the sting of a failed investigation.

CHAPTER FIFTY-TWO

The big cat was kept sedated after Pierce's men captured him at the top of Savage Gulf. He drifted into and out of consciousness and hardly recognized when they loaded him back into a cage at the Farm for the trip to Mississippi. The parts truck left the dealership and picked up the cage for its trip to the Delta late in the night. Because the truck was not air conditioned movement at night prevented the animal from being overcome with heat exhaustion. Pierce explained how valuable the cat was and how much they invested in the animal and its recapture.

Camp workers received the cage once it arrived in Greenville. A tow motor moved the cage to one side of the warehouse as far removed as possible from the cages in which the monkeys were kept. Even sedated and sleepy, the monkeys watched with apprehension if the tiger even yawned, so when he stood and began a tight pace inside the cage, monkey chatter grew more excited. The men who worked the barn were local but regular employees unlike the temporary staff who took care of the house and grounds around the house only when guests were in residence. They too, were fearful of the cat and kept a watchful eye.

The morning after he arrived in Greenville, the cat began to recover but did not eat the food placed in his cage because it had a funny smell. Something warned him there was something unusual about the raw meat. As if something was added to the meat giving it a sharp and bitter odor. The cat's hunger grew but his mind cleared and he became restless which set off an uproar in the monkey clan.

The desire to escape now overwhelmed the animal and he focused on his release. From the rear of the cage the tiger leaped at the door and felt it wobble. He stepped back and lunged again and again until the latch began to warp and give way. A few more attacks and the lock gave way forcing the bent door to open. The tiger stepped out into the dim lighting of the warehouse. There were doors at either end and a tall door in the middle. No one was in the warehouse except him and those damned monkeys. Slowly, the tiger stepped toward the monkeys and their agitation reached a new level of distress. Monkeys that hurled feces at him earlier in the day cowered in the remotest part of their cages and howled. The beast surveyed the stacks of monkey cages and glared at one monkey in particular who was one of the most vocal and who enjoyed hurling turds at the cat. The cat's large round eyes locked on the monkey and the level of monkey screams reached a frantic level.

The noise did not go unnoticed. Two of the warehousemen passing by on the drive outside heard the racket and decided to investigate for the safety of all the animals was part of their responsibility. As the door opened they saw the tiger batting a monkey cage around the room like a soccer ball. He swatted the cage and sent it crashing across the floor. Then the tiger leaped to the place the cage rested and struck it again sending the cage to ricochet off another wall. It looked as if the beast enjoyed tormenting the small animal for when he leaped at the cage again he roared. It was not a mighty jungle roar just a muffled throaty cat sound that terrified the monkeys. The cacophony of monkey voices echoed off the metal roof and walls amidst the rolling thunder of the tiger's call.

"God ahmighty," one of the men said and slammed the door shut as he took off running back to the office where the camp foreman was located. Within minutes additional support came running to the warehouse including a couple of men with tranquilizer guns.

"I ain't going in there," one worker protested.

"You will if I say you will," the foreman shouted.

"Let's see what we've got," the foreman said holding one of the dart guns and cracking the door slightly. At the other end of the warehouse room the cat continued to amuse himself with the monkey cage. When he turned to the noise of the door opening the frightened monkey jumped out of the cage and climbed on top of the stack of cages in which other terrified monkeys yelled and screamed and pointed at the tiger. The smell of excrement and urine was pervasive in the room.

The well-known threat signals pulsed through the tiger's mind and he turned to face the men, but they were prepared. Darts flew across the room and stabbed the tiger. Once again he fell to the floor his tongue hanging out as his eyes slowly closed to the sight of the monkeys pointing and screaming.

CHAPTER FIFTY-THREE

"Jack," Calvin said in a quiet voice he did not often use, "we need to talk."

"Go ahead," Jack said noting how somber Calvin's tone had become. It was almost, what? Humble?

"No, not on the phone. I am afraid my calls are being monitored."

"Monitored? Do you mean like wiretapped?" Jack asked.

"Could be. We need to meet face to face. How about lunch at the place we used to celebrate after exams?"

Jack checked his schedule and didn't find anything that couldn't be moved. This cryptic message could only refer to The Loveless Café. If anyone were truly bugging Calvin's communications the exact location of their meeting place would remain a mystery. The Loveless was a former motel just outside Nashville on Interstate 40 that had been converted into shops and a music venue. Its biscuits and country ham were to die for and it made all the tour books promoting "The best place to eat in the Music City." Dining at the Loveless presented a palate of southern treasures. During law school Calvin and Jack celebrated completing an exam with a

Sunday morning breakfast at the Loveless with their study group, homemade scratch biscuits piled high with country ham and red eye gravy or strawberry jam. For southern boys like Calvin and Jack it was a religious experience. After three years of law school, even some of the northern boys in their study group became Martha White converts. Meeting at the Loveless meant a three hour drive for Calvin and two hours for Jack.

"Sure," he said. Jack cleared his afternoon with his assistant Tammy, and texted Emily that he was going to Nashville to meet with Calvin so he would be late for dinner. Emily didn't immediately return his text.

That is how Jack and Calvin came to be having some of the finest fried chicken in Nashville on a bright fall afternoon. Jack sipped iced tea at a window table adorned with a red and white checked tablecloth when Calvin arrived. Not at all the polished obsidian litigator Jack was used to working with, this Calvin was distant and distracted. Rather than assume his seat in a controlled manner, Calvin seemed to collapse into it, a crushed man. Jack knew this had to be about the TBI investigation. He just didn't know how bad it could be.

Calvin began, "For some time I have been worried about my partner, Damascus Williams, about how easy the money is coming in and how much of it there is. The cash flow is great and means we don't have to finance our practice with bank loans and credit lines, but something is out of sync. In my practice, I have to fight hard and long usually for years before I am able to monetize a case. Corporate defendants and insurance companies don't open the checkbook when I file a lawsuit. It's just the opposite. They lawyer up and make me work for every nickel. Every skirmish we win during a case only inspires their lawyers to think up new defenses and new ways to make us worry about our case. So, when Damascus proposed we get together and start a firm I thought it was the answer to my prayers. He had a steady business practice that would help smooth over the dry periods for a litigation practice like mine. I guess I came to enjoy the easy money too much, because I stopped questioning the clientele." Calvin paused and rubbed his temples.

"You wouldn't believe how sleazy some of the people are who show up for Damascus to help them with a difficult business transaction. I'm talking about greasers with slicked back hair and three piece suits, not sophisticated business people. And, there's the Congressman, Dodge. While he looks like a cut above the sleaze bags, underneath, I don't think he is any different. I've never trusted him. He always has his hand out. Companies hire Damascus just to get to meet with Dodge, and I know big checks change hands, I've seen them."

Calvin paused again to drink more tea since his throat turned cracker dry. Jack remained silent listening and held Calvin's eyes as he continued with the story.

"I was raised to value honesty, loyalty and hard work, not to worship money. If you are good, the money will follow, but it's not the ultimate goal. Dad always said you can't compromise your principles, and I think for the most part I have succeeded in following that advice. Then I got to thinking about Damascus. He's bright enough, but we are all plus or minus ten percent. So, if he's not the sharpest crayon in the box, why do all these people come to him with big bucks to have him structure a business deal? That is the question I should have asked two years ago. All Damascus is really doing is putting up roadblocks he builds out of dummy corporations and trusts to hide what's swirling in the cesspool at the bottom of the ditch. Whose money is driving this deal? What in fact is the real deal?" Calvin ran his napkin over his bald head and wiped away the moisture. Jack realized Calvin was in a deep struggle within himself as his principles clashed with loyalty to his law partner. Calvin's path to this Loveless table was twisted and littered at the edges with broken glass, the remaining shards of his friendship with Damascus.

Jack could see in Calvin's eyes that the man was

whipped, like a prize fighter too proud to surrender and yet with enough strength remaining not to fall to his knees. His voice sounded of quiet desperation. Jack reached across the table and grabbed Calvin's forearm in a gesture he hoped conveyed empathy, friendship and help.

"Sins of omission are a lot easier to resolve than those of commission," Jack said. "Do you think Damascus is involved in illegal activities?"

Calvin nodded. "Up to his eyeballs. I went through some of our older files involving ACME Investments, one of his larger clients, and all I see is a lot of "begats". You know A owns B who owns C who has a piece of D, and so on. There is not a shred of any planning in any of the files. There's no tax research or memos discussing the tax advantage of this structure or any alternate structures. Those files have been sanitized. I laid open four or five and I couldn't tell you the name of a single human client. All the billing addresses go to P.O. Boxes or a UPS Store. That legal work could have been done by a paralegal. It's nothing more than a daisy chain, certainly not the work of an extraordinary lawyer."

"Tell me, have you done any work for ACME?" Jack asked recalling that Yogi mentioned ACME as the owner of the warehouses where the truck loads of birds were dropped off.

"Not that I can recall. But, they would be considered clients of the firm, and therefore there is a privacy right held by the client. That attorney-client privilege handcuffs me, and by the way, you as well." Jack hadn't thought of that angle. Since he became associated with the firm even on a part time basis he was subject to the same privacy rules as Calvin.

"I'm not so sure about that. I think the Rules of Ethics permit you to reveal adverse information relating to a client to the extent you believe it is necessary to prevent the client from committing a crime, or a fraud, or to prevent injury to a third party."

Calvin pondered that and said, "But, I don't actually know they have committed a crime. I am just suspicious and I see a lot of markers in that direction."

"What did Damascus say?"

"That maybe I didn't want to know too much," Calvin said looking up at Jack. That statement disturbed both of them.

"My first instinct would be to call the District Attorney," said Jack.

"Which one? I'll wager the Sequoyah County D.A. is beholden to either Cheatham or Pierce, or both. And, you're gonna love this, you know who the

Shelby County D.A.s best friend is? Try Congressman Dodge," Calvin said. Now that complicated things they both thought.

"You know what we need, Calvin?"

"What?"

"A lawyer."

Calvin gave a weak smile. "With your permission I am going to engage Allen Pence in Nashville. He's got a great reputation and can look at this more objectively than either of us."

Calvin said, "Good choice. I know Allen. I just wish he wasn't so much of a randy Republican." As Jack paid the waitress they rose and stepped outside pausing beneath the oak tree in front of the café.

"I would really appreciate it if you could spend a couple of days in Memphis right now," Calvin said.

Jack, however, was committed to seeing through the matter with Henri Jacques and would not abandon Emily this time. "Calvin, right now I just can't. I am involved in something at the school and Emily needs me there. I will stay in touch. Once I speak with Allen, I will call you. We should both get what the spy novelists call burner phones." Calvin's shoulders dropped and Jack wanted to reach out and embrace him, but he had chosen Emily.

"I will get us set up with Pence in the next day or so. What are you going to do?" Jack asked.

"I'm going to talk with Damascus. He said he was going to a meeting in Greenville something called the Wolf Creek Hunting Club. Thought I would drive down there and see if I couldn't catch him away from the office and shake him clean. I've still got family there so I can catch up with them as well."

"Our missing client, Lola Crockett?"

"Yes."

"She has family in Greenville. That may be where she ran to."

"Be careful."

"You too." The men shook hands and left in opposite directions.

CHAPTER FIFTY-FOUR

Near the back of the hunting lodge were a couple of oaken doors that Bailey unlocked at five minutes until three that afternoon. He then told each of the guests to get themselves something to drink and claim a seat at the table in the Boardroom. Larsen and David Ramparts were not invited to this meeting but received instructions not to wander off. Two very large and very dark men stood on either side of the door and were introduced as Hotel and Motel Booker. Neither man appeared to have a sense of humor and stared ahead glassy-eyed as if they could not see the men who passed beyond them into the Boardroom. Inside the room nineteenth century artwork depicting great hunts for boar and deer hung on the walls. Dogs raced in packs towards the prey.

Damascus did not know all of the men in the Boardroom. One of the men from the helicopter resembled the actor Jack Palance with his jutting jaw and squared body. He heard someone call him Pierce. Unlike Pierce who dressed like he just stepped out of a photo shoot for *Cowboys and Indians* magazine, the other tall man looked like a used car salesman complete with a string tie. Damascus knew this man from a prior meeting when others referred to him as "Wild Bill". The muscle stayed outside the room. Once everyone was seated, Bailey walked to a door at the rear of the Boardroom, opened it, and stood to the side as a tall Asian man walked in. The Asian towered making Damascus at six feet the runt of the litter.

"I trust your accommodations are adequate?" the Asian man asked in perfect English. He wore casual clothes over loafers and sat at the head of the expansive table.

"Yes, thank you, Mr. Wu," Cheatham said. He had met the man once before when he became part of the organization.

"Excellent. Each of you represents an essential part of our operations and I trust our financial arrangements have been mutually beneficial. Mr. Cheatham, you collect and transport the merchandise. Mr. Pierce you provide storage and essential maintenance services. And, Mr. Williams," Wu turned to Damascus, "your benefactor supplies warehouses throughout the south which have become the last destination before delivery to our clients. For obvious reasons the Congressman cannot openly attend these meetings, but he has assured us of your agency and that you speak as and for him." Damascus nodded but his mouth was dry.

"We are glad you could join us today because the Committee which I represent has become concerned that our distribution chain is not performing as expected." Wu let that sink in as his gaze passed from man to man.

Wild Bill Cheatham began to protest, "Mr. Wu, that incident with the tiger was only a speed bump. In fact, I believe the tiger was delivered here last night." He looked to Pierce for affirmation but Pierce was looking hard at Wu. Pierce was not amused at the tone Wu was using and felt threatened by this entire meeting. He agreed to come with Cheatham, but he wasn't putting up with threats or the rest of this crap. Who did this guy think he was? Slowly, he pushed his chair back and crossed his right leg over his left knee. The subtle movement did not go unnoticed by Bailey who adjusted his weight to a different foot.

"Mr. Cheatham," Wu responded, "the anonymity of our operations is critical which is why we picked Northwoods in the first place. From what we hear the escape of that tiger has received a significant news coverage, and several people have been killed. That, sir, is not remaining anonymous."

"So, just what are you saying?" Pierce asked.

"That none of you are so critical you cannot be replaced. Either you work within our system, or the system has no need for you," Wu said looking directly at Pierce. Neither man was blinking or willing to stand down. There was a harsh edge to Wu's statement.

"And if we choose to get out?" Pierce said his eyes moving from Wu to Bailey and back.

"Things are not that simple, Mr. Pierce. No one has ever left our organization," said Wu quietly yet with a firmness the tensile strength of steel. Pierce realized he had crossed the point of no return. He probably crossed that line long ago but failed to recognize the road sign. Cheatham had been less than straightforward with him about the end game and all the players who sat at the table. Pierce tensed and began to assess options.

"Mr. Wu, I want you to know my principal appreciates the relationship but he cannot tolerate any publicity that links him to this operation. I have concerns as well that my law partner has become worried about my involvement," Damascus said.

"Then deal with your law partner, Mr. Williams," Wu said.

"You don't know Calvin Greathouse. There's never been a more principled attorney. If he thinks something is wrong he will figure it out, and, quite frankly, I don't have the ability to control him," Damascus said.

"So, the Committee should intervene?" Wu asked sharply. "You expect us to take care of your problem?"

Damascus lowered and shook his head. He wasn't believing where this was going. Taking a little extra money for himself and the Congressman was one thing, but this guy, Wu, sounded like a completely different animal. Damascus felt a change in the atmosphere of the Board Room. A still coldness filtered through his mind. Something had changed. A new card from a new deck was laying on the table face up and it had the grim visage of death.

"Everybody take a deep breath," Wild Bill said in a laughing tone trying to diffuse the tension in the room. "We're all doing the best we can. It's all going to work out just fine. It's all getting back on track." The car salesman in Wild Bill was eternally optimistic. Yet, he could sense that Pierce was on a collision course with Wu, or his man Bailey, who looked as tight as Pierce. Wu reached the lip of the table top and depressed a recessed button. The two doors sprang open as Hotel and Motel exploded into the room, guns drawn. As everyone's head snapped in the direction of the noise, Bailey's hand emerged from his jacket holding a Glock pistol outfitted with a silencer. It was pointed directly at Pierce.

"Now, Mr. Pierce, we'll have your gun. Slowly put it on the table," Wu said and motioned for Motel to retrieve it.

"You see, our failure to check your bags was not an oversight, but a test."

Very carefully Pierce raised his pant leg and with two fingers extracted the pistol from his ankle pushing it in the direction of Motel Booker. Motel seized the gun in his left hand and slid it into his pocket then he and Hotel took Pierce by the arms and raised him out of the chair. Wu nodded as together with Bailey they escorted Pierce out of the room.

As Pierce's back cleared the room, Wu said, "Deal with him, Bailey, and the two who came with him." Wu rose and stared grimly at Wild Bill and Damascus before he left through the door at the end of the room.

CHAPTER FIFTY-FIVE

"My, if you ain't looking fine, child," the old lady said.

"Hello, Aunt Lettie," Calvin said as he took the frail woman in his arms and gave her a hug. "It has been too long since I've been back to Greenville."

"Thought you had forgotten about us, the little folks that raised you. Then you went running off to the big city," she chided him and admired Calvin Greathouse once more. "We miss you, Calvin, and it's not that far. You need to come see Lettie more often. What is it you say, How far is it from Memphis to Greenville?"

"About two hundred years, Aunt Lettie," Calvin said now chuckling. "I know, I know I need to visit more often. There's just so much going on," he said as she led him into her living room.

The room was neat with a side board at one end on which family photographs in frames collected like pillars at Stonehenge. On another wall hung a faded brownish picture of Jesus, and on another a picture of Dr. Martin Luther King. The room was as comfortable to Calvin as a pair of old slippers since his Aunt raised him after the death of his parents. Many hours were spent in this room watching the only black and white television in the house. From

Aunt Lettie and her sisters he was infused with the history of the Greathouse family and its humble roots in Mississippi. Here he learned it was not an easy climb out of slavery for the Greathouses. Calvin was a star athlete at Greenville High, but was clearly destined for greater things. Michigan State University football came calling his Junior year and he ultimately graduated as a Spartan before attending Vanderbilt Law School. Yet, in this room, in this house, he was just another beloved member of Lettie's extended family, all of whom save one, made something out of themselves. Calvin parked his fame at the front door. Nobody got the big head in Aunt Lettie's house or she would cut them down to size. Everyone was equal in Lettie's eyes. Calvin heard her preach the same mantra as his father over and over: find something you like to do and do it better than anyone else.

On the way to Greenville, after speaking with Jack at the Loveless, Calvin pondered what kind of man he was. Was he, as they said, a man of character? Did he have the guts to do what was right when the chips were down? It wouldn't be easy but down deep he knew he would have to do the right thing, else he would never look himself in the face again, or pull out the picture of his father he kept in his wallet, and look into that man's mournful eyes. It was all about character. He explained all this to his wife, Robin, who understood. She loved Calvin the man, not Calvin the great lawyer, not Calvin the entertainer, not the polished surface that was displayed for everyone else. She loved him at the core, and had taken his measure. Calvin explained it all to her that he might face disbarment. She nodded, then kissed and hugged him. Her love filled his eyes with wetness on the road south from Memphis.

Now in the embrace of Lettie's house Calvin began to relax and took a deep breath. This was a place of solitude, a sanctuary against evil. His aunt would not let evil in this place, and he was safe. Lettie brought him iced tea, for there was no alcohol in Lettie's house, and they talked for hours about what this or that cousin was doing, who married who, and how many young 'uns were running around. For the first time in days Calvin laughed, a good old belly laugh that reverberated around and filled the room. In Lettie's lined face Calvin found the same firmament that radiated from his father's eyes. There was a deep soul there flowing eternally like Old Man River.

After a while, the room got awkwardly quiet, and she spoke, "Now, tell Lettie, why you is really here."

Calvin shook what was left of the ice cubes in his tea glass and looked up at her. "Aunt Lettie, I am afraid my law partner may have done some bad things, things that I've got to help straighten out. What he's done will also reflect on me and will surely get me in trouble as well. I'm here to find him and see if I can talk some sense into his thick skull."

"Go on," Lettie commanded when she sensed Calvin was having difficulty getting his story out.

"I think he may be down here at a place called the Wolf Creek Hunting Club, and I was hoping maybe you could help me find it."

"Wolf Creek?" Lettie asked. "That is sho 'nuff a bad place Calvin. People goes out there and they don't come back. I heard stories of boar hogs the size of cattle and snakes bigger than a man's leg. There's something evil out there in those woods. Best you leave that alone." Calvin sensed Lettie's warning was genuine and borne out of fear. She shook her head denying the evilness of Wolf Creek.

"I can't ignore it, Aunt Lettie. If my partner, Damascus, is out there I have got to get to him before he heads back to Memphis. It may already be too late. Things are happening so fast," Calvin said holding his head in both hands as if he were afraid it would explode or maybe just fall off.

"There's a few local folk who've been hired to work out there on a daily basis. You know, cooking, cleaning and serving the white folks. Your cousin, Roosevelt, Minnie's oldest boy, works there. Maybe he could get you in." Calvin remembered "Rosie" as they called him. Rosie was a giant and would have played college football if he had not blown out a knee in high school. At six feet six and three hundred twenty-five pounds, Rosie had to duck and turn sideways to come into Lettie's house. Lettie called Roosevelt and he hurried on over heeding the beckon of the family's matriarch.

"Calvin, it's damn good to see you," Roosevelt said, then covering his mouth with his hands as Lettie wagged her finger at him. You see, Lettie didn't allow cursing in the house either.

Calvin explained some of the situation with Damascus and that he needed to talk with him.

"He's there shore 'enuf," Roosevelt added. "Saw him yesterday. We don't see many Black people wearing three piece suits out there."

"Can you get me in?" Calvin asked.

"Not looking like that I can't," Roosevelt said pointing at Calvin's fine clothes. "But, if we can find you some Duck Heads like I'm wearing, it's possible." Duck Head jeans were a staple in rural Mississippi for decades. "And, you will have to shuffle, and look down. They won't be tolerating no uppity Black folks out there."

Calvin nodded. He knew the drill.

CHAPTER FIFTY-SIX

Emily missed Jack's text message that he was headed to a meeting with Calvin in Nashville because she was deep inside one of the large sandstone buildings housing the administrative offices and the signal was blocked. By mid-afternoon she circled back to the Gallery and paused before the group of Severini paintings. Her eyes rolled from frame to frame finally resting on the last one. As she stared at the picture she duplicated she rubbed her eyes realizing it was actually her painting. Emily's heart raced and her eyes focused in disbelief on the mark she hid in one of the images, the singular swirl that was her mark, not Severini's. There was no question, this was her painting. Jack was right, Henri was an art thief. What else was he?

She removed her cell phone from her shoulder bag and snapped a photo of the Severini. Then she texted one word to Jack. As secretly as possible, she scribbled two words on a scrap of paper she clutched in her left hand. Turning, she almost bumped into Henri who came up behind her silently. In his face Emily saw something new, a look she had not seen before. The face barely disguised a subterranean greed.

"Why the interest in that picture, Emily?" Henri asked his eyes checking her left, then her right eye and back again. Under his arm was an aluminum tube approximately four feet long that could have contained a two piece Sage fly rod, but Emily suspected its contents were quite different.

"Oh, nothing. Just looking," Emily lied. She was not a convincing liar, and Henri continued staring at her face.

"You don't lie well Emily. Perhaps we should discuss this somewhere else," Henri said grabbing her arm. Emily winced at the force of his grip. "Don't make a scene, my dear. No need for anyone else to get messed up in this," he whispered in her ear. "Like that innocent girl at the front desk. Don't do anything stupid."

Henri guided her forcefully toward the door of the gallery and past the student proctor's desk. As they passed Emily used her body to shield Henri from the desk. She let the note slip from her grasp. It landed on the book open before the student who picked it up and read the two words "Follow me." Puzzled, the student read the message again and sought to catch Emily's eye as she and Henri passed. Then the student rose and walked slowly out of the gallery. She watched Emily and Henri as they exited the door at the end of the Old Library headed in the direction of the Administration Building. The student followed them nonchalantly from a distance until they cleared the Administration Building and moved more quickly along the gravel covered walkway at the end of the Quadrangle. From there a straight route took Henri and Emily toward the University's Cathedral, but any turns led to numerous possibilities. Henri guided Emily directly to the Cathedral where they disappeared into a side door. The student who also served as an acolyte for the Chaplain during regular services knew that entrance well. A left turn led to the room that stored vestments for the clergy, choir and acolytes. Straight ahead led into the altar area. A right turn went down a flight of steps beneath the church to what the student heard was a crypt and some rumored, a secret tunnel. It was from this direction she heard the thump as a heavy door slammed shut.

While he met with Calvin, Jack silenced his cell phone, and upon leaving forgot to turn the ringer back on. Once he reacquired I-24 heading east, Jack loaded the new Jason Isabel compact disc into his changer and was rocking with the former Drive-By Trucker when Emily's text arrived. Jack pulled off I-24 at the Manchester exit, commonly known as Greasy Gulch in honor of all the fast food population located there. He gassed up at the Mapco and bought a cup of coffee. As he began to pull away from the pump something reminded him to check his phone. He stopped at the edge of the parking lot and powered up the phone. Emily's one word message with the attachment waited from a half hour earlier. The image was a photograph of a Severini painting.

The message said "Mine".

Immediately Jack knew what it meant. Jacques substituted Emily's painting and took the original. He called Emily's phone over and over but she did not answer. Jack's mind raced and he feared somehow Jacques was on to Emily and that she was in danger. As he started to ascend the mountain his anxiety grew to near panic levels. Jack speed dialed his assistant, Tammy.

"Have you heard anything from Emily," Jack said hurriedly into the phone.

"Slow down, Jack. I haven't heard from Emily but a student who was working at the Gallery called and said Emily left with Mr. Jacques and dropped her a two word note that said 'follow me'".

"Did she?" Jack almost yelled, realizing he was passing every other vehicle blazing up the mountain at nearly ninety miles per hour.

"Yes. The student says they went under the church. Some kind of secret tunnel."

"Emily mentioned that tunnel a few days ago. Is Leon around today?" Leon was Tammy's husband who also worked for the University in the maintenance department. Like Yogi and Johnny Running Bear, Leon was part Cherokee and worked alongside them all in the Red Dagger events and in the case for the Cherokee Nation in the prior year.

"Yes, he's working today. Have you got his number?"

"I do. Catch you later. Call if you hear from anybody."

Jack then dialed Leon Allgood's number.

"What's up?" Leon asked. Like Johnny, Leon was a man of few words.

"Leon, it's, Jack. Are you familiar with a secret tunnel beneath the church?"

"Do you mean below the cathedral?"

"Yeah, I guess," Jack said. "I think Henri Jacques who Emily works with has grabbed her and dragged her into that tunnel."

Leon began, "I used to think it was just an urban legend until I found it one day while we were clearing trees out near Raven's Point. I dug around and found the school built it during the late 1960's as an escape route if students started a revolution over the Viet Nam War and seized the Admin Building. The tunnel would be used to get the faculty off campus secretly. They started from the far end so the dirt could be removed without attracting attention."

"Off campus? How long is the damn thing?"

Jack asked.

"About a half mile maybe longer, I guess," Leon responded.

"Can you find the end of the tunnel again?"

"Pretty sure, I can. So, you think they are in the tunnel?"

"Yes, according to a student. I am going in the opening up on campus. Can you cover the exit?"

"Leaving now. How much of a head start do they have?"

"Twenty minutes." Jack took the exit on top the mountain too fast and almost flipped the Jeep.

"They can't be out yet. I'll call when I find something."

"Thanks," Jack said as he raced toward the cathedral. Then, just as Leon hung up, Jack remembered he should have asked if the damn door was locked and where he could get a key. Jack hit the recall button to Leon.

"Leon, is that door locked?"

"I don't think so. Wouldn't really work as an escape route if you got there and found it locked," Leon said.

"But, it's been forty years or more since it was built. Surely, they just don't leave it open," Jack said.

"Trust me. Nobody even remembers it or knows about it except those nutty religious students who go down to the crypt to conduct Black Masses."

"Black Mass? What is all that about?" Jack asked wondering how much else he didn't know about his alma mater.

"Worry about that later. The door is at the end of the crypt. There's no light so grab a flashlight."

CHAPTER FIFTY-SEVEN

Hotel and Motel Booker along with Bailey escorted Richard Pierce off the porch to a side yard. Bailey pointed the barrel of his Glock at Pierce and said, "OK, hands behind your back."

"What in the fuck is going on?" Pierce said as Hotel grabbed his arms jerking them back and handcuffing Pierce with a zip tie.

"Mr. Wu said to introduce you to the hogs." Bailey said with a grin. There was something vicious behind his eyes. A shiver went up Pierce's spine. A man like Mr. Wu was not into agricultural pursuits so the porcine population must be retained for a different purpose.

"Hogs?"

"You know, the wild kind. One of those buggers got loose a couple of years ago and wandered out onto the main road. Deputies shot that hog two dozen times but not before he totaled two patrol cars by slamming them into the ditch. Real bad mamma jamma."

"Hey, I thought we were on the same team," Pierce pleaded wondering where in the hell Larsen and Ramparts were.

"Looks like you just got traded, bud," Bailey said.

"Where's your two boys?"

"I don't have a clue. I told them to stay close," Pierce said.

"We'll come back for them," Bailey said motioning Hotel and Motel to load Pierce into the Gator parked next to an outbuilding. Hotel got in the driver's seat while Motel drove up in a second Gator and picked up Bailey. The two Gators roared off into the woods and marsh in the direction of the river.

The all-terrain vehicles traveled a quarter mile when the side of Hotel's head exploded in a spray of crimson. The Gator veered off the road and kept running for several feet. A second shot rang out and a bright red spot covered the front of Motel's dark shirt. As he slumped into the steering wheel his big foot mashed on the accelerator and it too left the path crashing through the brush. Bailey could not reach the steering wheel since it was covered by Motel's massive chest and arms so he leaped out of the bouncing Gator and rolled into a tree which stopped his momentum. Lifting himself up onto his knees Bailey realized he lost his gun. The Gator carrying the now dead Motel continued to roll forward as the ground dropped off in the direction of the Mississippi River. Above the crashing of the two Gators now proceeding in different directions Bailey heard nothing so he began to carefully pick his way tree to tree back in the direction they came from. Blackberry thorns and green briar tore at his arms and legs but he knew staying in that place was not an option. If whomever shot Hotel and Motel didn't catch him, the boars would. He watched a man die once as the hogs tore him to pieces and Bailey shivered at the thought of the same fate.

After the second shot Larsen climbed down the tree and raced toward the Gator in which Pierce was a passenger. David Ramparts beat him there and succeeded in stopping the Gator before it went off into a small pond. Pierce was still in the Gator having wedged himself in tight. Cutting the tie that bound Pierce's hands, Ramparts said,

"You all right?"

"Yeah, think so," Pierce said as he stretched his big frame and rotated his shoulders. Larsen came running up still carrying the scoped sniper rifle.

"Now what?" he asked Pierce. "Do we go back and get those guys or get out of here?"

"Let's get back to the helicopter and beat it," Pierce said.

"In the Gator?" Ramparts asked.

"Too noisy. I think the airfield is just over in that direction," Pierce pointed to the east.

"We may have a problem," Larsen said.

"What?"

"When I went back to get this rifle our pilot was dead outside the copter. Bullet to the head."

"Shit," Pierce said. "Hell, I'll just have to fly it myself."

"Let's go then," Pierce said as he marched off through the woods in what he hoped was the right direction. The memory of the hogs was ever present among the men as they moved warily between the trees and underbrush.

CHAPTER FIFTY-EIGHT

It wasn't until they crossed into Mississippi that Yogi realized Bradley was still talking. By now his mind treated the incessant jabber as white noise and for the most part it worked. Looking into the back two rows of seats in the dark Yukon Yogi saw that the other TBI agent with Johnny Running Bear along with the two FBI agents had all crashed and were asleep so deeply Bradley's chatter was no more disturbance than that of a common housefly. Behind the last row of seats several gear bags were stacked and loaded with weaponry, NVG's and communications gear. It would be late afternoon by the time they pulled into Greenville making this mostly a night operation.

Bradley drove straight to the waterfront of the lagoon bordering the western edge of Greenville where a switcher tow boat idled at a dock. Switchers were used to ferry food out to tow boats or to remove a single barge from a tow and tie it off for a day or so until another boat picked it up for a different destination. The MV Evins Marie was already loaded with two four seat ATV's leaving just enough deck space for the six men and their gear. A young black teenager named Ha-Ha wore an oil stained orange PFD and helped them aboard with the gear. The Captain spoke with Bradley and the FBI agent in charge and backed the boat away from the dock as Ha-Ha loosened the rope holding the boat to the dock from around the cavel and then pulled it back onto the vessel. Without pushing anything in front of the boat like a small barge the Captain eased his way down the lake toward the river. Any excess speed forced the bow to sink and flooded the deck. After a half mile they were at the mouth of the lake and the Mississippi River lay before them. Yogi noticed that the Captain entered the current of the Mississippi the same way he and Jack peeled out of a river eddy and into the current of some mountain stream they were paddling in their open white water canoes. First, the skilled paddler aimed the bow into the upstream current stroking deeply, then let the natural force of the water turn the boat gradually as he leaned into the downstream force riding the water into a smooth and graceful turn. It was not unlike riding a bicycle into a curve.

Below Greenville the sand and mud banks reached from the water's edge up into the forest that looked impenetrable from a half mile out in the river. Late summer was dry that year and more so in the fall so more of the bank was exposed. Bradley climbed to the wheelhouse with his navigation maps and conferred with the Captain. When they were within the shoreline of the Wolf Creek Hunting Club property a few miles below Greenville, the Captain made a long sweeping turn and headed the boat back up stream once again using a ferry move to let the power of the river push the boat eastward toward the bank. As the boat pressed up against the bank Ha-Ha pushed four long boards from the front of the tow boat to the bank where the men unloaded their gear and the two ATV's. Fortunately, the sand and cracked dirt of the bank was stable enough for them to load the gear and drive off in the direction of the woods. At the edge of the woods Yogi saw the tow boat slide back into the river and slowly plow back upstream with Ha-Ha barely visible as an orange smear against the two tall bumper pads on the front of the boat.

Henry Greene, the FBI agent in charge, stopped his ATV as it entered the woods and climbed out with a topographical map of the Wolf Creek Hunting Club property. Before the mission, he searched for satellite maps but found nothing that worked much better than the maps available through the State of Mississippi geotechnical services. Henry laid out the map on the top of one of the gear bags in the dump area of the ATV and studied the topography as best he could. No trails were marked inside the compound but he knew the woods must contain game trails which they would seek to avoid creeks and ponds. He and Bradley discussed getting to within a quarter mile of the Hunting Club buildings and moving in from there on foot. Henry Greene carried a search warrant issued through the District Judge. While several of the men studied the map Johnny wandered up and down the shoreline looking for animal tracks.

"See anything?" Yogi asked as he wandered up to where Johnny squatted.

"Many deer, turkey, raccoons, otters, turtles, and hogs. Big hogs," Johnny said drawing a circle around a print with a stick.

"How big?"

"You know that tiger we've been chasing?" Johnny asked.

"Yeah."

"I bet they outweigh that cat. These are not dainty small wild hogs you can hunt with dogs. These bastards are huge boars. Do not get tangled up with one," Johnny said rising and looking solemnly at Yogi who nodded.

A gibbous moon appeared in the western sky casting a long blade of light across the river and penetrating into the forest until it too vanished in the darkness. For a little while they would have the benefit of the moonlight. Climbing into the ATVs the team pushed into the woods in the direction of the Wolf Creek clubhouse. Each man clutched a rifle and night vision goggles and gripped one of the support bars surrounding the cabin of the ATV. At first the going was rough as the ATVs lurched through thick brush. Johnny noted hog tracks were everywhere. A few hundred yards into the scrub the men encountered crisscrossing trails that from the evidence of tire tracks was proof the trail was used recently by other vehicles. They selected a trail that led in the general direction they expected to carry them toward the clubhouse and moved forward cautiously.

CHAPTER FIFTY-NINE

At four pm the evening crew of workers gathered at the gates of the Wolf Creek Hunting Club. Their vehicles were not allowed inside the compound and a guard at the gate searched each person with a wand. This group reporting for work consisted of six Blacks. Two tall men and four women waited for the indignity to pass so they could enter and work. Calvin Greathouse leaned on his college acting experience to imitate a man not quite so proud or upright as the real Calvin. This character slumped and shuffled and as with all good darkies, kept his eyes down, never meeting those of the white guard. As they waited for the Suburban from the clubhouse, one of the women in the group looked at Calvin intently and he realized he knew this woman as Lola from Northwoods! He heard her mention she came from this area, but now here she was in the same work detail. Lola thought she recognized Calvin but wasn't quite sure, thus the study she was giving his face. Calvin only briefly met her gaze then ducked his head and turned. She was thinking "It couldn't be Mr. Greathouse," but the similarity between the two men was striking. So intent was her stare, Calvin leaned into Roosevelt and said, "please ask that woman to quit staring before she gives me away." Roosevelt nodded and stepped over to Lola.

Quietly and in a soft low voice Roosevelt stepped

over to Lola and said, "Sister, we would ask that you not stare at my cousin or you will get him in trouble. We will explain everything later."

Lola took her eyes off Calvin and looked into Roosevelt's dark eyes.

"But, I think that's Mr. Greathouse," Lola said in a whisper.

"Perhaps it is, but you must remain silent." Roosevelt put his finger to his lips and stepped back over to Calvin as the Suburban arrived to carry the crew up to the clubhouse.

The gravel road wound through the dense forest until an opening appeared in the middle of which stood the clubhouse. The Suburban pulled to the rear of the clubhouse where a similar group of people were standing waiting to go off shift. They were encouraged not to talk with the other help so the loading and unloading process occurred almost silently. Wooden steps led up into a small screened in area on which sat a couple of metal trash cans. Beyond that lay the large kitchen area. Each of the women put on a white apron while Roosevelt took Calvin into a side room where a collection of butler's uniforms hung on a metal rod.

"There should be one here that will fit you," Roosevelt said.

As Calvin rummaged through the rack he said, "Did they have yours made at Greenville Tent and Awning?" Roosevelt just shook his head. He was a big man.

"How many guards does he have around here?" Calvin asked.

"I've seen eight, nine maybe, at one time. Two big ass boys named Hotel and Motel Booker. Guy named Bailey who sort of runs things. Guard at the gate, and a few more scattered around," Roosevelt said.

Dinner was in an hour and until then Calvin would be busy assisting Roosevelt set up the dining room and attending to anything any of the guests requested. The last part of his duties should give him an opportunity to leave the dining room in search of Damascus but until then Calvin busied himself following Roosevelt through the swinging door that separated the kitchen and dining areas. Roosevelt reported that one of the people at the Club was a tall Asian man named Wu who appeared to be running things. Calvin did not know this person. Another man was a tall Caucasian wearing a string tie and looking for all the world like a used car salesman. This, Calvin imagined, had to be Wild Bill Cheatham. The third man was a Black man, who would undoubtedly be Damascus.

"What about another White guy, dressed in western clothes, strong jaw, big rawboned guy?" Calvin asked, certain that Pierce was here somewhere, after all, they saw his helicopter leave the Mountain.

"He was here yesterday with two men, but we are only supposed to set place settings for three," Roosevelt said. What did it mean that Pierce was missing? Calvin wondered. When their work in the dining room was finished Calvin wandered off into the balance of the large clubhouse in search of Damascus. The sound of life abounded from the kitchen but the remainder of the house was as still as a funeral parlor. Calvin followed a hallway toward the front of the house and, turning a corner, walked straight into Mr. Wu.

CHAPTER SIXTY

Jack abandoned his Jeep in a no parking zone in front of the Cathedral and sprinted for the side door of the church as Leon reported. Flinging open the door he looked to the left and saw an acolyte in red and white vestments coming out of the door to the room housing the garments. The young man's mouth hung open for Jack must have looked like a crazy person. Ahead lay the chapel and to his right steps leading downward. Swirling to the right, Jack leapt two steps at a time downward as the stairs twisted to the right into darkness. At the bottom, he found another door leading into what Leon must have referred to as the crypt. Stone carved sarcophagi stood around the room entombing the remains of bishops long passed. Jack's flashlight played over the stones that cast shadows eerily around the room as the pomposity of bishops rested in eternal slumber. In the middle of the room he noticed a blackened stain as if a fire burned there at one time or some primeval liquid was spilled. On the far wall was another door matching what Leon described. Jack ran to that door and pulled but the door gave nothing. Again and again he tugged but nothing happened. The god damned thing was stuck. He was burning precious seconds. Now the blood pounded in his ears and he was breathing hard. As he played his flashlight over the door handle he noticed a small lever which when he pressed on it, released a latch and the door swung open.

Hurling himself through the opening Jack saw what looked like an endless mining tunnel before him. Exposed rock peppered the walls and sparkled with quartz and sandstone flecks of light. The ceiling was constructed of support timbers. Beneath his feet, a dusty dirt floor led forward into blackness. Jack yelled "Emily. Emily" but only received a hollow muffled echo in return. Only six feet high, the tunnel did not afford him much opportunity for speed but he ran as best he could make out hunched over, now and then yelling after her. He was overwhelmed by dampness and dust. Once he thought he saw Emily and Henri rounding a corner up ahead and the strangest déjà vu sensation washed over him. The feeling stopped him in his tracks and he wobbled until the wave passed. His mind told him he was here before but that was impossible. Then he remembered. The dream that tortured him in the hotel near the Vanderbilt Hospital when Emily collapsed after shooting Julian Browne flashed before him as he relived the nightmare in real time. In the nightmare Emily remained just beyond his grasp and he was not able to save her. Jack began to run again and continued yelling until he heard a faint response. A woman's voice. Emily's voice was calling from up ahead in a plea for help. There were sounds of a struggle and shouting. Suddenly, a gunshot rang out and Jack saw a spark flash from the rock ahead as the bullet ricocheted off the stone. Startled by the gunshot Jack dropped his flashlight which hit a rock and went dark. He crouched in the blackness running his hands over the floor desperately searching for the light but it was lost to him. Now he wished he grabbed Emily's Beretta along with the flashlight when he left the Jeep.

A little further along the tunnel and Jack realized he must be near the end of the passage but the outside day faded into twilight and offered no definition of the end. He heard another shot and a scream. With his right hand he touched the damp rock wall for bearing and held his left arm up as protection if he should run into anything. His thighs burned from the crouch he was forced to use to maneuver his way. The floor began taking a downward angle when Jack crashed into a wooden object knocking himself down. This must be the end of the tunnel he thought. He shook off the cascading sparkles that the collision triggered in his head and searched for a handle or anything to open the door. When his hand touched the metal handle he felt further. Just as with the other end beneath the handle was a lever that depressed to open the large oak door to the outside.

For a moment his eyes adjusted to the faint light provided. As his vision cleared he saw on the ground before him two bodies and neither was moving.

CHAPTER SIXTY-ONE

"And who might you be?" Wu asked catching Calvin with outstretched arms as Calvin rounded the hall into the great room. This room was outfitted in rustic furniture arranged haphazardly around a large stone fireplace where no fire burned since it was still early in the fall season. Heads of hogs were mounted along the walls their snarl of vicious teeth a warning and a sign that real hunters roamed these woods. Calvin stayed in character with his head down.

"Suh, my cousin, Roosevelt, axed me to see if any of the guests needed anything befo' dinner," Calvin said in a dialect common to north Mississippi. Wu looked him over closely since he had not seen this man before.

"What happened to Leroy?" Wu quizzed.

"Leroy, he be sick, and Rosie, that's Roosevelt, axed me to come help this evening," Calvin mumbled.

"What's your name, boy," Wu demanded.

"Lincoln, suh," Calvin responded.

"Your family likes the name of dead Presidents, I guess?" Wu asked.

"Yes, suh, they sho' do."

"We have a guest on the front veranda and another one about here someplace. Go see if they need anything, and ask Roosevelt to check with me when he can." Wu walked off in his silk jacket not amused that Roosevelt substituted a worker without getting permission and before they could completely vet the worker. Calvin, aka Lincoln, shuffled toward the veranda and saw Damascus in an Adirondack chair just staring off into the distant forest.

"Calvin! What in the fuck…" he exclaimed as Calvin approached.

"Be quiet. We have got to talk. I am afraid the shit is about to hit the fan and we are both standing in exactly the wrong place," Calvin said. Damascus just stared at Calvin but in his eyes Calvin saw despair and defeat.

"Listen, my whole life I have fought for the rights of the common man, the guy who gets stepped on by everybody. I have fought prejudice and impossible odds, but you know, I've been successful because I've done the right thing. People trust me, they know I don't lie or cheat. I don't advance a client's cause if I don't believe in him myself. That reputation has served me and my clients well. When I tell a jury I'm going to prove something, they can take it to the bank. When we got together I thought you believed the same thing and for the last couple of years things have clicked very well. But, in the last few days I have learned some very disturbing things about you and Congressman Dodge. And, even more disturbing things about your involvement with the people at this hunting club. Who's the tall Chinese guy?" Calvin asked pushing his index finger into the chest of his law partner.

"Are you sure you want to know?" Damascus said quietly.

"I'm here aren't I? I came for answers."

"Mr. Wu is the representative of a group known as the Committee who are business associates of the Congressman, Mr. Cheatham, and until recently Mr. Pierce. He is as ruthless as anyone I have ever met," Damascus continued.

"Why did you disqualify Pierce from the enterprise?"

"Because an hour ago, Mr. Wu fed Pierce to the hogs," Damascus said flatly.

Calvin gulped and shook his head. "Damascus, how deep in this shit are you?"

"All I see is brown, all I smell is brown and all I taste is shit," Damascus said.

"Tell me this," Calvin asked, "is there dirty money that has come into the firm?"

"Yes."

"How much?" Calvin pressed.

"All of it on my side of the ledger," Damascus said dropping his head.

"Damn it, Damascus, you know better than that. Why did you do this to us?"

"I guess, I did at one time, but the money was too good and too easy. It blinded me."

"And, in the process fucked me like a tall Indian," Calvin said growing more animated.

"Well, I guess," Damascus said defeat in his voice.

"Ain't no guessing to it, brother. I'll try to help you get out of here but we're done. You understand that, Damascus. Done. Not only have you got yourself and me in trouble but Jack Mathews and everyone else in our office. I've gotten legal advice from a Nashville attorney, Allen Pence, who says I am going to have to come clean with the Bar Association and the authorities if I expect to keep my license. He thinks he can finesse it but there are people at the TBI ready to fry my ass after that civil rights suit we won against them a couple of years ago, and I must move quickly. We have to get out of this place and out of whatever crap you have landed us in."

"I'm not sure there is a way out," Damascus said. "I've got no car since I came on Pierce's helicopter. His pilot is probably hog meat too and you cannot just go wandering off in the woods around here or those wild boar will eat you for sure."

"You think it's better to sit here wringing your hands?" Calvin asked his eyes darting back toward the entrance in case the big Asian reappeared.

Just then there was a loud clamor from inside the clubhouse and yelling overflowed. Damascus and Calvin hurried off the veranda into the front parlor in time to see and hear Bailey yelling for Mr. Wu. Like a spirit Wu seemed to float down the stairs.

"They shot Hotel and Motel," Bailey yelled.

"Who?" asked Wu?

"I guess it was those guys with Pierce."

"Alert everybody and be sure the helicopter is secured. Tell our guests that dinner may be a little late," Wu ordered.

Seeking to take advantage of the confusion Calvin grabbed Damascus's arm and said, "Come on at least we can look for someplace to take cover and wait for our chance." Damascus put up no resistance and moved with Calvin to the kitchen and onto the small porch. Calvin saw Bailey and three or four other men with weapons jump into ATVs and race off into the forest. Out of nowhere another ATV, one of the larger models, careened around the side of the barracks building at the hands of two Asian looking men who proceeded to the front of the clubhouse to pick up Mr. Wu. When he climbed in the ATV headed off on a trail heading eastward.

"What's in that direction?" Calvin asked.

"The airfield. That's where we landed. By the time we arrived, there was already another helicopter there, I assume it belongs to Mr. Wu," Damascus said.

"I'm not getting a good feeling about this," Calvin said his eyes scanning for signs of danger. "Why would they all scramble away from this building like they did?" Calvin seemed to answer his own question. He stepped back into the kitchen and said,

"Ladies, everyone out. Now. Let's go." His voice boomed and the women ran screaming for the porch almost knocking Damascus down the steps. Outside the house Calvin moved them all away from the house in time for a gigantic explosion to rack the house like a localized earthquake. One of the women screamed as all the windows on the top floor blew out and flames leaped out like fingers.

"Come on," he yelled. "Away from all the buildings. They may have rigged them all to blow." Roosevelt carried two of the smaller women in each arm and was running to a grove of trees along the road leading back to the front guard's station. Calvin felt a pair of hands locked on his arm and looked down to see Lola's terrified eyes looking back at him. As the party moved into the trees, Lola looked at Calvin and said,

"How did you know?"

"I've seen rats jump ship before." Calvin had dropped the shuffling routine and was back in his role as a man of action.

CHAPTER SIXTY-TWO

Johnny Running Bear watched the brush intently and had donned his night vision goggles as soon as darkness fell on the men from the river. He looked back at the river one last time and saw the carbon arc of a towboat's spotlight paint the opposite shore of the river as it pushed its tow down toward New Orleans. As the ATVs plodded toward the clubhouse the forest strangled all light with a humid blanket like a thick cloud. Whatever moonlight assisted them in the beginning now was completely absorbed in the forest. Running the ATVs without headlights all the men now wore NVGs. Johnny rotated his head in a 180 degree arc and saw blazing eyes everywhere and heard the grunts and squeals of the hogs. All the men were tense. One unanticipated consequence of their soiree into the forest was that it rendered Bradley mute. From the ATV seat behind him, Yogi saw that Bradley was scared shitless. Even trained law enforcement had no experience under these conditions. The Academy did not proffer a course on Hogzilla. They all knew that even an accidental fall into the brush would mean death by hog, and that they would be gored by the carnivorous tusks of the animals.

As they bounced closer to the clubhouse within what Henry Greene thought was three quarters to one half mile they stopped and listened. Just ahead the woods reverberated with a cacophony of insect drone and hog sounds like Hogzilla himself was throwing a porcine party. Each man chambered a round into the .45 caliber scoped rifles he carried. Yogi knew they could damn well stop a Jeep engine with a .45 shell. He hoped it would stop such a beast. Tentatively the two ATVs creeped closer as the sounds expanded into an upswell of grunts and gnashing teeth.

"Look," said one of the FBI agents pointing into the brush where the green and yellow coloring of the Gator were visible. The brush waved frantically and hogs swarmed like blowflies around the ATV. One of the agents jacked off a couple of rounds of buckshot into the hog pack which scattered the animals squealing in all directions.

"Careful now," Greene said coming to a stop and firing up his flashlight. Two of the agents stepped toward the ATV when one of them said,

"Oh my god." He turned and wretched into the bush.

"What is it?" Yogi asked. Johnny leaped from the ATV and moved toward the Gator.

"It used to be a man. A large Black man." Johnny said. Their search of the area produced no more bodies, but the hogs circled anxious to resume the feast. Their grunts and squeals announced an intent to finish what had been a glorious culinary moment.

"What a way to go," someone said as a cold shiver ran across each man's spine.

"Hogs didn't kill this one," Johnny said, "His head was blown off."

Another fifty yards and someone noticed the second ATV down a small decline at the edge of a small pond. This area was also infested with the hogs. More buckshot scattered the hogs just to the edge of vision, but the men all knew what danger lurked just there. The men from Johnny's ATV walked down to the second Gator.

"You want to go over there?" Yogi asked Bradley.

"Uh-uh," Bradley whispered. His rectum had an asshole grip on the seat as if it were set in concrete. Nothing would move Bradley from the ATV short of dynamite.

"Here's another one," one of the agents said standing over the partially eaten corpse of another large Black man. A commotion in the hog pack erupted and without warning a huge boar charged his tusks tearing into the agent's thigh and knocking him face down into the forest dirt. The boar began tearing at him in such proximity the other agents nearby were afraid to shoot for fear of striking their comrade. Reaching for the serrated hunting knife strapped to his leg, Johnny leapt onto the hog's back and began cutting and sawing his throat. The boar roared and bucked, squeals mixed with blood and sweat as the hog ran attempting to scrape Johnny off on the brush. Briars and brush tore and scraped Johnny's head and body but the boar wasn't planning on stopping. Johnny knew if he let go the boar would be on him so he continued to attack the throat of the beast until the boar went down on its front knees. Johnny jumped off and back and .45 caliber slugs tore into the boar putting him down. The Indian limped back to the ATV and helped Yogi get the injured agent up and back into the ATV where he applied a tourniquet. One of the agents who was trained as an Army medic pulled out an emergency medical kit and gave the agent a shot of morphine so he could bear the pain. His pants were slashed and blood oozed from the gash in his thigh. This man would need medical attention and soon. Johnny had scrapes and cuts but for the most part remained uninjured from the boar. He told the medic to attend to the man who was really hurt. The others looked at Johnny in amazement for who among them had the courage to engage in hand to hand combat with such an animal.

Regrouping the men loaded up when they heard the first of two explosions.

CHAPTER SIXTY-THREE

Jack stumbled forward and fell to his knees next to the first body. In the darkness he could tell the figure was a large man and something sticky pooled from beneath him. Rolling the body over he recognized the face of his friend, Leon Allgood. Leon's eyes were closed and if he was breathing it was coming very shallow. A quick examination and Jack found a weak pulse in Leon's neck. He also noticed the sticky fluid leaking from a wound in Leon's stomach. God damn, Jack thought, a gut shot. "Hold on, big fella," he prayed and crawled away to the second smaller body only a few feet away. Jack was now covered himself in blood and dirt.

Horror overcame him as he realized this form was Emily. She was only a lump on the ground but he knew in his soul it was his wife. He didn't see anything like blood around her body and gently rolled her over. She was also unconscious but breathing and with a pulse. Rage for Henri Jacques filled his mind as he pulled Emily into his arms and rocked her.

"Come on baby, stay with me," Jack repeated over and over. After a few moments in which he was terrified by the fear of losing her, Jack recovered enough to realize both Emily and Leon needed medical attention and fast. Unfortunately, there was no 911 service on the Mountain but Jack there was a single bar on his cell phone so he dialed the hospital emergency room, a number he stored on speed dial. An EMT ambulance which was staffed by pre-med student volunteers was immediately dispatched from the University. Jack explained as best he could where they were but he couldn't sight in any landmarks. Meanwhile, as he held Emily, Leon was bleeding out not ten feet away.

His second call went to the University Police office. Most of Sequoyah County was served by the Sheriff's Department in Northwoods, but by state law the University maintained a small police department on campus. It was so small there was no dispatcher and only two service patrol units.

"Police," the husky voice said as the phone was answered.

"Chief, this is Dean Mathews. I am waiting at the end of the tunnel that runs beneath the Cathedral. Leon Allgood's been shot and my wife has been hurt as well. Listen, the ambulance has been dispatched but I need you to apprehend a guy named Henri Jacques, the head of the art department whom I believe did this," Jack said excitedly into the phone.

"Jack, we're on it. Do you have any idea what kind of car this guy drives?" the Chief asked.

"I dunno, something small, flashy, Porsche maybe."

"Ok. Do I need to come to you?"

"I don't think so, the ambulance is on the way, if it can find us."

"I've been around here long enough to remember that tunnel. I know exactly where you are. I'll get out on University Boulevard and lead the EMTs to you."

"Thanks, Chief."

The world revolved on its axis so slowly Jack felt as if he were watching his life with Emily in jerky flashes of motion played on a nineteenth century stereoscope. He remembered their first date at Gizzard Creek, their first kiss and how tough she was when they were caught up in the events at the Forestry Cabin and the Red Dagger. How she dazzled everyone at the President's reception for the visiting professor, Julian Browne, and how Browne attacked them in Jack's home resulting in Emily shooting him. Then her long period of recovery that stretched for more than a year and still presented cognitive issues even today. Oh, baby, baby he whispered as he rocked her. What would this do to her mind, and how badly was she hurt? He was responsible for her involvement in this and for that could not forgive himself.

The growing charge of sirens broke the stillness

of the evening and Jack saw blue and red lights reflecting off the trees above him. He heard voices and men clambering down the slope with lights and stretchers. They wanted Emily, but he didn't want to let go. "It's ok, Mr. Mathews," a young man said. Dazed, he watched as medics lifted Emily onto the stretcher and began to carried her back up the slope. Others leaned over Leon trying to stabilize him. These were only kids, underclassmen who volunteered their services, Jack thought. Did they know what they were doing? In other times, he realized, kids the same age were medics in military service and combat saving the lives of their fallen comrades. Now he trusted they would save Emily and Leon.

"Up here, Jack," the old Chief called from above. Jack pulled himself up the slope on all fours until he reached the Chief who grabbed and lifted him in a bear hug.

"Come on, we'll follow the EMTs to the ER," he said and Jack followed him to the patrol car in a state of shock. He felt as if his soul had been torn away and blown off the mountain like a high cirrus vapor trail leaving him with nothing. The medical staff at the hospital was ready when the ambulance arrived. Emily's gurney was pushed to one emergency room and Leon to the other.

"Has anyone called Tammy?" Jack asked of the

Police Chief.

"What's her number?" Jack held out his cell phone and pushed the speed dial number while handing the phone to the Chief. He wasn't sure he could speak and if he tried, he didn't know if it would make any sense.

Numbness saturated Jack's limbs and he collapsed into a chair in the waiting room unaware of how much time passed when Tammy came running through the electric sliding door hesitating only long enough for the doors to open enough to let her pass. Tammy was close to hysterical herself and ran to Jack. After he told her what little he knew she ran to the nurses' station where Nurse Garland, a fixture at the hospital, waited. She had no information to share despite how much Tammy demanded. Finally, Tammy went back over and sat next to Jack. Their eyes met, but no words were spoken. Jack felt Tammy's rage that he was responsible for Leon's situation as well. Tammy knew trouble followed Jack, and as her old pappy used to say, even if there was only one cow in the field, Jack would step in the cow patty.

CHAPTER SIXTY-FOUR

Mr. Wu pushed the radio control button to detonate the bomb in the clubhouse as soon as he and his men were clear of the buildings and speeding toward the airfield. The fact that there were Black workers in the kitchen meant nothing to him. If his men secured the airfield as he ordered he would be up and gone in a matter of minutes. This place was too toxic, and the presence of the new Black employee troubled him. The man's eyes did not reflect the vision of a man used to taking orders, but of a man used to commanding the troops. Dispatching Pierce to the hogs was unfortunate but necessary. In fact, this whole supply chain was breaking down and the gutless Congressman made him want to puke. Plausible deniability his lawyer said time and again. With any luck that mouthpiece was in the house when the bomb went off. Good riddance.

As they neared the edge of the field and before they breached the tree line Bailey jumped out with one of the Asian guards and sprinted to the edge of the woods. One of their men stood with his weapon by the open door of Mr. Wu's Bell Jet helicopter and the other crouched behind Pierce's Sikorsky. Bailey assessed the threat and yelled at Wu,

"Let's go, now!"

The Asian driver gunned the engine of the big

ATV carrying Mr. Wu and it lurched forward lumbering toward the Bell Jet. In all likelihood they could have sprinted to the door faster. The bulky machine presented a very large target for a sniper with a night scoped rifle. Halfway across the field shots rang out. Wu's driver was knocked out of the ATV in a red spray illuminated in the ATV headlights and the halogen lamps that lit up the airfield. Wu rolled out of the ATV and came up running with the other Asian guard running step by step with him shielding his body. Bailey and the other men put down suppressing fire in the direction of the far woods from which they believed the gun shot originated. As Wu reached the helicopter its blades began rotating. More shots from the woods dropped the man near Pierce's Sikorsky. Now only Bailey and one man were left. They unloaded their automatic rifles into the woods and took off running toward the helicopter. A muzzle blast of fire from a tree cracked and the man with Bailey dropped. Then a second round smashed into Bailey rolling him several feet. Wu's helicopter screamed into the air and vanished over the trees before the sniper could jack more rounds into his rifle.

Pierce and Larsen emerged from the trees and sprinted toward the Sikorsky. That's when they noticed someone had badly damaged their helicopter both outside and inside. Metal panels near the rear engine were torn open exposing the inner guts of the machine. Wires dangled and it was clear moving parts were bent and smashed. Inside all the Nav and Com equipment was destroyed as well.

"I will be damned," Pierce yelled. "That son of a bitch."

Larsen looked around and realized David Ramparts was not with them. In fact, Larsen didn't remember Ramparts with them when the shooting started.

"Boss," Larsen said over the cussing Pierce was giving Wu, "I think Ramparts was a rat. I was going to tell you but then things started happening too quickly. When he was in the shower I found a tracking device in his shoe."

Pierce studied Larsen closely. "That's just great. If I get my hands on that asshole, he'll wish he hadn't fucked with me. No time for getting even just yet. We've got to find a way out of here and I don't want to be back in these woods at night. I think that delivery truck from the Chevy store is still behind the building where they are keeping that cat. If we can get to it first maybe it's our way out of this mess."

The two men then crossed the airfield in a trot heading back to where the storage buildings stood. Unfortunately for them, Wild Bill Cheatham had exactly the same idea and was already at the truck and storage building where his two men, Potts and George, stood guard.

"You guys ok?" Cheatham asked as he stepped into the building.

"Yeah," Potts said as another explosion shook the ground and rattled the metal building. Potts spoke through clenched teeth since his jaw was wired shut after his encounter with Johnny Running Bear. A second bomb took out the barracks. The door Cheatham entered by opened into a large room with a concrete floor. The overhead doors on one side signaled that this was likely the place the hunting club stored its vehicles when guests were not present. Tonight it housed a large cage in which sat the tiger whose orange eyes glowed following every move the men made and twenty or thirty cages of excited screaming monkeys. It was the first time Cheatham saw the animal up close and he was impressed with the size and regal bearing of the beast.

The tiger stared back taking only slow deep breaths. He was patient and waiting for his chance. He would win his freedom the minute his captors made a mistake. Adrenaline rushed through his veins as he planned to escape and return to the wild as was his nature. The tiger's hip still hurt and his vision was not completely free of the drugs the darts poured into his bloodstream. But, he was aware of the cage and how it was not meant to hold an animal such as he was. The bars were wide and afforded him the opportunity to reach through if necessary. The men at the hunting club did not expect to hold this animal for very long and used a cage on site that was available. The mere presence of the tiger and his throaty breathing filled the room with tension and scared the shit out of the monkeys who hurled more feces in his direction. Cheatham and his men saw the pictures the Sheriff showed them of the two boys the tiger tore up that first night. The first time George saw the tiger up close, he reflexively grabbed his testicles just to be sure they were still attached.

By now the smoke from the burning clubhouse and barracks floated into the building and Cheatham knew they needed to get away before someone reported a fire and locals from Greenville began to show up. The presence of the caged tiger was an anomaly that would attract a lot of unwanted attention.

As he explained this to Potts and George the door to the building slammed open then Pierce and Larsen stepped in their guns pointed directly at the three men from the dealership.

CHAPTER SIXTY-FIVE

The FBI and TBI agents with Bradley, Johnny and Yogi stopped when they heard gun fire off to their right. The roar of the jet helicopter told them someone was making an escape. What they would find at the airfield where the gunfire came from was not anything they would worry about just then. Earlier they heard the explosion in the direction of the clubhouse which was followed by the smell of black acrid smoke. When the second explosion erupted they began to move faster toward the buildings. Pole lights placed at the edges of the compound provided some illumination but the light was unreliable due to the building smoke and the fog that was creeping inland from the river. As the advanced closer they saw the Chevrolet parts truck parked outside one building and from the cover of the woods they watched two men armed with rifles kick open the door and run into the building.

Yogi and Johnny covered the right wing of the advancing law men. The big Cherokee was in his combat mode all his senses searching for whatever signs were out there. Yogi was a trained law enforcement officer but that training was nothing like what he observed in Johnny Running Bear who was a Special Forces tracker and an almost full blooded Cherokee. Johnny used as his senses and especially his gut to assess the situation. Johnny reached over and grabbed Yogi's arm and put his fingers to his lips, a signal for Yogi to wait and remain quiet. Johnny saw something in the woods just beyond, something invisible to Yogi who strained to see anything in that dark direction. Silently, Johnny faded back into the woods as Yogi crouched. Behind him lay the forest and the hogs. Ahead stood a group of buildings where armed men were making escape plans. The heavy smoke gathered and began to obscure the halogen pole lights. The glow of fire was visible ahead licking over the top of the buildings. To his right Yogi saw movement and swung his rifle in that direction as a man emerged from the woods his arms raised and behind him Johnny Running Bear.

Johnny nudged the man forward with the barrel of his rifle to where the rest of their group waited. Special Agent Bradley stepped forward and said,

"It's ok, Johnny, he's my inside man. Name's David Ramparts." Yogi remembered Ramparts from Pierce's Farm and asked,

"You're sure?" Yogi had not lowered his rifle yet.

Bradley said, "Positive. Who do you think pulled you out of that barn at Pierce's? The tracking device in his shoe allowed us to follow Pierce's helicopter here." Ramparts turned to Johnny who apologized and handed Ramparts back his weapon.

"You're good to get on me like that. Are you the one they call the Bear?" Ramparts asked.

"Yes. Are you the man with the other tracker, the Maasai?"

Ramparts nodded. "He said you were good also. Almost as good as him," Ramparts said.

Johnny grunted, "The old man wishes."

"What's the status?" Henry Greene asked as the FBI agents joined the group.

Ramparts said, "Big Asian guy named Wu just left on a Bell Jet 'copter. His men took Pierce out in the woods to feed him to the hogs. Pierce's man, Larsen shot the drivers and we freed Pierce trying to get back to Pierce's Sikorsky. Wu's men damaged Pierce's helicopter so Pierce and Larsen came back over here to get the delivery truck. I was following them when the Bear here jumped me." Johnny grunted.

"We saw two men enter the building over there. It must have been Pierce and his man. Are they armed?" Greene asked.

"Very much so. Larsen has a scoped sniper rifle and Pierce is carrying a fully automatic AR-15." Ramparts stepped over to the larger group.

Bradley said "we are looking for Cheatham also."

"He was here with two goons. His muscle, Potts and George," Ramparts said.

"Fat boy," Yogi and Johnny said in unison.

"We have unfinished business with those two," Yogi said.

Just then a thunderous roar exploded and blew out of the open door to the storage building. It was a primal animal sound, one heard for thousands of years in the Asian jungles but unknown to the Mississippi Delta since pre-historic times. It was the sound of a proud animal who was provoked beyond all reason.

"What in the hell was that?" one of the FBI agents asked.

"Something you do not want to mess with," Johnny said.

CHAPTER SIXTY-SIX

"Dammit, Potts," Cheatham yelled at his man who poked the tiger with a long pole. "Get your ass outside and watch. There's too many people left on this compound we haven't accounted for."

Potts dropped the pole and spit in the direction of the cage. The tiger stared back with death in his eyes. Just a little closer, he thought, but Potts moved away and stepped back outside. Potts was stupid, but not a complete fool. Taunting the animal from a safe distance amused him.

"We need to get out of here," Pierce said.

"All we have is the delivery van. Two can ride up front, but everyone else will have to ride in the back," Cheatham said.

"Have you smelled back there?" George asked. "That tiger shit and pissed everywhere."

"It will have to do," Pierce said. He and Cheatham realized they needed to cooperate and escape whatever catastrophic plans Wu put in place for the hunting camp. Two buildings had already exploded and were burning. From the highway they would appear as two lanterns or beacons that would attract a lot of attention very soon.

Greene and Bradley staged their men outside

the building when Potts emerged and lit a cigarette which he was able to painfully slide between his clenched teeth. Beneath the pole light Potts drew deeply on the tobacco until the end glowed brightly. Insects began a drone of high pitched noise as legs rubbed together defining territory and seeking mates. Lightning bugs blinked on and off in bursts of light that were quickly scattered by the smoke and fog. Johnny and Yogi were assigned the job of taking out Potts which was exactly what they hoped for but stealth was required. Any commotion of a fight would alarm the men inside the building and destroy any element of surprise. Using the delivery truck for concealment, Johnny began calling like a Barred Owl, not the regular "who cooks for you," but the broken fragments of the call such a bird might use if he were alarmed, injured or just screwing around. Throwing the call from behind the truck and low to the ground it sounded as if the bird were in fact grounded and very nearby. Potts responded as expected and stepped into the shadows between the building and the front of the truck looking for the distressed creature probably to kick or kill the bird. As he moved into the shadow Johnny inched backward and Yogi came forward around the right side of the truck until he was immediately behind Potts whose eyes were adjusting to the darkness. Before Potts could react, Yogi grabbed him around the neck tightly with his forearm and squeezed until the oxygen to his brain was cut off and Potts collapsed to the ground.

Johnny zip tied his hands and gagged him with a bandana. Yogi resisted the urge to piss on him and turned in time to see Greene, Bradley and the others burst into the building guns drawn.

At first chaos ruled as men on both sides shouted "Drop it." The swirl of bodies around the room were like blown leaves in the fall. When Johnny and Yogi joined the melee the law men outnumbered Cheatham and Pierce. Firing on the lawmen would have been suicide even though they could have taken out some of the agents. The reality of their situation began to sink in but neither Pierce nor Cheatham lowered their firearms. For a moment everyone seemed frozen. No shots were fired as each man assessed his chances of survival. Pierce and Cheatham, shoulder to shoulder backed away from the state and federal agents like rats chased into a corner. Their fatal mistake was failing to remember there was another danger in the room, one that was as savage and ruthless a killer as they were. Mindlessly, Pierce and Cheatham backed toward the cage assessing their options and focusing completely on the array of guns pointed at them. There must be some option Pierce thought, a way out of this. For an instant Cheatham considered bullshitting his way out, but that was sorrowfully only the used car salesman in him speaking.

"Boss!" George shouted, but too late to save

either man. In retreating Pierce and Cheatham came within inches of the bars of the cage when two gigantic arms reached out wrapping and securing the chest of each man. The throat of the beast and its face were pressed against the bars as it held the two men in an embrace of death. Claws flashed open and raked across each man cutting his throat. The downward sweep of the claws across the abdomen tore open each man so that his intestines poured out onto the concrete floor. Pierce and Cheatham were dead before they hit the concrete. The tiger threw his head back, slammed the cage and let out a roar that shook the foundation of the building. The lawmen stared in horror at the scene before them. The tiger glared from his cage daring the next man to approach. His teeth gleamed in the light as his tongue panted in the excitement of the kill.

"Holy shit!" George exclaimed dropping his gun and raising his hands high.

CHAPTER SIXTY-SEVEN

In a catatonic state Jack Mathews sat in the waiting room chair his elbows propped on his knees and his head in his hands. Tammy, no longer able to speak, moved away to the other side of the room. Jack guessed he was grateful for this because he could no longer tolerate the rage in her eyes for she blamed him as Emily blamed him, and Rachel as well. What right did Jack have to push others into danger? From time to time Nurse Garland came over and gave him a sugar coated report on Emily and each time he asked about Leon but she just shook her head. Then she went over and sat next to Tammy holding her hands as they spoke in low tones.

Sometime before midnight a doctor emerged from the hallway leading to the emergency rooms and approached Jack who stood.

"I think your wife is going to be fine, at least physically. She was concussed from a blow to the left side of her head but we found no other injuries," he said. Jack knew it was a small gift but since Emily was left handed, a blow to the left side of her head would affect her right side first. At Jack's insistence, the doctor read Emily's chart from the Vanderbilt Psych Ward which addressed her breakdown related to Dr. Julian Browne. The University ER and Vanderbilt had an affiliation. Medical records were available to doctors in either hospital on line.

"We don't know what the long term effects may be, but she is being moved to a private room where you can join her," the doctor said.

"Thank you," Jack said.

"Give us about twenty minutes and Nurse Garland will tell you when you can see her."

"Thanks. How about Mr. Allgood, he's my friend," Jack said.

A dark look came over the doctor's eyes, a look of despair that said some things we cannot fix. He shook his head and went back into the treatment room area. Jack walked over to Tammy and sat down.

"Tammy, I'm so sorry. I'm praying for Leon. He'll be ok."

She looked up at Jack when he touched her arm with wet and glossy eyes. Nurse Garland approached and motioned to him. Before leaving he squeezed Tammy's shoulder.

When Jack got to room 201 Emily was asleep. Because she was breathing on her own, she was not hooked up to the monitoring equipment. The room was strangely quiet reminiscent of her room at Vanderbilt. A steely silence greeted him. Jack collapsed into the chair beside her bed as his cell phone buzzed with an incoming text.

The first one came from Yogi and read: *Things pretty much resolved on our end. You won't believe it.*

The second text was from the Police Chief and read: *Mr. Mathews, the State Patrol apprehended Mr. Jacques outside Murfreesboro. Will fill you in later.*

Upon the receipt of each of these texts a sense of relief washed over Jack Mathews. He still burned with rage at Jacques but that asshole was in custody and thus someone else's immediate problem. However, he needed to let Yogi and Johnny know about Leon.

Jack texted back to Yogi: *Things are rougher on this end. I'm at the hospital with Emily. She has a concussion but should be ok. Problem is with Leon. He got shot in the gut and may not make it. Come to the University ER as soon as you can. Tammy needs you.*

The message came back instantly: *We are on the way.*

Johnny and Yogi drove straight through the night from Greenville back to the Mountain in Bradley's TBI Yukon blue lights flashing and ignoring the suggestion of a speed limit. Bradley agreed to ride back to his office with one of his men and wished them God speed. He had worked alongside Leon and knew him to be a good man of stout heart. On the road Johnny called back to the Cherokee Council in North Carolina and arranged for a medicine person to meet them at the hospital.

That night Jack was restless. Even though he dozed for minutes at a time, he continued to hold Emily's hand and prayed she would wake up, but she remained unconscious until the first light turned the sky from black, to purple, and then gray. Jack felt her hand stir and it shocked him awake. Emily's eyes fluttered open as she turned her head and looked into his eyes. Jack had no idea what to expect. Whether she would recognize him or whether she wandered in the dark, soulless place that called up phantasmagorical images he wouldn't know and dared not speculate. For now, just to have her awake was enough for him. Emily's gaze moved around the room and came back to rest on Jack.

"You ok?" she asked. "You don't look so good."

Jack's heart raced as he pulled her hand to his face and kissed it. Jack stood and kissed her. Her eyes were focused and bright.

"How do you feel?" he asked.

"I've got some bad headache but I think I'm ok. How's Leon?"

"He's not good. What do you remember?"

"The last thing I remember was Henri opening the door out of the tunnel and there stood Leon. Henri shot him in the stomach. When I screamed I guess he hit me."

"Leon's not doing well. The bullet tore him up on the inside and he lost a lot of blood," Jack told her.

The door to Emily's room opened with Nurse Garland tapping lightly on the door.

"Mr. Mathews," she said softly.

"Yes," Jack replied.

"There's, uh, an Indian in the waiting room asking for you," she said.

"An India Indian, or like a Cherokee?"

"A Cherokee."

Jack gave Emily another kiss and said "I'll be back in a few minutes, this may have to do with Leon."

Nurse Garland led the way downstairs and back to the ER waiting room where an Indian in full tribal dress was standing. Jack shook the man's hand and introduced himself.

"I am, Henry Tall Oak," the man said. "The

Bear called me to help Mr. Algood. I am a healer and Mr. Algood is a member of the Nation."

Jack checked his cell phone and realized he missed a text from Yogi which said they would arrive around 5:30 am and for Jack to expect a Cherokee named Tall Oak who was a healer. Jack looked up at the Indian and said, "Yes, I received a message to expect you. Do you have plans for some sort of healing ceremony for Mr. Allgood?"

Nurse Garland raised her eyebrows at this suggestion. "Mr. Mathews, Mr. Allgood remains in critical condition, I am not sure the doctor would allow…" Before she could finish Johnny and Yogi came barreling through the automatic door of the ER catching only the end of the conversation. Johnny pulled Henry Tall Oak aside and they discussed what he planned.

"A ceremony would require a sweat lodge and although I know you have one near, this man cannot be moved. I have brought in my medicine bag pieces of cedar, pine, spruce, laurel and holly, the plants that did not sleep during the creation. These plants have strong powers. I can administer a small potion for him and speak healing words," Henry Tall Oak explained.

"Nurse Garland, may we have a few minutes with Mr. Allgood?" Johnny asked. She was obviously conflicted but replied,

"Yes, but I don't want any fires or smoke."

"That will not be necessary," Henry said.

Nurse Garland led Johnny, Henry, Yogi and Jack into the Intensive Care Unit where Tammy sat asleep next to Leon's bed. The beeping sounds of the monitors explained that Leon was on life support and monitored closely. His big head and dark hair rested on the pillow and his eyes were closed. Jack gently shook Tammy's shoulder. As she woke Johnny explained about Henry Tall Oak and that he was a Cherokee medicine person. Henry explained the nature of his work and the power of the important native plants that stayed green year round guarding the souls of the people. When Nurse Garland was confident no one would start any fires, she backed out of the room quietly.

Henry mixed a small amount of the various plants in his medicine bag with a mortar and pestle and added water from another container. As Johnny placed a small amount of liquid on Leon's mouth Henry began speaking in the native Cherokee tongue because the healing words were powerful only when spoken and then only in the language of the People. Johnny understood some of what the Healer said but none of the others had any hint as to the actual words, although they all understood the prayer was an entreaty to the Great Spirit to spare Leon's life. If the Great Spirit claimed Leon's soul the words would carry him along to the spirit world.

When Henry finished everyone was quiet. Jack put his arm around Tammy and she leaned into him, now perhaps finding forgiveness in her heart. The heart rate monitor attached to Leon began to pulse more quickly as the sound strained to keep up with the heart beats pounding in Leon's chest. They took it as a sign that his body and soul were fighting the injuries and would win the eternal struggle.

Then the monitor gave a long monotonous sound and the heart rate monitor flatlined. Leon expired and was now a ghost, lost to Tammy and the world of man. He was now travelling on the path of souls. The three Cherokee men, Tall Oak, Running Bear and Yogi dropped to their knees as Tall Oak began a chant, a song that would carry the brave Leon to the west and the Great Spirit along the path of souls all men must one day follow or they would wander as lost spirits forever. They joined in the song collectively, and Jack felt the song roll off his lips at the same time.

CHAPTER SIXTY-EIGHT

One flight of stairs from the ICU at the University Hospital to Emily's room felt to Jack as if he climbed the Empire State Building carrying King Kong on his back. Emily read in his face that something awful was present.

"What's happened?" she pleaded, although she knew straight up it was Leon.

"Leon, he didn't make it," Jack said as he slumped to a sitting position on the side of her bed.

"Oh, Jack," Emily said as her eyes filled with tears. She reached and laid her hand on his arm. "Leon was so brave. He saved me. When Henri jerked me through the door at the end of the tunnel, Leon was there and told him to let me go. That's when Henri shot him and then he hit me. What will Tammy do?"

"I'm not sure. She's not real pleased with me right now." It was more than Jack could process at that moment. The relief over Emily's survival was rapidly replaced with the overwhelming sense of loss over Leon, and how he let Tammy down.

Later that day Emily was discharged and Jack took her home where Rocket, their Golden Retriever, waited and threw herself at the two of them. Almost two days passed since Jack was home or slept. Relief flooded over and out of Rocket as she scrambled out and into the yard. In spite of the concussion Emily seemed better than she had in months and continued to improve in the days that followed. Jack watched as she moved around her painting gallery with a quizzical look on her face as she wondered where in the world some of those images had come from. The Emily that searched these paintings did not appear to be the same person who created them. If he was forced to trade a little artistic inspiration for the return of his wife, Jack would make that trade any day. Jack took Emily's wonder as a good sign.

The events at the University and at the Wolf Creek Hunting Club put many objects in motion. The FBI launched a Most Wanted search for Mr. Wu, which of course was not his real name. The tail number of his helicopter that David Ramparts recalled was traced to a rental fleet and then leased to an untraceable corporate entity. As expected, he vanished into the wind.

Calvin and Roosevelt got Damascus and all the work staff off the club property with the help of Henry Greene and Rockie Bradley. Jack and Calvin with their lawyer, Allen Pence, met with the State Bar Association, the District Attorneys in several counties, and the TBI. Calvin retained his license but received a private reprimand from the Bar Association. As this is being written Damascus has had his license suspended and is cooperating with the authorities. The Congressman has engaged new counsel and claims he hardly knew Damascus and denied any knowledge of the shell corporations Damascus created. Rumor was that he might move to New York state and run for Congress there if things got too hot for him in Tennessee. There was precedent for this.

It was reported that Potts suffered significant injuries when he resisted arrest and was subdued by TBI agents on the transport back to Sequoyah County. Both he and George are being held in the Sequoyah County Jail under acting Sheriff Yogi Baker. Sheriff Mark Brown occupies the cell next to Potts and George.

On the first Saturday in October Jack and Yogi tied their open canoes to the racks on top of Jack's Jeep and drove the four hours over to North Carolina for a canoe trip down the Nantahala River on a splendid fall day. Both agreed it had been too long since their last paddling trip and the beauty of this river seemed to relax them in ways not even a fine massage would accomplish. Launching above Patton's Run they navigated around the rocks, caught as many eddies as possible and surfed the rapids until they reached Ferrabee Park for lunch. This park was the most popular place to take off the river for a break and the grassy area of the park was busy that day as the overhead sun shone straight down into the Gorge. The name "Nantahala" meant the Land of the Noon Day Sun for a reason. Jack and Yogi were stretched out under a broad oak tree resting their heads on their pfds, almost napping and watching high dusty clouds race across the sliver of sky that hung between the ridges on top of the gorge.

"So how's Emily?" Yogi asked.

"I hate to say it but that bump on the head she got did her some good. And, if you ever repeat that I said that, I will have to kill you. I don't know how or why but she is clearer than she's been in a long time and back to the woman I married. How about Rachel?" Jack asked.

"I'm going to marry that girl, Jack. After she got beat up I knew I had not treated her right. Maybe it was something about my line of work that kept me from acting, but I can't live without her."

"That's good to hear. Soon?"

"Yep."

"I heard those thugs from the dealership had it a little rough on the way back to jail," Jack said.

"Yeah. Too bad about that. Those TBI boys didn't like it much when I told them what they'd done to Rachel. Payback can be a bitch. I just wish Johnny and I had a little more personal time with them before we left."

"Real shame."

"What about you and Calvin?"

"We're going to be fine. I've got to make some big decisions about practicing law or remaining a college administrator. Leaning more and more toward the law. Honestly, there's something about the roar of the greasepaint and the smell of the crowd, I like. I only wish people didn't get hurt. Leon was a good man, and we are going to miss him a lot. One good thing from all of this is that Calvin talked a lot with Lola while they waited at the hunting club and she agreed to follow through with the lawsuit. We issued an attachment against Pierce's Farm and the plan is to get a big judgment then seize the Farm and relocate all the homes in Hard Bargain out there and use the main house as a community facility. Wouldn't that be special? Some of the Hard Bargain folks want to continue to raise the Belted Galloway cattle so we'll see. Buster's death may not have been in vain. I suspect no one will show up to contest Lola's claim so it looks like a workable plan."

"I hear you. Bradley has offered me a position with the TBI so I've got some thinking to do as well. If I can put up with Bradley's bullshit, it might be a good career move for me. He seems to attract lightning about as much as you do and the equipment and resources of the TBI are something special."

Neither of them spoke for a few minutes until Yogi said,

"You know I've been wondering. How's the old Ranger Jarret and what's the deal with the tiger?"

Still looking up at the crystal blue sky, Jack said, "Once he got out of the hospital Jarret took retirement. 'Rangering is a young man's game,' he kept saying. That explosion busted him up pretty badly and he could see the writing on the wall even if he didn't want to. I heard he and Jonas Rodgers were planning to build a cabin together over by Savage Gulf. Not that they are gay or anything like that, just two older guys who spent their entire lives in public service protecting the land and the animals. Neither one ever got married or had kids. So, good for them. People have a right to be happy. The Fish and Wildlife Service took custody of the tiger and the Ranger worked hard to get him in a sanctuary for big cats in Colorado. In the end however, they decided they just couldn't turn loose a man killer like that even in captivity. That cat didn't deserve what happened to him through no fault of his own. There was something fierce and brutal about that animal."

Yogi said, "You should have seen his eyes up

close when he was in that cage. Those eyes were pure rage and he would have killed any of us that got close enough for him to reach. Looking into those eyes scared me. All I saw was hate and revenge. I hate to hear that because he was a beautiful animal."

"Well, Fish and Wildlife put him down, and I put in a bid for a taxidermy service to restore the animal to his beautiful natural state. Since the mascot of the University's athletic program is the Bengal Tiger, we arranged to have the stuffed animal displayed at the Student Pub. No one believes he was really rampaging down in Savage Gulf, except of course, that Callicott kid who can't go back in the pub without pissing himself. I hear even old fat sixty year old former athletes are returning to the Mountain to have their picture taken with him. Can you believe it?"

Yogi chuckled and they decided to finish the river before the light disappeared too far behind the Gorge because when it got dark, things were not what they seemed in the daylight. Things were so intense for each of them over the past few weeks, they prayed for a bit of quiet time to recharge their batteries and reconnect with their loved ones. Neither of them anticipated they were about to be cast into a burning cauldron of white hot sin as the ivory colored body of a mutilated teenager was discovered pinned beneath a rock in Gizzard Creek.

THE END

AUTHOR'S NOTES

The Savage Gulf Wilderness Area is one of the great public treasures in Tennessee and offers spectacular vistas during all four seasons. While this is a work of fiction, and as far as I know a Bengal Tiger has not escaped into the Gorge, if you visit the Student pub on the Mountain, somebody pat the Tiger for me, and thank Sluggo for the inspiration.

ABOUT THE AUTHOR

Jim Cameron is a practicing lawyer in Nashville, Tennessee. He graduated an English major from the University of the South at Sewanee and later Vanderbilt Law School. He and his wife, Margaret, live with a host of dogs and cats outside Leiper's Fork in Williamson County. This is the third in the *Sewanee Series*.

www.ingramcontent.com/pod-product-compliance
Lightning Source LLC
Chambersburg PA
CBHW060145260626
47160CB00001B/128